KJ Kelly

HOWEVER LONG *the* DAY

A_T_P

Artempo Publishing

Cover and interior design by Monkey C Media
First Edition
Printed in the United States of America

ISBN:
978-1-7347458-2-5 (trade paperback)
978-1-7347458-3-2 (epub)

Library of Congress Control Number: 2025902385

For those who have gone before.

CHAPTER 1

◆

What butter and whiskey won't cure, there is no cure for.

Lorna rushed along the wooden walkway, chiding herself for not sprinkling sea salt in the corners to chase away bad omens after Patrick killed the gull. In front of the brick storefronts near Ironwood City Hall, she slid on the slick pathway, plummeting onto the lane the mule trains recently plowed through. She slammed her fist in the mud and cursed the heavens for sending a deluge just when she needed help.

After passing a mining manager's gingerbread-trim house, she charged up the walkway to Dr. Larsen's house, her footsteps squishing on the puddled dirt and gravel. She pounded on the door and stepped back, adjusting her bonnet tossed askew by the wind.

An air of annoyance swirled around the doctor as he opened the door in his shirtsleeves, a napkin tucked in the neck of his shirt. Apple pie aromas followed him out onto the porch.

"Grace is really sick." She clasped her hands in prayer pose.

"Couldn't it have waited till morn?"

Brushing iron-red mud off her cheek, her gaze narrowed to a squint. "Her neck swelled like a bull's and blood's coming out of her nose."

He tossed his napkin on the floor. "Florence," he called to his wife, "Need to go out. Don't wait for me." With coat and satchel in hand, he led Lorna to his coach house and livery. As he hitched up his buggy, the horse neighed, ill-tempered, for being taken from his cozy stable on a frigid night.

As they started down the street, Lorna asked over the rattling carriage, "What's wrong with her?" For him to leave dinner and rush out, she feared it was serious.

"I need to examine her before I can say." He drew the reins up, making a straight trip from the bit. "You say her neck swelled?"

"True as day. I thought it was a winter bug. But she got hoarse and couldn't swallow more than a few drops of water." Lorna ran her thumb over her rosary beads tucked inside her pocket. "Patrick made his mother's syrup. Told her she'd be fit as a fiddle. But now blood's coming out her nose."

"Blood-tinged nasal discharge," he mumbled. "What was in that syrup?"

"He simmers a bottle of beer and licorice until it's like molasses. Swears it's the nectar of the gods and good for sore throats."

Dr. Larsen raised one eyebrow. "Old-fashioned remedy."

"Is it typhoid again?" Thoughts of the last epidemic's devastation crowded Lorna's mind. The city closed the mines and cordoned off parts of the Location, the settlement where they lived near the mining company headframe.

He shook his head.

Diphtheria was Dr. Larsen's diagnosis.

"Your other children are susceptible. Is there somewhere they can stay?"

Lorna grasped Patrick's arm. "Ask Mrs. Hag if she'll take Ellen and Andrew."

"Mighty sure the fine lady will," he said, taking his flat cap off the peg near the door.

"Pelting rain out there," the doctor said. "Take your slicker." After Patrick left, the doctor handed Lorna two blue glass vials. "Willow bark for fever and opium if she's in pain. Feed her liquids and gruel, if she can take it."

Holding the vials to her chest, Lorna said, "They call diphtheria the Strangling Angel of Children."

"Old women's gossip. Do you no good to think that." Before he left, he placed a diphtheria placard on the cottage door.

Patrick returned with Mrs. Hag. She handed Lorna a freshly baked *Hönökaka*, her Swedish flatbread specialty. "Don't worry none. I'll keep them as long as you need."

After Ellen and Andrew left with Mrs. Hag, Patrick removed the medallion of St. Christopher he wore on a crude leather cord and placed it around Grace's neck. "You're named after Queen Grace O'Malley, the fiercest ruler of the waves." His voice wavered as he whispered, "You're brave and strong like her."

All night Lorna bathed Grace's forehead with a cold cloth. *You'll not be leaving me now, child. Not after all we've been through. You pulled through before and you'll do it again.*

Lorna thought back five years to when Grace was born at four in the morning on a blustery day in mid-December, weighing only two pounds. The doctor and Mrs. Novak—her sister-in-God, the neighbor who talked her through the birth— didn't think she'd live the night. They told Lorna to keep her comfortable. She was so bitty Lorna couldn't put her in the wooden crib her older daughter Ellen had used. She cushioned a shoe box with netting and cotton flannel, and placed her in it, feeding her with an eyedropper. Day and night she prayed her child would live. Still, she and Patrick feared she wouldn't survive. They baptized her at St. Ambrose, the church down the hill from their house, to guarantee her entrance to heaven. As the weeks passed, Grace struggled to take Lorna's breast. She slowly began to latch on well and gained weight.

"Truly a miracle baby," Mrs. Novak said. "Not many low-weight children survive."

Lorna believed she was a miracle as she watched Grace grow into a beautiful, angelic child, never whimpering or fussing too much, with strawberry-blonde hair the color of Patrick's.

When Dr. Larsen returned the next day. Grace was still hot with fever and as white as the sheet she lay on.

"Any improvement?" Lorna said, clutching at her blouse.

"Have to wait longer. Keep praying."

Two days later, Dr. Larsen told Lorna, "Her fever's dropped. She'll recover." He took Grace's pulse. "We won't know the extent of damage until later. It's possible she may not walk again."

Lorna trembled and dropped to her knees beside the daybed. "*Tabarnak*. Why did you say that?"

Dr. Larsen turned red and sputtered, "I won't give you false hope."

"There's no such thing as false hope. Everything's possible."

"You'll do well to respect my training and knowledge, which is better than relying on the town's charlatans."

"She's going to walk, I tell you. My daughter's going to walk."

"There's only so much you or anyone can do to save your daughter." He lowered his head. "Let me know if she relapses."

After he left, Lorna sat next to Grace and stroked her damp hair fanned across her forehead. "Don't listen to him. He's not God. You're going to be fine and when spring comes, we'll go to the woods and pick your favorite forget-me-nots and lilies of the valley." She tried to quell the animus she felt toward the doctor because he was tending to her daughter. But she refused to idolize the man; he only knew what he'd seen, and what Dr. Larsen had seen had nothing to do with Grace. Her daughter was a survivor; she had a strong core, and she'd walk again.

Lorna put her hand over the pearl-ribbed photographic brooch that held a picture of Grace, as if the mere act could protect her child.

When Patrick returned from his ten-hour shift that evening, Lorna had readied a bucket, a bar of soap and a bristled brush beside the sink for him to wash. He took off his sweat-stained shirt and lathered up, scrubbing his thick-skinned hands, arms and neck; the iron dust accentuated their deep crevasses and turned the glistening suds the color of gunmetal.

As soon as he finished, Lorna said, "I'm going for Bishop O'Neal. He's here from Saint Cloud, ministering to the Chippewa." She pointed to two pasties on top of the stove. "Your dinner's there." The Upper Peninsula's baked pastry, filled with diced beef, sliced potato, rutabaga and onion, was her standby when she didn't have time to prepare a full meal. "Watch over Grace until I get back."

Patrick put his hands on her shoulders and held her firm. "Nay, darling, fresh northern front coming. Wait till morn."

She pushed his hands away. "Can't. Don't know how long he'll be on the reservation and we need help now."

"I'll not have you buried alive in a snowdrift." He locked eyes with her. "If you're set on getting him here tonight, I'll go."

She shook her head. "You're worn out. And the holy man will talk you into waiting."

"Well, hope he's not like that old priest from Cork—the one with the sing-song accent," Patrick said. "If he comes for a wedding, he'll wait for the christening." He took a coin from his front pant pocket and handed it to Lorna. "This will make the buzzard's eyes shine."

Lorna placed the coin inside her glove and flung her hunter-green wool cape over her shoulders. "This god-forsaken place," she muttered, opening the door.

"A little fire that warms is better than a big fire that burns."

"You and your Irish blarney. Always an answer for everything."

A while later, Lorna returned with the bishop. Bundled in a coarse brown wool coat and cape that covered his mouth and nose, the heavyset man went straight to the metal wood-burning stove and took off his gloves. He warmed his hands, turning them over and down as if flipping flapjacks. When he took off his hat, thin white shocks of hair stood on end, making him look as if he'd seen an apparition. He sat on the chair next to the daybed where Grace lay and made the sign of the cross over her. After rubbing his hands together, he touched them to his ruddy face to test for warmth and then placed them on Grace's head. He closed his eyes and said an Our Father and several incantations. After he finished, he called Grace's name. She opened her eyes and blinked a few times. In a gentle but firm voice, he said, "Next week, you'll walk."

Even though anxiety gnawed at her, the bishop gave Lorna hope. *Hope, the last thing in us to die.*

After the bishop left and Grace slept, Lorna put the teakettle on for her and Patrick. "I know you don't like to talk about it, but I've given you seven years in this wretched place. First typhoid and now diphtheria." She flung her hands up.

"I have to keep saying it?" Patrick picked at the black soot under his nails. "We're not moving."

"It's brutal here, Patrick. Dangers in the mine, freezing winters, rowdy miners—"

"I'm shift boss. Anywhere else I'd have to prove myself again. Or they'd say I'm too old."

"Plenty would want you with all your experience." Lorna poured water over the leaves, steeping the tea.

"Cobwebs in your brain." He caught Lorna's eye and pointed his finger at her. "Stop thinking a move is going to solve all that ails."

"And the fires—burned half the town. It could happen again with the constant explosions."

"That was no explosion—faulty chimney at Dwyer's. And they rebuilt it before you could say Muckanaghederdauhaulia." Patrick took his tobacco pouch from his shirt pocket. "Codes now for restaurants, so don't worry your pretty head."

"You don't fool me," she said, narrowing her eyes. "You're the one complaining about the throttlebottoms on the town council."

"Does a body good to complain." Patrick grunted. "Still don't remove those animal carcasses fast enough. Stinks up the place."

"Because they're busy with all the drunks and cussing in public we have to put up with."

"Infringing on our rights is what they're doing."

Lorna shot him an irritated glance as she poured two cups of tea and pushed the honey pot toward Patrick. As he twirled the honey dipper, she studied his face. He appeared older than his forty-two years. But then, his life had never been easy. Born two years after the potato famine, he was obligated to help his family and pay his own way. He started working when he was nine years old, hired as a crossing boy who swept the roads clean of horse-dung and rubbish left by the horses that pulled carts and carriages.

"You said you didn't always want to be a miner—wanted a more comfortable life."

"Me, a sworn bachelor, bamboozled into marriage. 'Tis true—a man's bothered until he's married, and after that bothered entirely." He stroked his handlebar mustache and gave her a sly grin.

"You're the one who wanted to marry. Saying you regret it?"

"Lordy, woman. As annoying as you are, I do love you." He ran his knuckle down the side of her face. "Why did you marry me, my little colleen?"

Lorna looked away to hide a smile. Thoughts of earlier times filled her mind, times when Patrick charmed her with his stories and took her to performances at Pierce's Opera House and the Alhambra Theatre. She liked he had many friends and varied interests, like his membership in the Knights of Pythias at the Odd Fellows Hall, or his helping with practices of the 16-piece Hibernica Band at Mullen's Hall. "Guess I fancied you. And thought I'd make your life easier, take care of you."

"I figure I'm the one taking care of you." He stirred his tea with his finger. She slapped his hand and gave him a spoon.

"You forgetting my garden?" Lorna said, referring to the plot of land she had carved out behind the cottage and planted green beans, beets, potatoes and carrots. Whatever they couldn't eat or can for winter, she sold, setting up a stand alongside the horse-drawn vegetable wagons that came weekly from local farms.

"Your pay's never enough—two dollars a day." Lorna let out a humph. "After they take out rent, electricity, medical, doesn't leave much with butter going to thirty-seven cents a pound and ham fifteen." She hesitated, but only for a moment. "New Brunswick's temperate. If we go there, the children can know their grandparents and my father can—"

"Lordy, faraway cows have long horns. I've told you I know nothing about seafaring." He scowled as he rolled a cigarette, his nostrils flaring.

"Doesn't have to be seafaring. There're other things—manage a store, farming, work on the railroad."

"Can't do something because you think I can." Patrick took a few puffs on his cigarette and started coughing.

"See, the cough again—all that powder and smoke in the mines." Out of a corner of her mouth, she blew at a lock of auburn hair that had fallen on her forehead. "Aiyee, should have listened to my parents and lived the life of a lady."

Patrick's left eye twitched and he gazed at her as if wounded. He catapulted off his chair, speaking haltingly with barely contained fury. "Blessed Mary and Joseph. That excuse is nearer to you than your apron."

"Hush. You'll wake Grace," she said, swatting the air between them to get him to sit down.

The momentary silence amplified the crackling of burning wood in the stove. He wiped his lips with the back of his hand and grabbed his jacket and snow shoes.

"Where are you going this time of night?"

He didn't answer and before the door slammed shut, Lorna gave him a chin flick, like her mother used to give her father when he annoyed her.

"*Osti.* Godspeed, you old goat."

She sat immobile, reproaching herself for bringing up moving again. But he had to know she was suggesting it for his own good and for the good of the family. She thought of all he did to provide for them, working all day in the dark tunnels, some seven levels deep, alongside a drill the miners called the Widowmaker. As the mine became more important, work was more dangerous with deeper, poorly lit mines, and so little oxygen candles wouldn't burn. She lived with the constant fear of an explosion, fire or cave-in.

But more than anything, Lorna regretted insinuating she would've had a better life back home. Did she really believe she'd have a better life married to a man she didn't love? Well, one thing about marrying Patrick, even though life with him was a struggle, she did love the man.

As the minutes crept by, she fretted he was out too long in the frigid cold. He was spent after his shift. What if he fell asleep in a snowdrift and froze to death? The thought of going after him scurried across her mind, but she had to watch over Grace. And she had no way of knowing which way he went. By now the wind had scattered his footprints to the far reaches, erasing all traces. *It's a long road that has no turning.*

CHAPTER 2

◆

Waiting by the window, Lorna watched the snow fly sideways, coating the house and hickory trees with frozen fluffs. She couldn't stop upbraiding herself for pressuring Patrick. It would do her and the children no good should he pick up and walk away. Some men in these parts had done that, leaving behind grieving families who struggled to scrap together enough to leave the mines.

"Aiyee," she muttered, "he'll be chilled to the bone." She placed bricks on a baking sheet and heated them on the stove.

As she was tidying up the kitchen, she heard Patrick stomp his feet against the door frame, shaking off the snow. He came in without a word, his arms clutching his abdomen.

"Bricks ready for you."

He wrapped the warm clay blocks in a dishtowel and brushed past her, his face averted. As he slithered to the bedroom, he griped, "No more of your nonsense."

After checking on Grace, Lorna joined Patrick. He was cold and shivery. She nestled close to him and fell asleep, her arm draped over his shoulder.

The next day, the wind continued to whip through the trees, wailing and hurling clumps of last-night's snow from the upper boughs. To keep out the bitter streams of arctic air blowing through the cottage, Lorna placed towels along the window edges and a hook rug across the doorsill. She stoked a roaring fire in the stove to keep Grace and the house warm.

At three o'clock a code of whistle blasts from the company foreman's office announced the next day's work schedule. Though Lorna was accustomed to these blasts, today they irritated her, her nerves taut like a warp strung out on a loom. Not only did she have Grace to worry about, Patrick left that morning still miffed, forgetting the water canteen he wore around his neck. "Damn whistles. Rule our lives," she grumbled. "Could use some peace and quiet."

Thoughts of her childhood home transported her back to New Brunswick and its calming sounds: the waves lapping against the shore, the grunting foghorns, the singing warblers and tree swallows. In her mind's eye she saw herself siting on the porch of her family's gabled two-story house, looking out over the bay, while winds whipped inland from the Gulf of St. Lawrence, ruffling the water.

She glanced at Grace to see if the whistles woke her and saw she had a tad of color on her face. As Lorna came closer to check, Grace's eyes gently opened. In a hushed voice, she said, "Momma, can I have some soda bread?"

"Of course, my little moppet. I'll bake your favorite with caraway seeds." Signs of an appetite certainly meant Grace was feeling better, but Lorna tempered her elation as things had a way of reversing. Hadn't Dr. Larsen mentioned a relapse?

"Can I see Ellen and Andrew?"

"If you're better in a few days, they'll come home." By then, Lorna figured she'd know if Grace was truly on the mend and no longer contagious.

While Grace rested in bed, Lorna kneaded the bread, humming for the first time in a while. Her melodic voice rang throughout the house, a medley of Irish and Scottish tunes—and her mother's favorite, "I wandered today to the hill, Maggie." Looking out the window, her eyes lingered on the deer tracks in the fresh snowfall, near the web of hemlocks where they nibbled on the branches. She caught her reflection in the glass; like

Patrick, she looked older than her years. Worry and hard work will do that to a person.

As she transferred the dough to a cast-iron skillet, she wondered if Grace's recovery was due to the bishop's blessing or if God had answered her pleas. It didn't matter; her daughter was getting well. A sense of relief seeped into her until she remembered the doctor saying Grace might be paralyzed. She had to know now or else she'd be sick with worry another day.

After Lorna finger-traced a cross an inch deep on the top of the bread, to bless and score it, she held up an ice pick and called to Grace, "Come help me let the fairies out."

Grace struggled to sit upright in bed and place her legs on top of the bedcovers. Then she pulled up her white cotton stockings, eased her legs over the side of the daybed and lowered them to the floor. As she tried to stand, her body went limp. She slumped to the floor. Lorna started toward her but stopped when she saw Grace, on hands and knees, scoot to the chair and pull herself up. She tottered as she took a step, then another, continuing onward. With the back of her flour-covered hand, Lorna dabbed at the tears running down her face. When Grace was nearly at the table, Lorna smothered her with kisses.

"It's all right, Momma," Grace said, "don't cry."

Lorna helped Grace up on the chair and handed her the pick. She watched as the child punched four holes in the dough, one on each side of the cross, to set the fairies free. "Good girl. Now back to bed. See if you can catch the fairies dancing in the sunlight." As she watched Grace's eyes roam the room for the mythical creatures, Lorna was as certain as ever the harsh life here was not good for the family, especially Grace, who might be weakened from her illness. The Location had perils and there were many weeks of cold season before them, weeks that more often than not, brought flus, bronchitis, and ear infections. She had to protect her children.

Winter set in hard. Fortunately, Lorna had taken in enough staples to last until spring. Her mother Maggie taught her well how to can and pickle the summer and fall vegetables she grew, and her jars filled the larder shelves. Like her mother, she could make a meal out of nothing, a handy trait when snowbound. She also rationed her food to ensure there'd be enough until the thaw, praying there wouldn't be late winter storms to sink supply ships.

One afternoon, Mrs. Hag visited to exchange some of her butter cookies and Kringle for Lorna's canned vegetables. "*Daily Advocate* says waves on Lake Superior froze and ships couldn't dock."

Lorna nodded. "Can't depend on the railroads."

"Not with mining supplies having priority," Mrs. Hag said. "At least the dogsleds are getting the mail through, even with those snow drifts."

"Patrick said some in town were over two-hundred inches high."

"So they say." Mrs. Hag put the canned beets and green beans in her jute bag. "How's Grace doing with all this cold? Any lingering effects?"

"Only that little limp."

"You barely notice it."

"She wanted to go tobogganing and skating with Ellen and the neighbor kids, but I didn't think she was strong enough. I told her she could only go on those sleigh rides the company organized." Lorna looked out the window with a vacant stare. "But Patrick said I shouldn't coddle her. So, I gave in . . . worried the whole time she was out."

"I did the same with my Tuva after she broke her arm. Tried to persuade her not to do things, afraid she'd injure herself again."

"I try not to hover and make her think she's still sick. But I'm hovering."

Mrs. Hag placed her hand on Lorna's shoulder. "It's called protecting our children, dear."

After New Year's Patrick stopped coming straight home after work, arriving an hour or two later, after a few pints with his friends. Lorna didn't say much at first, knowing he had a large coterie of friends that vied for his company. She was glad people wanted to be with her husband, who, she had to admit, could be a charmer. And she figured he needed a break after working long hours in the darkness. It might also be a release after being anxious about Grace when she was sick. But she worried it was becoming routine, not good for his health, and he was using money she needed for the household.

There was also the incident with Ian McDonald, the 'Terror of Scotland,' as miners called him.

"What in heaven's name happened?" she said when Patrick came home one night with a swollen and bloody nose.

"Got in a row with Ian at Kane's. Badgered some of my pals and I told him to bugger off. He smashed my nose."

"Lordy. He could've hurt you like he did Tim Delaney," she said, referring to Tim's shattered left eye socket and lost vision.

"Ah, it's nothing. I gave it back harder. Elbowed him under his ribs and there he was, bent over and groaning. Pushed him to the ground and gave him some good kicks."

"Don't you say it's better to be a coward for a minute than dead for the rest of your life?"

"If he messes with my guys again, I'll lay him out straight so they can measure him for the coffin."

"Well, get down on your knees and thank God you're still on your feet."

At the end of January, Lorna and Patrick attended the Scottish celebration for the birthday of Robert Burns at the tin-ceiling community hall. The townswomen festively decorated it with tree boughs and pleated crepe paper streamers. Tables made from planks of wood held oil lamps that cast the room in a golden glow. Cinnamon sticks stewing in the hot cider scented the room. Along a back wall, a long table held foodstuffs the Location residents brought: mincemeat pies, pickled goods, jams, beef jerky, venison, mashed potatoes and an array of homemade breads and local brews. After Lorna set down the baked beans she simmered for hours with molasses, she joined Patrick and the men he worked with at the Norrie mine. A bank employee with an ear trumpet sat next to her and asked her to repeat everything said at the other end of the table. She complied out of kindness to the man the others ignored, figuring it was the Christian thing to do.

A miner at another table showed off his new Kodak box camera, the first many had seen. He gathered his friends for a group photo.

Lorna grabbed Patrick's arm. "Let's have him take our photo."

"Always wanting your picture taken."

"Got my new frock on." Patrick looked befuddled. "I put new lace around the collar."

As they posed side by side, Lorna saw a spider crawling toward her. She clutched Patrick's arm. "Get it."

Patrick squashed the arachnid with the heel of his shoe. "Lordy, woman. You don't mind a snowstorm, but go into a tizzy when you see a bug."

A short time later, people in the hall locked arms together and started singing "What Shall We do With a Drunken Sailor." Lorna swayed to its jaunty tune, her shoulder nudging Patrick's. With a lack of women, some men danced with each other, a few wearing scarfs to show they were temporary 'ladies.'

After a few rounds of the song, Mrs. Cameron from the Scottish council asked Lorna to play some church choral songs on the piano. "Before they sing their salty versions."

Before Lorna could answer, Ian McDonald entered the hall. He tossed his cap on the antler-ear coat rack and crept cat-like behind several men milling around a corner.

"Ask me later," she told the woman, sneaking glances Ian's way. She prayed he wouldn't come in their direction, but he did, a slight stagger to his gait. Lorna poked Patrick's side.

"I saw the bugger."

"Don't let him get to you," she said, sliding her gold cross back and forth along its chain. "Tell him he wouldn't want to dishonor his country's celebration."

Patrick scraped his scuffed boots with side buckles against the side of the bench and smashed a nail protruding from the floor. "If he tries anything, I'll have my crew lay into the jackanapes."

"Hey, you, Ryan," Ian said, pointing his finger at Patrick, a nasty grimace on his face. "Got some unfinished business."

Before Ian could utter another word, Patrick swung his arm back and slammed it into Ian's face, knocking him to the ground.

"What a sockdolager," one miner said, shaking his fist in the air like a club.

Patrick was about to jump on top of him when three of his friends grabbed his arms and held him back as he sputtered something unintelligible.

A crowd gathered, and several men who had vendettas against Ian pelted him. Two vigilantes who enforced the laws of the Location grabbed Ian. As they escorted him out, a miner yelled, "Don't let him back in."

"You should have let me at him. Could have taken him.," Patrick said, shaking his friends away.

"Gammon and spinach. Pride's the author of every sin," Lorna said, noticing some women glaring at them and silently tsking.

"I need a drink," Patrick said, walking toward the drink table.

Lorna gave him a chin flick and kept an eye on him. He was angry and it would do no good to try to stop him. After a few rounds, he staggered over and sat down next to her, planting a kiss on her cheek.

"Look at you. You can hardly stand upright. It hurts me to see you like this."

A smile crept up his ruddy face. He rested his head against her breast. "A nice cozy bed's waiting at home for some cuddling and snuggling."

She gave him a grieved glance. "I've been trying to figure out why you're drinking. Friends enticing you? Need a break after being cooped up all day? Are the children too rambunctious and you can't relax?"

"Little darlin's," he said, slurring the ending of the word. He shrugged his shoulders. "If you're looking for a husband without a fault, you'll be without a husband forever."

Lorna's father's words rang in her head: *Lusty lot those Irish, drinking and carousing. Aiyee, thirst is a shameless disease.*

Patrick didn't abandon his sorties after work and one Tuesday in early February, Lorna waited up the entire night for him. When he hadn't come home by morning, she feared the worst, even though there'd been no word of an accident. She doubted he'd be lying face down in the middle of the street—his friends would have carried him home. Midmorning she inquired about him at the mine office, but no one had seen him and he hadn't reported for work. She shoved her pride in her apron and went to Kane's saloon. He wasn't there either. She stewed all day, refusing to believe he'd abandon them.

After the shift finished, Colin, a friend of Patrick's, came to the house. "Sorry to be the one to tell you, but Patrick's in jail. In Bessemer."

It took a few moments for Lorna's disbelief to turn to anger. "Jail?" Colin nodded. "What was he doing in Bessemer?"

"Sometimes we go to nearby towns."

"Taverns, you mean."

"Oh, no. Not always. We went there once to hear old "silver tongue" William Jennings Bryant."

"Did you now." She took a moment to calm down. "What did he do?"

"Arrested for drunk and disorderly conduct. Sheriff hauled him before the justice of the peace. Fined him five dollars and court costs." Colin wrinkled up his bulbous nose. "He refused to pay."

"Aiyee, the *Sidhe*," she muttered, referring to the Irish spirit she blamed when things went wrong." She rested her hands on the back of a chair and taped her fingers on it. "Stubborn old coot."

"Judge incarcerated him for thirty days."

"Thirty days?" She sat down and absentmindedly twirled a strand of hair as Colin's words sank in. *And I was worried something terrible happened. Locked up like a common criminal. Osti, what will I tell the children?*

Colin put down his empty bag with *Dupont Explosives* written across the front and handed Lorna a fistful of coins and a few dollar bills. "Me and the guys took up a succor collection. It's not much but may help. If you need more, you could ask for alms at church."

"Never. I was raised you work for what you need."

In a pique after he left, she tore down the pinecone- and fir-bough garlands draped around the parlor and threw them on the floor. She scurried into the kitchen and took her conical tin from its hiding place behind the flour and sugar, and counted its contents. If she managed well, there was enough to cover the month's expenses. If not, she could sell some of her canned goods. However, she hated to part with any since they had another eight to twelve weeks of winter ahead. But as her mother used to say, *Enough and no waste is as good as a feast.*

She might have enough to pay Patrick's fine. But if she was ever going to put a stop to his drinking, it was now. He might do some thinking while locked up. She wouldn't spend money getting him out of jail when she could use that money for new shoes for the girls; the winters had dried and cracked the leather and the soles were splitting off. *May you be afflicted with the itch, Patrick Ryan, and have no fingernail to scratch it.*

Transfixed, she stared at the water damage that darkened and frayed the edges of the wallpaper. She thought of her mother, and how she must have fretted when her father was at sea. She never knew if a storm would capsize his ship or take him off course, if they'd get stuck on a sandbank, or if a fire in the hull would destroy the wooden vessel.

All wives are tormented by thoughts of disaster.

CHAPTER 3

◆

A goose never voted for an early Christmas.

Patrick returned home after his one-month confinement in Bessemer. Every time Lorna brought up his incarceration, his conversation turned to grunts, and he'd avert his eyes.

"Go ahead. Slink away. But you know you can't lollygag anymore with your pals after work." She didn't want to be a taskmaster because it was in Patrick's nature to socialize. But someone had to set boundaries.

In the coming weeks, Lorna thought he seemed changed. She told herself she did the right thing by letting him stay in jail, even though she second guessed her decision daily while he was away. Now he spent more time with the children. After dinner, he'd listen to Ellen read from her primer, help Grace draw on her chalkboard, play Button on a String with Andrew with an empty spool of thread. It became a ritual for him to tell them a story before bed. One of the children's favorites was the tale of Little Girl's Point, a lovely spot in the Upper Peninsula with maple, hemlock and birch trees. They'd gone there one summer to catch glimpses of hawks, rabbits and ruffed grouse—and swat away horseflies, deerflies and mosquitoes. As Patrick told the story, there was a Chippewa hunter who lived on the shores of Lake Superior. He had a daughter who climbed the highlands to gaze at a place called Sacred Grove, a pine-forest-covered sliver of land where fairies dwelled.

Patrick's voice went down an octave when he told of the girl's parents, fearing bad spirits had enticed their daughter, forbade her to go to the Grove. But she went anyway. And one day a towering tree with branches splayed wide told the girl to think of him as her lover. The daughter was about to be married to a man chosen by her parents, but on the day of the wedding, she disappeared. No one could find her. Years later, several fishermen passed near the Sacred Grove and saw a female figure clad in green, standing near the shore at the point—it was the Chippewa maiden.

The tale unsettled Lorna. An inner voice hinted she was here in Ironwood, not that far from Little Girl's Point, to remind her of what she'd done. In all her years away from Maritime Canada, she'd never been able to banish her guilt. She knew she was right to not marry Mr. Winthrop, but did she do the right thing by running away?

The young men in town never interested her, the ones who tried to get her attention by laughing loudly or mock fighting with a friend. Unlike the rest of the girls who lived for the day they could be called Missus, no matter how bad the match, Lorna never had qualms about telling her mother she wasn't happy her father promised her in marriage to Mr. Winthrop. But her father convinced her mother she'd have an easier life married to the city's lumber mill baron. They figured it wasn't good for Lorna to remain unmarried too long; it was better to clinch the deal while she was in her prime.

For every objection Lorna had about the marriage, her mother had an answer. When Lorna said Mr. Winthrop was too old, Maggie said a husband should always be at least ten years older; older men tended to be more considerate toward their wives and less inclined to have a roving eye. When Lorna wrinkled up her nose and said she didn't care about his money, Maggie reminded Lorna she really didn't know what hard work was, and she'd get plenty tired toiling away night and day, if she had to help support a family. And when Lorna said she couldn't stand the thought of him touching her, Maggie only said that most of the time he'd be busy with his work. And being older, he'd get tired easily.

She found it difficult to blame her father. He was a good man and only wanted the best for her. He often said Lorna reminded

him of Maggie as a young woman. She was spirited and robust—
or healthy-looking, as the men in town said, which really meant
good for having children and working hard. He'd smile when he
watched her talk, her hazel eyes dancing, her hands conducting
an imaginary orchestra. He'd stroke her auburn hair that
cascaded in waves down her back. She remembered he once said
when the sun hit her tresses the right way, streaks of strawberry
blond and burgundy emerged, as if caressed by a Renaissance
master's brushstrokes. But he also complained she could be a
bit of a 'mouth' and he'd tell Maggie to tether her. But Maggie
never wanted to set too many limits. She wanted Lorna to be the
woman she was meant to be, never imagining she would assert
her independence so young and go against her father's wishes.

Lorna often played games with herself, imagining what life
would have been like married to Mr. Winthrop. She'd be a 'lady'
as her mother used to say. Her life might have been easier in
some ways, but she married the man she loved.

In June, when floral-wreathed Swedes celebrated *Midsommar*
with outdoor meals of herring, new potatoes and strawberries,
Lorna was certain she was pregnant again. She hoped it wouldn't
worry Patrick; she didn't want him to revert to drinking.

One Monday evening, after he placed his lunch pail and
miner's hat on the kitchen counter, she watched him pump
water at the sink. The waning daylight filtered through the
trees and the window, bathing the hand pump and washbasin
in a glimmer the color of angel wings. "How did it go today?"
she asked.

"Stunk like crazy," he said, referring to the worst day to go
down after miners spent the weekend drinking and did not
brush their teeth.

"Well, I've something to tell you that will take your mind off
it," Lorna said.

He looked sideways at her. "Hope it's good." He waited for
her to say something. "Quit stalling. What is it?"

"After you wash up and change."

Patrick returned to the kitchen and rolled up the sleeves on his favorite tattered sweater. "You're going to tell me you've had it and you're going back to Canada—going to find that old Mr. Winthrop and beg him to take you."

"Phooey, how can you think such a thing?" She pierced the last of her potatoes to test if it was cooked through. "You're going to be a father again."

"This isn't a ploy to keep me sobered up, is it?"

Now that Patrick was home more, Lorna hoped life would get easier. They'd made it through Grace's illness, the last bitter winter and his drinking. She convinced Patrick to build a chicken coop because she wanted to purchase a flock of hens from her garden earnings. They'd supply them with fresh eggs, and hopefully lay enough to sell some to the grocer where they often went for thirty-two cents a dozen. Her chickens grew plumb with the cracked corn and bonnyclabber she fed them. They also provided entertainment as they stirred up dust for a bath, squabbled with each other, and foraged for bugs and grubs inside the heavy duty, double-screened pen that kept the local bears, wolves and roaming dogs and cows from raiding her peep.

All was going well until the end of summer. Lorna was putting Andrew down for his nap when she felt a shock wave and heard a blast. She dashed outside and saw Mrs. Hag gesticulating.

"Hope it's not Norrie," she called out to Lorna, the blasts from the alarm whistles muffling her voice.

More neighbors were out in the street now as rescue brigades rushed from different directions, heading toward Norrie and Aurora.

Lorna placed a hand on her stomach. *Please, nothing can happen to Patrick. He has to know his child.* Starting down the grassy slope, she said to Mrs. Hag, "Watch Andrew. I'm going to see what happened."

Mrs. Hag beckoned her. "Stay here. You have the baby to think of. I'll tell you when there's news."

When Lorna reached the street, a man passing by said, "Go back. You'll only get in the way and could injure yourself."

Lorna stared at the man with a look of bewilderment. *I should have put on my stockings inside out this morning. That would've ensured luck.* The man turned her around and pointed up the knoll. "Go now."

When she arrived home, Andrew was still asleep. She knelt next to her bed and tried to say the rosary. But worry crowded out her Hail Marys. She flung her rosary on the bed and went into the kitchen. She filled a bucket with hot water and vinegar and started cleaning the parlor window. Her cloth zig-zagged across the pane, faster and faster, keeping pace with her thoughts.

After she finished the parlor and was working on the kitchen window, Mrs. Hag knocked and came in. "Heard it was a windy shot. Exploded a thousand-feet down. Imprisoned forty men working that section. It was Norrie."

"Was it Patrick's crew?"

"Man didn't know. Recovery teams are removing tons of ore and dirt so they can drive down pipes to where they're trapped."

Lorna's thoughts made her mute. She picked up yesterday's newsprint and started buffing the window.

"You don't have it in you to cook. I made a big pot of *Ärtsoppa* and I'll bring you enough for your dinner."

Mrs. Hag returned with a large bowl of her pea soup and a plate of pancakes as the girls came in from school.

"They let us go early," Ellen said, taking off her flat-brimmed straw hat.

"Told us to go right home," Grace said, unbuttoning her ruffled-edge pinafore.

"There was an accident," Lorna said. "We're waiting to hear what happened."

Ellen flung her book bag towards the sofa and missed, breaking a porcelain dish on the side table.

"Look what you did. That was my mother's," Lorna said. "Must you be so reckless."

Ellen hung her head and pulled her knees together. "I'm sorry, Momma."

"She didn't mean to," Grace said. "It was an accident."

Lorna looked down, her hand to her forehead. "I know. I'm the one who's sorry. Didn't catch my temper in time. 'Tis only a stepmother who'd blame you."

When Patrick came home hours later, his wide and terrified eyes greeted Lorna. It was the first time she saw fear in them. She put her arms around his neck and tried to hold him close. He broke free and wandered into the kitchen.

"You're not hurt, are you?"

He shook his head and gripped the edge of the sink, staring out the window. "Ten died. Lots with third-degree burns." He wiped away the beads of sweat glistening on his upper lip. "Killed Johnny Hennessy."

"Oh, Lord, not little Johnny." The image of the eight-year-old boy filled Lorna's mind. She remembered how proud he was to work as a trapper to help his family, opening and closing the trap doors inside the mines to allow air to flow in. Sometimes he waited hours in the darkness to let the ore tubs through.

Patrick paced in front of the sink. "Trapped down there. Debris flying everywhere. The heat, smells."

"Sit down and rest. Try not to think about it."

Without answering, he went outside and kicked at pebbles and twigs. He stomped on the grass, turning his revenge against the lawn as church bells tolled for the dead.

Lorna's sense of relief and gratitude was tempered as she thought of the families that lost someone. *I can't celebrate our good fortune while others suffer.*

After a fitful night, Patrick got up early and told Lorna, "Going to see if I can help clear things out and stabilize the area."

"You hardly slept. Stay home. The recovery men know best." As she said it, she knew she couldn't prevent Patrick from going.

Later, as Lorna prepared a bag of canned vegetables to take to the Hennessy family, Mrs. Hag came over and handed Lorna a folded pile of black crepe. "Had this left over. You can use it for your door."

Lorna stared at the fabric and rubbed it between her fingers as if checking for texture and drape. "Hate to put this up." She turned and looked at Mrs. Hag. "Reminds me none of us are immune."

"The inspector's there now," Mrs. Hag said, "making his report. And the managers are reviewing safety procedures."

"Are you going to the vigil for the dead and wounded tonight at St. Ambrose?"

Mrs. Hag nodded her bowed head. "Such a shame. More widows and fatherless children."

When Patrick returned, grimy and tired, he told Lorna, "Paul Flanagan was injured. I told him he can stay here till he gets better."

"What ails him?" Lorna asked, knowing it was customary for families to take in unmarried men to care for them after an accident.

"Burns and some injuries from flyrocks. Can't let him go to the almshouse."

"I'll make up the daybed for him."

"Some men are threatening a strike," Patrick said. "Demanding better work and safety conditions. Said they're going to destroy equipment and kill anyone who tries to stop them."

"Don't get involved."

"Have to stand up for what's right. Those deaths can't go unanswered."

"Have you thought about us if you're injured—or you lose your job?" When Patrick didn't answer, she continued, "Didn't think so."

Patrick hammered out his words, "And all this time, to hear you tell it, you're the one supporting us with your vegetables and chickens. Could've fooled me."

Colin came over that night and told Patrick, "Company contacted the state militia. Said it would fire anyone who participated. It unnerved plenty of the men. Strike's off."

Lorna raised her eyes to the heavens. *Thank you for making them come to their senses.*

The community held two large funerals. Fraternal orders helped prepare the bodies for burial, build coffins, dig graves and organize the ceremonies for the dead. They also supplied pallbearers. The Hibernica Band led the funeral parade through town, playing a dirge on the way to the rugged hills surrounding the mines, where wooden headstones popped up. The mourners wore their best clothing, many with a black crepe rosette on their left breast.

Mrs. Hag and her husband stood with Patrick and Lorna at the gravesites as the priest led prayers and committed the bodies to their eternal resting place. On the way back to town after the service, the band played a jig called *Merry Men Home from the Grave.*

"Let's stop at Kane's to toast those we lost," Mrs. Hag's husband said.

Patrick's shoulders slumped. "Best not," he said, glancing sideways at Lorna. "The burned child fears the fire."

Lorna let out a quick snort. "As true as the gospel."

CHAPTER 4

♦

It's difficult to choose between two blind goats.

Not long after the explosion, and before Paul was well enough to go back to his boarding house, Patrick talked to Lorna about the Gold Rush in Canada.

"They say miners are discovering gold and getting rich."

"A story without an author is not worth listening to," Lorna said. "I've heard those rumors. Pickings are meager for the average man."

"You're thinking of California. This is a new field in the Yukon."

"You sure your dream's not a delusion?"

Patrick gave the table a whack. "My pretty colleen, I'm going to give you your wish. Give you that life of a lady you say you could've had."

"Nice words don't butter turnips." Lorna looked hard at him and thought back to the mining accident, wondering if the explosion had induced more fear than she realized. There were no guarantees he'd strike gold, but it'd get him out of the mines.

"Got to recognize opportunities when they come." He leaned forward and pinched Lorna's cheek. "Company approved my leave. OK, Lorna, darlin'."

"What do you mean, OK? *Osti*. None of that saloon talk with me."

"And none of your old French swear words."

After Patrick set off for Canada, Lorna focused on keeping the family afloat. She stuffed her pride in her apron pocket again and went around the Location, asking unmarried miners if she could take in their laundry at twenty cents a pound. By the end of two weeks, she had enough paying customers to maintain the household while Patrick was away. She also had her vegetables and a new batch of chickens whose eggs she sold at the weekly market.

Months passed without word from Patrick and Lorna stewed, fearful something terrible had happened, or worse, he'd abandoned them. But he'd never been one to shrug his duties. Wasn't he off to Canada to make a fortune to better take care of them? Can't blame a man for that. And hadn't she been pleading with him to do something else? If she had to blame someone, it should land on her shoulders, hard as it was to admit.

While he was gone, the vibrations and noise from the mines, always shaking Lorna to her core, drove her mad. Some days, she thought she couldn't take any more. Every Sunday she planned excursions for her and the children to get away from the Location and the smell of metallic ore. Sometimes they went to the lake shore where they gathered agates and driftwood she used for the stove. Occasionally, one of Patrick's friends took Andrew trout fishing in a nearby stream, sequined by sunshine. While they fished, she and the girls hunted for mushrooms, blueberries and thimbleberries in the thickets at the forest edge.

One blustery day in late autumn, Lorna stood over the stove doing laundry. As she stirred the clothes soaking in soapy water, a man she didn't recognize came into the cottage.

"Leave your bindle there. It'll be ready in two days. If you need it sooner, costs five cents more."

The man's tattered pants hung loosely from his frame. Bunched up around the waist, a loop of twine prevented them from slipping down.

The man placed his bag on the floor and said, "Even a good horse can't keep running."

The voice carried an unmistakable cadence and timbre. Lorna put down the stick she stirred the clothes with and stared at the man. As she traced the outlines of his face, she felt her heart swell. "You grew a beard," was all she managed to say.

He went to Lorna and buried his head in her neck. The embrace was tender, with a sense of closeness and comfort. Lorna felt tears forming in the corner of her eyes.

"Don't see gold flakes flying off you, so suppose it was slim pickings."

Patrick stepped back with eyes downcast. He was silent.

"Best we get you out of those clothes and into the tub. Then I'll give you a nice shave and you can sleep before the girls get home. Later, you'll tell me more."

The following days, Lorna coaxed information from Patrick about his trek, but he was more forthcoming when he discussed it with Colin.

"Eighty some thousand prospectors. Best Klondike fields staked," Patrick said with a shake to his head. "What was left was not profitable."

"At least you tried," Colin said. "You could've been one of the lucky ones."

"Mounties made us carry a year's worth of supplies. Had to trudge through wilderness with hundreds of pounds on our backs. Horrendous." Patrick lapsed into sullen pauses. "And bloody cold. Slept outside. Sometimes next to horse and pack-animal carcasses—they called it 'Dead Horse Trail.'"

"Suppose many men also died," Colin said.

"That they did. And some went insane." Patrick rubbed the back of his head. "Got afraid of shadows, heard voices, talked to the dead animals, thinking the beasts knew where the gold was."

Lorna placed her closed fist to her mouth.

"A physical and mental struggle for sure," Colin said.

"Food was scarce," Patrick said. "Had to ration what little we carried."

"We can see from your scrawny frame," Lorna said. "I'm fixing to take good care of you—plenty to eat and a lot of rest."

"That she'll do," Colin said to Patrick. "A good woman can beat the devil."

Patrick sat silent, his eyes fixed on the red and white tablecloth. "There were times after an animal died, men split open their bellies and put their feet and hands inside to keep warm."

The image of freezing men, warming their limbs in the entrails of the dead animals, seared onto Lorna's mind. She wondered if Patrick had to do it. Seeing the painful expression on his face, she couldn't ask. She didn't want him to dredge up memories he was trying to forget.

"Desperate times," Colin said. "Have to do what you have to do."

"Ask him how he got that scar that zigzags across his forehead," Lorna said to Colin. "He won't tell me if he fell, passed out from exhaustion, got into a brawl."

"Been meaning to ask," Colin said. "How did you?"

"Doesn't matter."

"Yes, it does," Lorna said. "Makes it worse not knowing."

Patrick frowned and scooted his chair away from the table. He picked up his tobacco pouch and went outside.

"I'm worried, Colin," Lorna said, after he left. "What else is he not telling us?"

After Patrick's gold search foray, as Lorna called it, he resumed his position as shift boss underground. After a few months, he regained his strength and was less restless, but still had bouts of the doldrums. Fretting he may have an accident during one of his spells, or take up drinking again, she said novenas and rosaries throughout the day and as she fell asleep. If the past taught her anything, she needed to prepare for the worst. And it pained her to think she could be stuck in the Upper Peninsula for all her known days.

Another brutal Michigan winter greeted the Location in January. Lorna, nine months pregnant, was snowbound at home with Patrick and the children. A harsh northern wind battered heavy snowflakes against the crystal-fringed windows, creating drifts that inched halfway up the side of the dwelling.

"Bursting with frigid air tonight," she said to Patrick. "Good you boarded up the windows and put sawdust down."

"Should have gone to the general store before this hit."

"Our inkwells at school froze," Ellen said, looking up from her spelling book.

"You would've found empty shelves," Lorna said to Patrick, referring to suppliers unable to deliver their wares. She was glad she had the foresight to sell and slaughter the last of her chickens before the worst hit; she preserved the meat she kept with the lard she also used as a spread on bread. "I'll lay a good table with what's in the larder. And there's enough flour, bacon, butter and milk to make my baking-powder biscuits you love."

As they baked, she sang her mother's song, "I wandered today to the hill, Maggie," and rested at the kitchen table, her hands stroking her protruding stomach. Patrick helped Andrew ride his burned-wood rocking horse, its head outreached and tail flowing; Grace was reading *Our Little Ones*; and Ellen, her hair bound about her head in two braids, practiced her letters on her slate school board. She wondered if the new baby would be a boy or a girl. It didn't matter because they'd love the child. But she hoped for a son so Andrew would have a brother. Soon she'd have a newborn to tend to along with her other household duties. She'd manage as she always did. But would it ever be possible to leave Ironwood with four youngsters under the age of eight? She couldn't pressure Patrick again. As her father used to say, she had to see that her ship berthed in a calm port.

Their son, Daniel, named after Patrick's brother, was born three days later.

A few days after the Polish Ducking Days Festival on Easter Monday, when the Poles at the mines drenched one another with water and handed out colorfully decorated eggs, Lorna felt her prayers were answered. Patrick started talking about Butte, a place where some of his friends from the Ironwood Hibernica Band had recently settled.

"Michael wrote they're looking for skilled miners, preferably Irish. They run much of the town and the mines. No shortage of work, he says. Need copper for the electricity they're putting in homes."

"We can go when school ends," Lorna said.

"Whoa, castles are built by degrees. Thinking out loud, my little colleen." Patrick lit his cigarette and laughed. After the first puff, his laugh turned into a wet, phlegmy cough.

"You can work in an office. Get away from dust. Better for your cough." Patrick shook his head. She knew what that meant: there was pride in being a miner. Miners were the elites and got more respect; the men who worked above ground were considered unskilled laborers. But working the mines didn't provide extra benefits or privileges, and it didn't lessen the risks.

"Three dollars and fifty cents a day." He coughed again and expectorated, spitting into his large hankie.

"That's plenty reason to start planning," she said.

"A windy day is not a day for thatching. Time and patience bring a snail to Cork."

Despite Patrick's hesitation, Lorna intuited they'd leave Michigan, especially if Patrick had friends there. And so what if it was to a place called Montana? It had to be better than Ironwood. They'd be moving farther away from New Brunswick, making it impossible to see her father again. Like her coming to Michigan meant she never saw her mother again. Maggie died three months after Daniel was born. And her father, nearly sixty years old, no longer plied the high seas. He was content to stay home and read his Gothic novels and whittle, carving wooden owls, fish and spoons.

She thought about taking the children to meet their grandfather before they left. Yet, if she delayed, Patrick might find an excuse to stay put. He always told her to forget about Canada; he and the children were her family now, not relatives in faraway places. As hard as Lorna tried, she needed to cling to hers. If she lost them, she might lose a part of herself.

As she thought about her childhood home, she wondered if mornings were warmer now that summer was near, and if the marshes were full of yellow and white lilies. Were there chanterelles to pick in the woodlands where lupines and Queen Anne's lace sprang up? Were the raspberries in the roadside brambles as sweet as before? And were seagulls flying over the dancing whales with their tail flukes high? If only she could see it one last time.

That night Lorna found it difficult to sleep, envisioning how it would be out West with homesteads miles away from town and its wide-open lands that cowboys herded cattle across. People still talked about fighting the Indians, but she thought the talk exaggerated; the last Indian war was way down near Mexico. And was it true all they said about outlaws, gunslingers and vigilantes? Her mind churned as she listened to the howling wind. It would be difficult to leave her good friends, especially Mrs. Hag. But she wouldn't miss living at the mine with its caves that could gobble up a child with no one knowing. Nor would she miss the itinerant men who drank on Saturdays, keeping the Location residents up all night. But if mining was the principal occupation in Butte, she would likely face more of the same— except she could hope for less paralyzing winters.

As Lorna foresaw, Patrick decided to move to Butte once his friends assured him of work. But he wanted to wait until after Ironwood's Fourth of July celebrations.

"Promised Andrew he could race with his friends in the three-legged race and the bike races," Patrick said. "Two-dollar prize for the winners this year."

Lorna nodded as she gazed at the chalk squiggles Andrew had drawn on the wall. *A last hurrah to this vile place*, she thought to herself.

The Norrie Band and the Curry Rifle Cadets led off the morning parade that included cowboys and clowns. There was an extra feature this year—Uncle Sam and a group of men, supposedly Cubans, leading some Spaniards in tow, to mark the beginning of the end of the Spanish-American War.

Patrick told the children to wave at his friends when the Sons of St. George, the Scandinavian Society, and the Knights of Pythias marched by. After the races in front of the Curry Hotel, Patrick and Andrew watched the broad jump, high hurdles and wrestling matches, while Lorna and the other children wandered among the vendor booths on a main street.

Patrick and Andrew were chopping on watermelon slices when Lorna joined them. "Colin won the drilling contest. Drilled down a foot in twenty minutes."

"Stop swallowing those seeds," Lorna said to Andrew, "your appendix will burst."

Andrew turned and spit a seed onto the wooden walkway.

"Won twelve dollars," Patrick said.

"Then he has no excuse not to come to the supper at St. Ambrose tonight."

"What about us going to the Grand Ball at the Armory?"

"Phooey, Patrick. That's for people who don't have a baby."

He smiled his lopsided smile and flashed his eyebrows. "For a while, my darling colleen. Let me give you a twirl." He took her hand and squeezed it. "It's been too long since it's just you and me out on the town. Ellen can watch Daniel. I promise not to keep you out late."

Patrick won her over and years later, Lorna would think back to this evening and treasure it. It was as if they were young lovers again, savoring each moment in the other's arms. She recalled feeling a lightness, a hope for a new life. That night, their lovemaking had an intensity that harkened back to the days when they were first married, an insatiable desire to belong to each other. Had she known then what the next years would bring, she would have stretched out the seconds longer.

35

CHAPTER 5

◆

May you die in bed at ninety-five, shot by a jealous wife.

As they'd heard, half the population in Butte was Irish. Thinking it would be more agreeable, what Lorna found was a loosely structured Western town where anything went. Morals were lax with a large red-light district and many saloons. And the noise was worse than at the Location.

The town was not as prosperous as Ironwood, nor did it have as many amenities. Instead of communities built around the site of mines where the miners worked, in Butte they were segregated by ethnic community. Each lived in their own area with rules posted in sixteen languages. Patrick rented a cottage in an area called Corktown, next to Dublin Gulch. As much as Lorna disliked the wretchedness of Butte, she wouldn't allow herself to complain, for she had encouraged the move. It was up to her to make the best of it.

In Butte, "the Richest Hill of Earth" as they called it, Lorna once again found their lives controlled by the mines, some of which went twenty-two miles into the earth. One difference was that the mines closed on Irish holidays like St. Patrick's Day and Robert Emmet's birthday.

Patrick was glad to be reunited with his mates, especially Michael, who was also his companion in the mine; all men were required to work with a partner. He no longer held the rank of shift boss, but the pay was better and the men better organized.

Shortly after they arrived, Michael told Patrick and Lorna, "You must join the Ancient Order of Hibernians. You'll get the best jobs and benefits. All the top men are members."

"Blimey, Michael, the initiation fee is too much. Then those yearly dues."

"It'll pay off. But you need to do it straight away. Sick and death benefits don't kick in for six months."

"Have to take my chances. The move here took our savings."

"Ask if they'll postpone the fee. Do it for your family. The Order sponsors picnics, athletic competitions, song fests, poetry readings. And other events that'll make Lorna and the children feel they're a part of things here."

"Kids doing fine. It's an adventure for them. And the Order's Ladies Auxiliary already came round, wanting Lorna to join."

"Are you going to?" he asked Lorna.

She intertwined her arm with Patrick's and leaned close. "Told them with four children I hardly have time to comb the cobwebs out of my hair."

After they'd been in Butte a few months, Lorna often found Patrick staring into space, mumbling under his breath, or forgetting things. She wondered if the arduous trek in British Columbia did more to his psyche than she realized. But she pushed this thought aside and convinced herself it was because he was adjusting to the new job and having to prove himself—until Michael put things in a different light.

"Thought I should tell you, Lorna," Michael said, fingering the metal lamp on his hard hat. "Patrick gets disoriented. Yesterday he wandered away from me underground. It's a labyrinth with all the tunnels that connect the mines. Easy to get lost."

"It's not the drink, is it?"

"Zounds, no, Lorna. The copper collar is like the devil's work. Fear's always with us. Not that strange to see men go off."

See men go off echoed in Lorna's head. She told herself to not say anything to make Michael think she was also concerned, which might prompt him to tell the shift boss. But she understood his concern; no miner wants a partner who cannot be trusted underground.

"He's probably worn out. I'll see he goes to the doctor. No harm in that."

That Sunday, Lorna watched Patrick as he tried to fix a railing on the rocking chair. He fiddled and fiddled with the broken piece. Then he let out a long sigh, sat back and glanced around the room.

"Can I help while you glue it?" Lorna asked, noting this was not the only simple task it took him longer to complete.

Patrick scowled and curled his fingers. "Don't need help."

"You aren't still having flashbacks to Canada, are you?"

He poked his tongue into his cheek and shook his head.

"Must say, you've seemed absentminded. It's been a while since you saw the doctor. Might be good to have a checkup."

He forced a laugh, a slight tremor in his lip. "Ever think you're the problem?"

Patrick never saw the doctor and in late April, when they'd been in Butte less than a year, he didn't come home for dinner one night. Lorna worked herself into a frenzy, fearing he'd reverted to his old ways of meeting friends for a few pints after work. When she later heard footsteps near the front door, she mentally prepared poisonous words to sling at him. But it wasn't Patrick. It was Michael. He asked her to come out on the porch.

"Couldn't come earlier. Patrick's in hospital."

Lorna's anger vaporized. "Is he hurt? He's not dead, is he?"

"No. They found him wandering near the mine shafts." Michael tapped his temple. "He didn't know what he was doing there. Couldn't remember his name." Michael hesitated and fiddled with the handle on his two-tier metal lunch container. "The doctor committed him to Warm Springs, the Psychiatric Hospital."

Lorna felt her eyes widen as panic swept over her. "Psychiatric Hospital?" She rocked her head. "No, no, no."

"It's ten miles outside town. Here are the directions." He handed her a piece of paper, marred with ore dust. "They need you to go and give his personal information."

After Colin left, she sat at the kitchen table, wondering how severe his condition was and trying to imagine what he was going through. Grappling with why this was happening now when they were starting a new life, she questioned if the move was too much after the Yukon. It might've been better for him to stay in the place he knew best.

"Well, I can't sit here and fret. I have to help him," she muttered to herself. And she needed to tell the girls. She practiced a few phrases but when she sat them down, all she said was, "Your father … h-he n-needs to rest."

"Are you OK?" Ellen asked, bewildered by Lorna's garbled words.

"I'm fine . . ." Lorna took in a big breath. "Your father's in hospital."

"What's wrong with him?" Grace asked.

"You've heard us talk about miners with too much silica in their lungs." Both girls nodded. "It's happened to your father."

At first, Lorna was surprised the girls retained their composure. *But they've already been through much in their young lives. They're resilient.*

Lorna arranged for a neighbor to take care of Andrew and Daniel the next day. When she arrived at the General Office of the State Hospital, the receptionist told her to go to the doctor's cottage where he was writing up his notes from rounds. The steep gabled, ivy-covered shingled house was close by. She waited on the long wraparound porch until the doctor's wife escorted her to a small room that served as his home office.

"Born in Ireland. Forty-four last birthday. Did a bit of drinking, but that's behind him." She stared at the anatomy chart on the wall, her eyes scanning without seeing the stripped away man. "Hunted gold in Canada. Took the spittle out of him for a while." She dug in her sleeve for her handkerchief and dabbed her nose. "Maybe more than I knew."

"He displays signs of apathy and a loss of motivation. This isn't necessarily caused by emotional distress, intellectual impairment or diminished level of consciousness. We see these symptoms in miners who are exhausted, worn down by harsh lives."

"He's always worked hard and we have four little ones at home." She took a deep breath and gulped at the air. "When can he go back to work?"

"He won't. He could make a mistake and cause an explosion or a cave in." The doctor shifted in his chair. "Could get lost and run out of oxygen in deeper depths."

As the doctor's words sank in, Lorna stroked the black lace and faux flowers on her hat that rested on her lap. Her cherished hope of a decent, if not easy, life in Butte flickered out. If Patrick was unable to work, she'd have to be the sole breadwinner. In Ironwood she had her vegetables and chickens, but here she had nothing.

"I suggest you don't see him yet," the doctor said. "Wait till we stabilize him."

"He'll be all right here, won't he?"

The doctor nodded. "We'll supply comfort and support."

On the way back to Butte, she again blamed herself for pushing Patrick to leave Michigan. But she'd done what she thought was best for him and the children. The hardship of ten to twelve-hour shifts, six days a week, and the responsibility of the family would crack the strongest man.

After word got round Patrick wouldn't be returning to the mines, Lorna asked Michael where she could find work.

"He should've joined the Hibernians. They'd be taking care of you, if he'd done it."

"No use dwelling on that. Have to find a way to take care of the children."

"Heard a manager at the mine needs a household servant for cooking and cleaning. Has a couple of kids. Name's Hugh Walsh."

Household servant slapped Lorna in the face. She never imagined she'd be anyone's servant. She could have been a lady, isn't that what her mother said? But if the man would have her, she'd have to do it until she figured out something else.

That evening she set the three oldest down and told them, "Your father has to stay in hospital longer."

"You said he'd come home soon," Grace said, curling her arms over her head.

"It takes time to get all the silica out." She didn't like lying, but she worried they wouldn't understand the real reason. "I have to get a job to take care of us."

"What will you do?" asked Ellen.

"A manager needs a housekeeper. Hopefully, it won't be for long." Lorna stroked her brow. "I'll try to find something to do from home—like I did in Ironwood."

"I can work," said Andrew.

"Sweet boy, you're only four. It's your time to be a child," Lorna said. "But I'll need you girls to take care of your brothers and the house." She watched their reactions; they sat solemn as monks at the altar. "I don't like you missing school and having so much responsibility."

"It's fine, Momma," Ellen said. "I can do it and Grace can stay in school."

"Hope Daddy gets better soon," Grace said, picking up one of the paper dolls she and Ellen made from Sears Roebuck catalogs.

Lorna didn't tell them she prayed against hope Patrick would recover. And her hope allowed her to believe her children's lives wouldn't be affected without their father.

Pride was filling up her apron as Lorna entered service for Mr. Walsh. Over the next months, she visited Patrick each Sunday, her one day off. He often seemed in a dream state, barely aware of his surroundings. Her chest tightened when she saw him in his ward filled with white cots lined up against the wall, one next to the other. She consoled herself he was better off than patients in another area who slept on thin mattresses on the floor and had physical restraints on their wrists, ankles and waists—and screamed and howled.

One Sunday, as they walked on a pathway around the side of the building, she said in the most chipper tone she could muster, "The children are doing well. They're growing fast. You won't recognize them when you come home."

"Little darlings."

"We miss you and can't wait for you to come home." She took his face and turned it toward her. "I'll fix you a good old Irish coddle." He closed his eyes and nodded. "How are you doing?"

"Bloody monotonous. Same routine every day." He shielded the sun from his eyes with the back of his hand and squinted up at a sycamore tree. "Coarse food. But the staff likes me and treat me well. The doctors like me, too."

"Who wouldn't like you, you big old lug," she said, her voice breaking. "Oh, a giant water bug." She grabbed Patrick's arm and shied away from the creature.

"Three things hardest to understand; the mind of women, the work of the bees, the coming and going of the tide." He picked up the bug and flung it across the yard.

Hearing him utter this saying, Lorna dared to think he might get better.

But then he stood still as a boulder and looked around the grounds, as if searching for something. "I'm afraid to die."

For a moment, Lorna was at a loss of what to say or do next. "You're not going to die. What makes you think that?"

"Death doesn't take a bribe."

"Listen, you're going to be fine." She stroked his forehead, her fingers tracing his scar. "You'll come home and we'll all be together."

The journey home, Lorna couldn't stop wondering if Patrick was giving up. He'd drawn inward, never asking how she was managing, and she never told him she was working for a family that gave her leftovers and used clothing. She didn't want to offend his pride should he have some lucidity. She couldn't help but compare his diminished state to how vital and charming he once was, the Patrick Ryan she fell in love with.

There had to be a way to encourage him and help him stop thinking morbid thoughts. *I have to get him home, even if he's not all there. Better than wasting away in this lifeless place. The children need their father.*

When Lorna arrived at the Walsh home one morning, Mr. Walsh said, "I need to speak to you. Please come into my study." As he motioned for her to sit down, Lorna felt a flurry of panic as she tried to think if anything had gone wrong the last days, or if she did something he didn't approve of. But there was nothing she was aware of.

"Yesterday afternoon, the hospital informed the company Patrick escaped."

Lorna reared back in her chair. "What? Weren't they watching him?"

"I'm told they have strict security measures and a vigilant staff, but it takes only a moment for someone to wander off."

"They said they'd take good care of him."

"The hospital and local officials started searching as soon as they discovered he was gone."

"What can I do?

"Pray. Plenty of experienced people are looking for him."

Lorna could barely sleep, nor focus on her job and the children while they searched for Patrick. Constant worry distracted her; she singed one of Mr. Walsh's dress shirts; one of his children nearly choked on a marble while she was tending them; she broke one of the rosettes- pierced, gilded Spode dessert dishes the family used for entertaining. Lorna feared she'd lose her job and didn't know where she'd turn next to find other employment.

Realizing how inattentive she was, she had to help look for Patrick or she'd cause more mishaps. She asked Mr. Walsh if she could take a day or two off.

"I know it's stressful," he said, "but I don't know if there's much you can do."

"A wife's intuition."

Mr. Walsh silently nodded. "If it'll make you feel better."

She decided it was no use looking around the hospital because they'd searched that area well. So, the next day she set off for Anaconda, the town nearest the hospital. She visited every establishment and stopped every person she encountered, showing them a photo of Patrick. No one had seen him.

Her hopes dashed after a few hours of roaming the streets, she needed to rest and plot a new strategy. She went to the new Hearst Free Library. As she poured over a map of the town, she overhead the librarian telling a man the history of the nearby smelter plant.

"They process the copper from Butte. It's up near Deer Lodge Valley. They built it there so the winds would carry the gasses and smoke away from the city and farms. Can't miss the big smokestack and the smells."

After the man left, Lorna approached the librarian and told her about Patrick. She asked the woman if she had any suggestions of where she should look next.

"Miners like to be around mining," the woman said. "It's where they feel a connection. I doubt he'd stay around here. Head back to Butte."

It made sense Patrick would return to the places he knew best, and fruitless for her to spend another day in Anaconda.

When she arrived home, Ellen asked why she was home so late. She hadn't told the children their father was missing, so she never told them she went to search for him. "Extra ironing today." Lorna removed her hat and plopped on the sofa. "Did you eat?"

"Ellen heated up the stew from yesterday," Grace said. "Know what, Momma? My teacher selected me to recite 'The Owl and the Pussycat' in front of the class. I memorized all of it. Do you want to hear it?"

Lorna nodded and rested her head on the back of the sofa, closing her eyes while Grace rattled off the poem, complete with hand gestures and swaying hips. After she finished, Ellen said to Lorna, "We left some stew for you."

Lorna didn't answer. She was sound asleep.

Two days later, they found Patrick wandering outside the Pabst mine in Butte.

"Slept outside and was dehydrated," the doctor told Lorna. "The staff and I discussed Patrick's prognosis. We don't think he'll ever function in society again." Lorna's hand flew up to cover her mouth. "There's always the chance he'll improve, but from my experience, it's unlikely."

Lorna riveted her eyes on the brass balance scale and weights on the doctor's desk. "Will he return home?" she said in a voice so low it was almost a whisper.

"Probably not."

She wondered how much credence to give to the doctor's words. Hadn't Grace recovered when the doctor told her she wouldn't. She looked up at the doctor with an unwavering eye. *I'll manage. I always do. I don't know how, but I will.* And she thought of her father. *Calm seas never produce able sailors.*

CHAPTER 6

♦

Death leaves a heartache no one can heal,
love leaves a memory no one can steal.

Ellen kept up on her studies and included Grace, reading nightly about the fundamentals of arithmetic, grammar and U.S. history. Though the girls were diligent, Lorna decided it wasn't fair for Ellen to miss school, and for both girls to be saddled with so much responsibility. She hated to admit it, but she needed help. Perhaps the Hibernians or the parish priest could suggest something.

Doubting the Order would give her more than sympathy, since Patrick never joined, she first went to Father Collins at St. Lawrence's. His was the largest parish, and she figured it would have the most resources. The pastor lamented he had limited means and many parishioners to care for. Next, she saw Father Lynch at St. Patrick's, the church she and the children attended. He consoled her and his response was the same. But he suggested she go to Sacred Heart. "It's a smaller congregation. But it has a new priest who recently came from Helena. He might have an idea."

When she met with Father Casey, he was silent for a few moments before saying, "There's an excellent boarding school in Helena. Run by the Sisters of Charity. I'll talk to them. This way, you can keep your job and they'll get the education they need."

"The boys are too young for school. I don't want them separated."

"All ages are there. They'll stay together."

"You say it's a good school?"

"One of the best. The Sisters consider St. Joseph's their mission in life. They'll be well cared for."

She answered with a small nod. "I have no other choice."

"I'll see if they can be admitted next week."

"Only until I work something out—I don't want to be away from them."

Arriving in Helena, Lorna quickly found St. Joseph's. The large fenced-in brick Gothic building, with its multiple chimneys to let out steam heat, was in the center of town. The large cross on top stood out against the neighboring hills.

Cradling Daniel on the edge of her hip, she leaned forward to read the brass plaque next to the door. Her heart sank to her knees. She straightened up and took a step back. "Made a mistake. This isn't the place." Lorna tightened her grip on Andrew's hand and started back down the steps. "We're going home."

As she was walking away, a nun called out to her. "Hello, I'm Sister Catherine."

"The priest made a mistake. I'm taking my children to a boarding school."

"This is the right place. We're expecting you."

"You don't understand. My children have a father and mother."

"Many of the children here have parents. It's only until you're able to have them with you."

Lorna felt a tightness inside. Her children were not being forcefully taken from her, but it felt as if they were. For a person without choice, everything seems like a violation.

"Come in. I'll show you around," the nun said, fingering the edge of her white bib. "You'll see how nice it is, and your children can meet some of the other students."

"Momma," Ellen said. "Let's go in." Ellen, in her eight-year-old wisdom, also knew they had no choice.

As Sister Catherine escorted them into the building, she said, "We are one of the finest institutions in the West. We purchased the land seven years ago and built St. Joseph's with money donated by companies, business managers and friends of our Order."

"It's pretty here," Ellen said.

Lorna feigned a smile. She imagined Ellen and Grace would marvel at living in such a grand place after their little cottage.

"This building houses the girls and young children up to age five," the nun continued. "The older boys live in a separate building next door. All your children will be together in this building." The Sister patted Andrew on the head. "Some children have no surviving parents and we maintain them with food, clothing, shelter and education. We ask for small contributions from those who have parents."

Lost in thought, the nun's words blurred into nothingness for Lorna.

The nun pointed out a large window to a plot of land alongside the building. "We plan to cultivate land around here to supply some of our needs. Boys who are large enough for farm work will do their share."

A bell went off and the halls filled with neatly dressed children, the boys in navy pants and jackets with a wide white collar, and the girls with belted navy dresses and the white trim at the collar. The youngest girls wore white dresses.

"While the children are on recess, let's see our chapel. It was a donation from a local family." She took them into a darkened room with a marble altar. The sister genuflected and made the sign of the cross. "With all the temptations in the world today, we guide the steps of our children here along the righteous path of life."

"I want you to know," Lorna said with pursed lips, "I've taught my children well. They're already righteous."

"I didn't intend to insinuate they weren't. Oh, here comes Sister Stephanie. She'll take them to their rooms."

Lorna grasped Andrew's hand tighter as Sister Stephanie took Daniel from her.

"We'll be fine, Momma," Ellen said. "We can play with the kids, and Sister is nice."

Lorna looked first at Ellen and then Grace, her gaze lingering a moment on each of her daughters. "It's only for a while. I'll visit as much as possible."

After the children were taken away, Lorna hid in a recess near the staircase. She gripped a fistful of her blouse and doubled over, her body shaking as she trapped sobs in her throat. *Why this now after losing Patrick?* She crumpled to the floor and put both hands over her ears, rocking back and forth. *Get up,* she told herself; *no one must see you, especially the children.* After wiping her tears, she gathered up her skirt, teetering as she rose. She stood there fixed for some moments, her eyes boring into the tile floor. Then her expression hardened and she looked ahead. *I'll never tell Patrick his children are in an orphanage.*

As Patrick became more lethargic and less able to communicate, Lorna stopped going to Warm Springs each Sunday. She rested up to travel once a month to Helena, some forty-eight miles away. While visiting, her children clung to her but they appeared happy, eager to tell her all they were doing and learning. They rarely complained and assured her everything was fine. She often thought they comforted her more than she did them. On one of her visits, the Mother Superior asked to see her.

"Grace is having debilitating headaches," Mother Barbara told Lorna. "Sometimes she's so ill we have to send her to bed."

"She had diphtheria when she was five. Could it be from that?"

"A residual effect? I don't know. But they're interfering with her studies."

"She's a sensitive child. She's worried about her father."

"They don't know how sick he is?"

"I don't want to tell them. It's hard enough being separated." Lorna crossed her arms and her expression went slack. "I haven't told them I had to give up the cottage. I want them to think they have a home to come back to."

"Where are you living?"

"With my employer and his family." Her voice broke as she continued, "I never thought they'd stay here so long."

"You made the right decision," the Mother Superior said. "You did it as an act of love. You're giving your children the best opportunities during difficult times."

The next time Lorna visited St. Joseph's she was shocked to see Grace's long strawberry-blond hair had been shorn.

"Holey Moley, what did they do to your beautiful curls?" Lorna bellowed, calling to mind how she'd often brush Grace's hair a hundred strokes before bed.

Grace wrapped her arms around herself and looked down. As Ellen watched her sister, she cracked a knuckle and said, "We were getting in bed and Sister Jaqueline came with scissors. She said she had to cut her hair because it was too long and making her sick."

Grace glanced up at Lorna. "I said I'd never have another headache if she didn't cut it."

"She kept telling Sister she was sorry," Ellen said. "I asked Sister not to do it. But she wouldn't stop. I told her you wouldn't like it."

"Darn right, I don't. Those blasted nuns always have their bowels in an uproar."

Lorna flew off to find Sister Jaqueline.

"How dare you cut Grace's hair without my permission. You want everything to be dull and drab."

Sister Jaqueline fiddled with the rosary beads hanging from her belt. "We do what's best for the children."

"Balderdash." Lorna resisted the urge to pull off the nun's veil. "Long hair doesn't give you a headache. What poppycock. Don't you so much as tie a ribbon in their hair."

On her way back to the children, the clacking of the nun's rosary beads hammered in her head. *Dear God, why this now?* She had something else to mourn—the loss of Grace's hair that later grew in darker.

The beginning of September, Lorna received word the hospital doctor wanted to see her. A premonition of impending misfortune gripped her.

As she waited for the doctor in his office, she felt she was suffocating. Did Patrick escape again? Was he injured? Was his condition becoming more hopeless? She tried to still her mind, but she was cemented in a state of alarm.

The doctor entered and after some pleasantries, he took a folder from a desk drawer. "I'm very sorry to tell you Patrick had a cerebral hemorrhage and passed away."

Lorna felt the ground beneath her vaporize. She sat back and shook her head. "No. No. It's not true. It can't be."

"It was sudden," he said. "We don't think he suffered."

Tears formed as she clutched her cramping stomach.

The doctor handed her the death certificate. Through a fog of denial, Lorna scanned the document. "It doesn't say hemorrhage. It says exhaustion."

"Exhaustion was the underlying cause that led to the chain of events that resulted in his death. His hemorrhage was the immediate, final cause of death."

"He was supposed to get better here. You let him escape."

"His escape was unfortunate, but it didn't change his condition. We did all we could."

She stared at the paper in her hands. "I wanted him to come home. That kept me going. What do I do now?"

"If you recall, I mentioned we didn't believe he'd be able to rejoin society."

Lorna was still for a few moments. "How am I going to tell the children? They love their father."

"So much love never ends a life. The moments you had with him will always live in your hearts." The doctor came around the desk and put his hand on Lorna's shoulder. "The staff will prepare his body for burial."

For a long time that night, Lorna sat on her bed in her dimly lit room, paralyzed by the uncertainty of what lay ahead. She felt empty and alone. Her hope of being a family again had evaporated like filaments of smoke from a candle. She wondered if she had the strength to carry on. But she had to—for her children.

Michael held a wake at his home the night before the church funeral Mass. Patrick's body, clad in his Sunday suit, was laid out in a wooden coffin in the parlor. Lorna placed a rosary in his hands, and on his breast, she put a crucifix and his bowler hat. She remained next to the coffin, her hand resting on his, as mourners offered condolences. Their words of comfort fell on deaf ears. How could any of them understand how adrift she felt?

"His vast vocabulary gave him more curse words than most learn in a lifetime," Sean Cassidy said, saluting Patrick's body.

Michael had stopped the clock and turned the mirror toward the wall as a mark of respect. Lit candles sat on a table, alongside bread, meats, whiskey, pipes of tobacco and snuff.

"Here's to your fairy tales, your horror stories and Irish myths," Paddy Brady said, raising his glass of stout to Patrick first and then to Lorna.

Lorna felt some consolation with Patrick's friends and their families gathering to celebrate his life and ensure he had a good sendoff. She hoped Patrick could look down and see all of them honoring him—so many, they overflowed into the street.

Tommy Cahill moved to the center of the room. "He used to say, *The quiet one's often guilty*. But we'll never say that about old talkative Patrick. May you be half an hour in heaven before the Devil knows you're dead."

Because they considered his death a significant loss, leaving behind a wife and children, the mourners wailed and keened. Their muffled sobs remained with Lorna for weeks, as did all they said about her Patrick.

After high Mass the following day, Lorna buried Patrick in the church cemetery without a headstone, without identification, in an unmarked plot of land that told no one of the man who had lived and been loved.

Lorna went to Helena the following Sunday. Sitting on a bench outside, she gathered the three oldest around and hoisted up Daniel on her lap. The boy rested his head against her breast and sucked his thumb.

Lorna stroked the cross around her neck and said, "The doctors couldn't get everything out of your father's airways." She looked away and was silent. It was too painful to speak of Patrick's death. As she struggled to continue, she felt a warm wind on the back of her neck. It was as if his presence lingered, telling her to go on.

"His hardscrabble life took a lot out of him. It was hard for him to keep fighting the sickness." She paused. "He died and is in heaven now."

Silent tears formed in the eyes of the girls. Seeing them, Lorna felt her eyelashes get damp. "Always remember, he loved you more than anything." Her voice cracked as she continued, "He'll always be with us and we'll always love him and keep him in our hearts."

And she thought back to the Grand Ball at the Armory.

CHAPTER 7

◆

*Firelight will not let you read fine stories, but it's
warm, and you won't see the dust on the floor.*

As Lorna toiled for the manager of the copper mine over the next two years, she tried daily to devise a way to bring home her children. Each year Mr. Walsh increased her salary an extra two dollars per week, but it was not enough to save up to rent a place and start a business. After much internal debate, she concluded the only way to bring her children home would be to marry again. It wouldn't be easy. Few men were willing to take on another man's children. And she couldn't be picky this time.

She looked in the mirror and ran her hands down her silhouette, pausing briefly at her tiny waist, proud of her curvy figure after four children. Spotting a few gray hairs, she plucked them out.

A few of Patrick's friends invited her out, but she never accepted, nor encouraged them. In some strange way, she felt it wouldn't be right—like she was being unfaithful to Patrick. In Butte, the Irish had an informal dating service, but she didn't contact them. She didn't know if it was because she was wary of marrying another Irishman, or because one may remind her too much of Patrick. At least in Butte it wasn't unusual to select a partner from outside one's community, which didn't happen in other mining towns.

One day, Lorna dressed in her best frock with its tight-fitting bodice and pinched waist and went to one of the local photography studios. On her head, she rakishly perched what looked like a man's top hat and looked straight at the camera, a confident smile on her face. She told the owner to place the photo in his storefront window until she came for it.

Not long after, a fireman at the mine sought Lorna out. As she took in his stocky physique and semi-hooded eyes that suggested hidden inner thoughts, she couldn't help but compare him to Patrick—her tall, handsome Patrick with sparkling eyes that hinted of romance and adventure.

Max invited her to a performance at the Curtis Music Hall and practicality won over desire. She didn't spurn him.

After the performance of six-act skits of comedy, magic and singing, they meandered up Park Street to the Board of Trade Saloon and Café. The main clientele were miners. When Lorna entered, a man motioned to her. She frowned and kept her gaze down as she followed Max to a table. As she sat down, another man winked at her. She asked Max, "Why bring me here? Doesn't seem fit for women."

"There are women here." Max pointed to two other women sitting nearby. But these women didn't concern her. It was the ones who hung over men's shoulders, tickling their faces, sitting on their laps. She overheard one of them say, "Two dollars for the works."

The owner came over and Max ordered two plates of the daily stew with biscuits, and requested he bring two ales at once. "Biscuits are the best here."

"Humph, probably not as good as mine," she muttered. A man sitting catty corner to her puckered up his lips and made smacking gestures. She looked away and told herself to not overreact. She'd been around mines long enough to have seen these men who sought companionship, and even love, amid the uncertainties of a mining life.

While they waited for their meals, Lorna asked Max, "How long have you been here?"

"Butte—five years." He took a gulp of his beer and used his sleeve to wipe foam from his mouth.

Lorna recoiled. *My Patrick would never do that.*

"Came from Bavaria with my family when I was five. Lived in Pennsylvania. That's where I started in the mines."

"Where do you live here?" She took care to keep suspicion out of her voice.

"At the Thornton."

Lorna knew of these houses that boarded the men who worked in shifts, many occupying a bed that a worker had emptied as he left for the next shift.

He told of his work as a fireman in the mine, explaining the various safety measures used to protect the miners. Lorna listened, but found her mind wandering. He gave the impression he was rigid in his habits and loathe to speak of anything intimate. Always talking about himself, he never asked her much. He knew she was a widow with four children, but didn't inquire further. The exact opposite of Patrick. She missed Patrick's sayings. Where once they drove her mad, she now yearned to hear them with their sprinklings of wisdom, sarcasm, or wit.

When the evening ended, she doubted she'd see Max again. She hadn't flattered him or feigned interest. It surprised her when he invited her the following Saturday to the local dance hall. She accepted. It might be a while for another man to come around.

At the dance, a local band filled the air with lively tunes. Miners dressed in their best attire gathered alongside women in simple dresses. The atmosphere was carefree, a respite from the hardships of the mines. As the music played, Lorna and Max twirled and swayed, and Lorna saw another side to Max. Perhaps she'd been too harsh with her initial impressions.

The following weeks, she saw Max nearly every Saturday night or Sunday. While conversations still focused on him, she found there were other facets about him she enjoyed. When they walked in the hills outside town, he'd tell her about the latest Mark Twain book he'd read, and showed her some of the wooden animals he'd carved. He'd also made his own bladder fiddle, or bumbass as he called it. The raw, earthy music he played on it seemed to have a personal resonance, one that transported him back to childhood.

And Max was reliable. She could count on him to meet her when he said he would, and he followed through on things he said he'd do, like pick up the darning needles she requested.

After a brief courtship, Max asked Lorna if she'd be willing to marry him. Marriage was what she wanted but she wished she could wait longer. Her mother warned her about men's wiles and how they can put on an act and hide their genuine characters for a while. But it was difficult for them to keep it up for a year. However, if she waited, she'd be without her children longer. It was also possible Max wouldn't wait. She sensed he was tired of being alone, tired of living with other riotous miners, and he wanted someone to take care of him, cook his meals, clean his clothes. *The older men get*, she mused, *the more they want a mother*. She decided to gamble if it meant being with her children again. Wasn't this what she'd been praying for? She could not turn down God's answer to her prayers.

"I'll marry you only if all my children live with us. And you have to promise to treat them as your own."

Max's eyes roamed from her waist up to her ample breast. "I'll do that."

With this assurance and a prayer, Lorna, at thirty-four years of age, married Max in a simple ceremony at City Hall. They moved into a company cottage in Finntown, near Finnish friends of Max's with whom he'd forged a strong bond owing to their shared dangers and fear of death. As soon as she settled their rented house, she brought the children back from Helena. They were happy to be with her, but wary of Max; he had not been around children much and their playfulness irritated him.

"*Osti*. Can't be worse than those hell-raising miners you lived with," Lorna told him when he complained about the noise the children made.

"The screeching and running around rattles my nerves."

"They're children. They're supposed to run and make noise. You'll get used to it."

"Why me? They should learn to be quiet."

Lorna wondered if Max and the children would ever adjust to each other. She soon realized she needed to plan should something happen to Max, or another unforeseen calamity befall her. She could depend only on herself. And to do this, she needed her own means.

"Max, I should start a business to help with expenses. The kids are growing and need more, and I can't expect you to do it all."

"What do you have in mind?"

"A daily lunch service, like the ones in Ironwood. Standard fare. Boiled meat, corn, potatoes and bread. Fifty cents a meal, if paying in advance."

"You sure you'll have time? There's the house and family."

Ha, Lorna thought, *worried I won't be paying you the attention you think you deserve.* "Adding a few more meals to my cooking won't take much. But I'll need you to set me until I have enough customers."

Max pressed his lips flat and let out a slight growl.

"I'll pay you back with interest, if that's what it'll take."

Max had Lorna sign a promissory note, and within several months she paid him back. By the beginning of the new year, she was doing well enough that when a frame stable on Grand Street Alley in town came up for sale at a good price, she purchased it. It was a bit on the flimsy side, but she rented it to a local doctor for his horse and carriage. She didn't tell Max about the property until she had the deed in her hand. When Max found out, he said, "That piece of junk? You should have asked me before you bought it?"

"I don't need your permission. I bought it with my earnings and it's a good investment."

"You're a woman. What makes you think you know a good investment?"

She gave him a chin flick. "*Osti.* Don't go thinking you know more than me."

One Sunday morning when she returned from checking on her stable, she found Max in his button-up, long-sleeved wool undershirt muttering, "Shite, shite." He was standing over the stove holding a cast-iron skillet, his head turned sideways to avoid the splattering grease.

"Burner's too hot for melting," she said, trying to hide her annoyance. "What in God's name are you doing?"

"I can get my breakfast without you." When the lard liquefied, he poured it into it the bowl of dry ingredients he'd readied on the table. She watched as he added boiling water from the kettle and mixed everything together with a round-bladed knife. She grabbed the flour from the pantry, but before she could sprinkle it on the table, he said, "Off with you. I'll make my own."

She plopped the bag on the table and thrust her fists on her hips. "Will you be having marmalade or huckleberry jam?"

"Eggs." He rolled out the dough, and cut out the oatcakes half an inch thick, careful to keep the offcuts he could re-roll to make more. After placing the cakes on a greased baking sheet, he turned to open the stove door. He hit the edge of the baking sheet straddling the tabletop and tossed the oatcakes across the room. They crumbled into hundreds of pieces.

"Guess you showed me alright."

Max hurled venomous words at her.

She closed her eyes and pinched the bridge of her nose. *Fine stew. What if he gets up and leaves?* "Sorry I wasn't here to fix it for you." She forced a smile, signaling all was right between them.

Even if life with Max was a compromise, Lorna believed she made the right decision to marry him. He was agreeable enough most of the time. And she could tolerate his annoying habits like when he blew his nose into her cloth napkins, or answered in one-word replies, or his reluctance to bathe regularly. The one thing that bothered her to no end was Max treating her girls better than the boys.

"You're imagining things. I discipline them because they need it—drowning those kittens."

"The Wilson brothers did that. They only tagged along."

"Pissing on the porch, spitting in the sink."

"They never did that." She gave the end of her sleeve a hard tug." The nuns and I taught them good manners."

"Better to shape them up now or they'll get into real trouble later."

Holding her impatience at bay, she said, "Don't be an overlord. I don't want them being afraid of you."

"Advice not asked for, advice poorly heard." He folded his chubby hands over his belly. "Like that Spaniard told me; *Cría cuervos y te sacarán los ojos.*"

"You'll be telling me, Max, what that means," Lorna said, arms akimbo.

"Raise crows and they tear your eyes out." Max leaned back in his chair, tipping up the front legs.

Lorna grabbed one of the chair legs, flinging Max onto the floor.

"What's wrong with you, woman?"

"*Osti.* I raised my children well." She swatted his arm. "Nincompoops, you and your friend."

"You've spent too much time around mines. You're as crude as a coal miner."

Lorna focused her gaze to the side and gave Max a *Tabarnak.*

Daily life in Butte changed little the next two years. The population increased as the mines were supplying around one-third of the copper for the country. And Lorna continued to build her lunch business. As she increased her clientele, she tried to follow her mother Maggie's maxim: *Take the world nice and easy, and the world will take you the same.*

"Have to say, woman, you've done built yourself a fine little business with those lunches."

Lorna smiled. It wasn't often Max complimented her. But she learned from his friends he was proud of all she'd accomplished. They'd tell her Max called her the best business lady of the mines, and he talked about how hard she worked to bring in extra money and ease their lives.

It was another weekday like any other when Lorna went to the dry goods store to get sugar and flour. While she was talking with the proprietor, she heard a commotion coming from the street. A minute later, a man flung open the front door and popped his head in. "The old stable on Grand Alley's on fire. Need all the help we can get."

Lorna stiffened and froze. "That's my stable." She left her items on the counter and rushed out, a frisson of fear surrounding her. She heard the fire's crackling sounds before she saw the flames shooting out of the windows and door. Several men formed a line and passed buckets of water to douse on the blaze. Off to the side, she saw two men standing next to the doctor's carriage; singe marks accented the edges of its black leather top.

"Rushed right in and got the carriage out," a man next to Lorna said. "Mighty brave."

"Where's the horse?" She asked the man with a tremble to her voice.

"Figure it wasn't there. They wouldn't have left it."

Lorna hoped the man was right and the animal was safe. Helplessness weighed on her as she watched as the fire gain strength and fan out rapidly inside the stable. Thick plumes of black smoke billowed into the sky and the crackling and popping sounds intensified. She placed both hands on her face and shook her head from side to side as the roof collapsed, raining down debris.

She heard a clanging bell in the distance and saw the fire department's horse-drawn hose cart turn the corner. As they were hooking up their hose, flames swallowed up the structure. The walls splintered and crumbled under the intense heat. Jets of water arced through the air as the firemen contained its spread to the neighboring wooden buildings. It was a total loss.

"What caused it?" Lorna asked one of the firemen as he doused the burning embers.

"Can't say for sure. A spark from a lantern, or someone threw a cigarette. Could've ignited the dry hay and old wooden beams."

After everyone left, Lorna remained, staring blindly at the charred debris and smoldering embers. "Tarnation, *Sidhe*," she muttered, "you lost me my income."

She tried to remember what else was in the building besides the hay and feed. There was a set of rubber-tired wheels the doctor kept there, a hammer and nails, a chair, a bench, and a brush and feed bucket for the horse. She dreaded telling the doctor and lamented she'd have to return part of that month's rent. She gave her head a toss. She'd manage, just as she'd managed before.

When she told Max about the fire, he said, "Before you buy another stupid ramshackle building, you talk to me."

"It wasn't stupid. It gave us good income. If I had to do it all over again, I would." She titled her head up and raised an eyebrow.

Later, when she received thirty dollars from the insurance company for the fire, Max's demeanor changed. "It's an omen," he said. "Means we should leave here."

Lorna knew employees at the mines often could not work beyond their mid-forties, and Max's job as a fireman had additional risks. His nightmares about getting crushed or falling down shafts were getting worse. He worried each day may be his last.

"There's this offer from Northern Pacific." He pulled a newspaper advertisement from his back pants pocket and handed it to Lorna. "Cheap passage to the West if you settle there. Plenty of money-making opportunities."

The ad to Puget Sound told of farming, forest work, fishing and mineral wealth. And to lure people into populating the area, the railroad offered to sell the land they owned near the towns they built near the Pacific Ocean.

"Your insurance money will get us there."

"What will you do there?"

"I'll find a way." He took the ad back from Lorna. "I'm sick of you cursing this place under your breath. You think I don't hear, but I do."

"I'm not going to another hellhole."

"Didn't look at the picture on the other side, did you?" He handed back the ad.

Lorna's eyes locked on the artist's sketch of mountains, forests and water, under the heading: *Tacoma, City of Destiny on Commencement Bay. Terminus of the first railroad to the Northwest.*

Could it be more like her childhood home? It would mean uprooting her family again, but she wouldn't be sad to leave the physical and psychological violence of Butte. And there was no mention of mines.

As Patrick used to say, *May the road rise up to meet you.*

CHAPTER 8

♦

'Tis true, many a sudden change takes place on a spring day.

The Pacific Northwest was everything Lorna hoped for. It reminded her of Canada: breezes off the sea; ships moored in the harbor; fresh seafood and fish, apples and myriad berries. At the railroad terminus in Tacoma, people touted the opportunities farther north where there was a need for loggers to mine trees, farmers to till the fertile land, and fishermen to augment the growing canning industry. After a few nights in Tacoma, Lorna, Max and the four children headed north.

In Everett, known as the City of Smokestacks, Max found work in one of the mills on the waterfront that made shingles for houses. The owner of the company, a Mr. Kearny, arranged for them to move into his apartment house. The Kearny Court Apartments was a three-story frame house with a suite of rooms for the family, and extra units for Lorna to manage as a boarding house. For one of her first duties, she prepared a detailed list of House Rules and Regulations: Rents must be paid promptly in advance; no dogs or cats allowed in the building; no sleeping overnight of guests; radio must be turned low at ten p.m.; no loud talking or laughing in the halls; do not raise windows above shades, allowing them to flap.

They had more than enough to cover living expenses with both of their jobs, but Lorna also took in laundry to save extra. She wanted to send Ellen and Grace to secretarial college, imagining a better life for them.

As in Butte, Max worked long hours and socialized after work with the Swedes, Norwegians and Croatians that settled in the area to work as lumberjacks, mill workers, and fishermen. On Sundays, Max rented a horse and carriage, and he and Lorna established the habitude of riding around town; he in a suit and top hat, and she in her finest frocks and wide-brimmed hats.

Life settled into a comfortable rhythm for Lorna, except it still bothered her how Max often treated Andrew and Daniel.

"Boys can't go fishing this weekend," Max said one night. "They didn't take out all the trash yesterday, and they left streaks when they washed the windows."

"What are you talking about?" Lorna crossed her arms and gave him a sharp look. "They're going fishing."

"Didn't look at the windows good, did you?" Max said. "They should take on more chores instead of lazing around."

"Is this the way you grew up? Strict discipline and work all the time?" She finger-tapped on the tabletop. "I never hear you go on about the girls."

Max didn't say anything for a few moments. "Men need to be strong. Wait and see how fine they'll turn out."

Controlling her tone, she said, "They've already turned out fine and don't need your crazy dictates. They need to enjoy life while they're young."

He looked in the mirror and fussed with his hair. "The man of the house sets the rules."

"I'm their mother and I decide what's best." Her nails bit into her palms. "Don't you drive my sons away."

Lorna once feared her children would feel she'd abandoned them. But they never showed any lingering negative effects from their years away from her. As hard as it was, she had to admit they were probably better off at St. Joseph's because the nuns fostered their growth and academics. Besides the basics, the nuns taught Ellen and Grace to sew and they cultivated her daughters' artistic abilities. They discovered Grace, besides drawing well, had a lovely voice. The nun in charge of the choral group gave her singing lessons and she joined the older students at the singing of Mass in the chapel. The nuns also gave the boys a sense of responsibility and discipline. As they grew older, they did minor jobs at the orphanage, giving them a head start on their peers.

She did the best she could and she was certain Patrick would've approved. He'd be proud if he could see them now. None had the feisty temperament she and Patrick had. Maybe things like that passed a generation. They all were generous, adaptable, kind and fun to be with. She wouldn't change a thing about any of them.

As soon as Ellen graduated high school, Lorna enrolled her in Acme Business College. Grace followed a year later. Along with learning new skills, their social circle grew and they kept busy with badminton, sailing and copying clothing from fashion magazines.

After Andrew's graduation, Max found him a job at the shingles mill. Mr. Kearny hired him to place sections of red cedar logs into the machine that sliced them into tapered wedges.

Andrew reminded Lorna of Patrick. He was charming and good looking, and like his father, he had many friends with whom he played billiards, camped near the ocean or in the mountains, and attended traveling vaudeville shows.

After Andrew was on the job less than a year, he and Max came home one evening and found Lorna in the kitchen. She dropped the mop she was wiping the floor with when she saw Andrew's bloody bandaged right hand. "Oh, my good Lord. What happened?"

"Machine cut off the tips of his fingers," Max said.

"The *Sidhe* again. Tarnation." She let out a quick, disgusted snort. "How bad is it?"

"Ah, it's nothing. Only cut off two," Max said. "You should see the guy last week, lost three fingers—left only his thumb and index finger."

"I'll be fine," Andrew said. "Going back tomorrow. Don't want to miss a payday."

"No, you're not," Lorna said. "With your hand like that, you could have another accident."

"No job can guarantee he'll be safe," Max said. "Don't treat him like a weakling."

"You'll have me worrying all day," Lorna said to Andrew.

"Worrying's like riding a hobby horse," Max said. "Gives you something to do, but gets you nowhere."

Lorna swatted Max's arm. "Andrew, the neighbor lady told me they need workers at North Coast Casket. It would be safer for you."

"Who wants to think about dying all day?" Max said. "Pay's better at Kearney's."

Lorna couldn't convince Andrew to stay home and he returned to work with a bandaged hand. But Mr. Kearny was concerned he wouldn't have the dexterity required to operate the machine. He transferred Andrew to the bundling area, which meant a decrease in pay.

In time, the entire family was working when Daniel started delivering for Owl Drug after school. Ellen found employment at the telephone company when she graduated from secretarial school, securing a job there for Grace a year later. Along with the girls' wealth of school friends, suitors started coming to the house. One evening she sat them down for a talk.

"With these men coming round, I figure it's time to talk about a few things," Lorna said.

"It's kind of late for that," Ellen said, glancing at Grace. "We already know, Mother."

Lorna raised her voice. "Of course, I know you do." She pulled the skin at her neck. "I don't want you to see one man exclusively. You learn about men by meeting and seeing different types, different characters. What appeals to you now, when you're young—the athlete, the handsome one, the one with a new buggy—doesn't appeal to you when you're older. Consideration, companionship and reliability are the most important things."

"We have no intention to see only one," Grace said. "It's more fun to go out in groups."

"We've been living around miners, friends of father's and Max's," Ellen said. "I'd say we're pretty discerning already."

Lorna cleared her throat. "Glad to hear that." Lorna shifted her weight and sat up taller. "Another thing. You've got to do and see all before you settle down. Travel, buy everything you need—new corsets, hairpins, gloves. Once you're married, you're married for a long time and all your money goes to the kids and the household."

"Glad you mentioned travel," Ellen said. "Grace and I were talking about how we want to see new places—Vancouver, Seattle—"

"San Francisco," Grace said. "We heard it's grand."

The following year, believing things had turned a corner and all would be right in her world, Lorna was optimistic only good fortune lie ahead. Ellen had a new position working for a law firm, and Lorna imagined it wouldn't be long before she and Grace, and also Andrew, would be out on their own. Then Max could retire. She started thinking of how she wanted to spend the rest of her years.

"Max, wouldn't it be nice if we got a place near the water when you stop work?"

"Um, don't know. Haven't thought about stopping."

"Not yet, but you will," she said, figuring he needed time to get used to the idea. "Imagine sitting and looking out to sea, walking on the water's edge. I used to do that back home."

"Nothing's ever enough for you," he said, ramming his hat on his head and dislodging his brass rim spectacles. "Nothing but constant blabber."

Lorna rubbed her chin. *What got into him? Everything I do is for the family.*

Before she could discuss a place by the sea again, Max didn't come home after work one night. Dread returned, like it did when Patrick went missing.

"You sure you saw him at work today?" Lorna asked Andrew.

"I saw him at lunch, but didn't see him later. But I usually don't until we come home."

"What if he had an accident—or he's stuck somewhere?" Lorna said.

"Mother, stop imagining the worse," Grace said. "He's probably out with friends."

"Check with his friends at the billiard hall," Lorna said to Andrew and Daniel. "And the back room of Young's. Could be playing cards."

The boys checked around town, at the mill and with some of his friends, but no one had an inkling of where he was.

After three days, Lorna went to the police and filed a missing person report.

"No knowledge of him," the police officer told her. "And no unclaimed bodies."

"How can I find him?" Lorna asked.

"Not much you can do. We'll keep the report on file and let you know if he turns up."

Two weeks later, with no word from Max, Lorna realized he'd deserted her and the family. Without warning and without a word. "*Osti*," she cursed, "may you be badly positioned on a windy day, Max Stern."

She believed she'd get by with the combined earnings from her managing the apartment building and the children's salaries. However, with Max no longer at the mill, Mr. Kearny asked Lorna to leave. He was giving the apartment to another worker and his family.

"Not only did he abandon me, the old scoundrel," she cried out to Ellen and Grace, her voice bitter. "He hornswoggled me and made me lose my income from the room rentals. *Tabarnak*."

"We're earning good salaries," Ellen said.

"It's better without him," Grace said. "No more yelling at Andrew and Daniel."

"No more listening to him drone on about politics and how his boss exploits him," said Ellen. "No more snoring that shakes the house, no more leaving cupboards open."

"No more smelling like sardines and picking teeth with a pocketknife," Grace added, with a laugh. A moment later, all three broke out in laugher.

"And no more of him asking me why I'm still in my nightdress at six in the morning," Lorna said. She stared out the window. Was his leaving so terrible, apart from her wounded pride? The girls were right. Things might be better now. Max was the means through which she got her children back. He did that for her. But she was perfectly capable of managing on her own. And did she really want to put up with him until the end of her days?

"With God as my witness," Lorna said. "I'll never marry again. I'll never let another man treat my sons badly."

Lorna rented a three-bedroom cottage on Hoyt Street, near the Public Library, and continued to take in laundry. Three months after they moved to the new home, Ellen moved to San Francisco, a vow she made after her trip there with Grace. She found work as a stenographer in another law office.

Grace took over Ellen's position at the Everett law firm and supplemented her income with tinting photographs at a local studio. Several nights a week, she also sang at the local movie house before the silent films began.

Lorna was pleased Ellen was following her dream and, in her own way, doing what she herself had done, though the circumstances were different. Some days, she still pondered what her life would have been like had she stayed in New Brunswick. But she led the life she was supposed to live. With Max gone, she hoped for a quieter and more content life. And then came December.

Before the Christmas holidays, Andrew went to a roller rink with his friend Henry, a bugler and a caretaker at the armory that quartered the Coast Artillery Guards. They stayed late, playing cards, and spent the night in a gas-heated ante-room in the armory. During the night, the stove overturned and gas gushed from its rubber tubing, asphyxiating both boys.

Henry's father discovered the boys the next day when he went to search for his son, who hadn't returned home. Overcome with an overwhelming outrush of gas from the room, he brought the coroner to the scene.

Since the cock was turned off, the coroner surmised that one of the young men in sleep knocked over the stove and disconnected the gas pipe.

"Your son," sputtered Henry's father to Lorna. "Always careless. Henry told me."

"How dare you," Lorna said, trembling with outrage.

"Got his fingers cut off—that was reckless. And Henry told me how they nearly got swept away by a riptide when your son insisted on swimming near Marysville."

"If you think blaming Andrew will make your grieving any easier, you're wrong," Lorna said. "I will grieve until the end of my life, and so will you."

The *Everett Daily Herald* featured the accident on the front page. An outpouring of sympathy helped Lorna cope as she was still trying to carry on after Max's abandonment. *Even a small thorn causes festering*, her mother Maggie used to say. As Lorna questioned why she had to have more than her share of thorns, fate struck another blow—the shock of Andrew's death made her hair start growing out white.

After fifteen months, there'd been no word of Max. The Snohomish Sheriff's office issued a *Return of Not Found* document. Lorna hired a lawyer to file a request to dissolve her marriage to Max in the Superior Court of the State of Washington. She also requested a release from "every obligation of the marriage contract.' Max had "deserted and abandoned her without cause, and against her will or consent."' Lorna also requested the Court return her to her former name of Lorna Ryan.

The newspaper published a summons for Max, requiring him to appear within sixty days. He never responded or appeared. The Court rendered a judgement against him and granted Lorna's demand. She resumed her life as Mrs. Ryan, erasing all traces of Max.

Being Lorna Ryan again rejuvenated her spirit, like days of long ago. It transported her back to Ironwood, a place that she once detested but now held potent memories. It was where she and Patrick created a family. The place she nursed Grace through her illness and where they survived brutal winters and mining explosions. A place that tested her mettle. And a place of love and family.

CHAPTER 9

♦

A friend's eye is a good mirror.

Asunny weekend the summer after Max disappeared, Grace and her friends, Rose and Genevieve, picnicked on a grassy knoll in Howarth Park. While Rose placed ham and mustard sandwiches on plates, Genevieve asked Grace, "How's the new house?"

"Not much difference from the last one. At least it's in the same neighborhood." Grace propped herself on her elbows and extended her legs. "Do you realize how many places I've lived in my life? You'd think my mother would get tired of moving. I sure am."

"She's being mindful of expenses," Genevieve said. "And you had no choice but to move out of Kearney's after Max left."

"You still haven't found out what happened to him, have you?" Rose said as she handed out the sandwiches and napkins.

Grace shook her head. "I think mother tries to find him. But she's secretive and won't admit it."

"Wonder why he left," Rose said, passing the bottles of ginger ale.

Grace shrugged. "To do what he pleases, to be free from obligations—or away from my mother."

"Or another woman," Genevieve said.

"Possible." Grace looked across the Sound. "We may never know and it doesn't matter."

"Did you see the article on Mary Pickford in this month's *Parisienne?*" Rose asked. "She's one of my favorites. I wish they'd write more about her."

"What did you think about the latest fashions from Paris?" Genevieve said. "Mother and I loved the pleated front dress with the big cape."

"Your mother favors anything from Paris," Rose said, with a smile.

"Speaking of mothers," Genevieve said in her lilting voice. "Mine says the three most important things between a man and a woman are the hands, the looks, the timbre of the voice." She extended one of her elegant hands with its perfectly shaped nails and half-moons.

"Your mother says the most delightful things," Grace said.

"What do you expect?" Rose said. "She's French."

"Bien sûr," Genevieve said with a tilt of her head. "She also says one must have the perfect number of guests at any soiree—less than the Muses and more than the Graces."

"If you want to see a swell dress, look at that woman," Rose said, pointing to a nearby bench. "Isn't the cummerbund waist grand?"

Grace and Genevieve turned and saw a woman fashionably dressed in a navy dress with side closure, accented with a multi-color sash at the waist. The woman noticed them looking at her and approached.

"Hello. Sorry to bother, but do you know how I get to the beach at Jetty Island?"

"It's not easy," said Rose. "The ferries don't run often."

"Check and see if you can find a man with a boat who will take you," Genevieve said.

"It does sound difficult. Can you suggest another place?"

"Are you new here?" Grace said.

"I'm visiting from Tacoma. Here on a short holiday." The woman smiled and gave a slight nod. "I'm Clara Tschida."

Grace introduced herself and her friends. "If you like, you can spend the day with us and we can give you tips on places to go. Later we're having dinner downtown and you're welcome to join us."

"That would be lovely. I'd like that."

Two days later, Grace invited Clara to dinner at her home.

"The stew's delicious, Mrs. Ryan," Clara said, resting her fork on her plate. "It reminds me of my mother's cooking. She's also a superb cook. Dishes she learned in the old country—both my parents are Germans from the Austro-Hungarian Empire."

"What does your father do?" Lorna asked.

"Decorative plasterer—he studied sculpture in Europe." Clara leaned slightly toward Lorna and smiled. "He's worked on all the important buildings in Tacoma—Union Station, the Tacoma and Temple Theaters, the Elks Temple. We're very proud of his work."

"Hmm. And you're a nurse, a good career," Lorna said. "And your siblings?"

"Marta's still in high school, and Joseph recently graduated from St. Martin's College in Lacey. He's working in the office of an import/export company." Clara let out a laugh. "If my parents have their way, he'll get married before long. They have a woman picked out for him."

"Did he agree to this matchmaking?" Lorna asked, trying not to sound too inquisitive.

"He says he's not interested. But my parents can be relentless and they have some idea about marrying your own kind." Clara turned to Grace. "You should meet him. I think you'd get along fine."

"Wouldn't want to upset your parents with another lass," Lorna said, dabbing her mouth with her napkin.

"Friends of mine visit all the time. It's not a problem." Clara reached for her water glass. "Really, I'd love for Grace to come down and spend time with me and my family."

Nearly a month later, Clara's brother, Joseph, took the Intercity Transit to Everett one Sunday. Grace fretted for days what to wear. After trying on various outfits, she decided on her burgundy georgette blouse with frog closures and lace trim, accented with a matching burgundy headband.

Sitting near the parlor window, she peered through the coarse bobbin-made-lace curtains, to get a glimpse before he came in. His debonair air instantly intrigued her; handsome with dark hair and eyes, nattily dressed in a fine-tailored suit, and white celluloid-collared shirt. He was different from the other men who courted her, with a stride that radiated confidence and seduction. Her eyes knew. She turned to her mother. "That's the man I'm going to marry."

"Lust at first sight, eh." Lorna pulled back the curtain and looked out. "So that's Joseph Tschida. A hell of a name to go to bed with."

As they sat in the parlor, Lorna kept her gaze on Joseph. With lips slightly parted, his eyes roamed over Grace, pausing momentarily at her bust line and then at her feet. She noted Grace sat up straighter than usual, and made frequent eye contact with the young man.

"Clara told us about your job. Import/export, is it?" Lorna said.

"That's right. I'm learning the business. Later, I'll look for something else to broaden my experience."

"Clara mentioned you do amateur theatre," Grace said, touching the nape of her neck.

Joseph stroked his tie and nodded in Grace's direction. "I did theatre in college—along with football and baseball." He wet his lips. "Now I play for the Catholic Order of Foresters' baseball team." Joseph smiled at Lorna and then turned to Grace. "I was wondering, if you'd would like to take a walk and show me around. I've never been here before."

Grace sprang from the sofa. "We can go downtown. It's a short walk."

A few feet away from the house, Joseph said, "I hope I wasn't rude suggesting we leave, but I wanted to talk to you alone."

"I'm glad you did. My mother would've kept peppering you with questions."

"My parents would do the same." Joseph kept his gaze down as they walked on. "I wasn't certain you'd want to see me. Clara told me you have many beaus."

Grace smiled and shook her head. "She exaggerates."

"I was glad you said it was fine." Joseph turned toward Grace and leaned in. "She told me only good things about you. Said you were kind, beautiful—talented with a lovely voice."

"She came with me one evening when I sang at the movies."

"She said we both have the spirit of an artist. Guess she was referring to my acting."

When he lightly touched the back of her waist, Grace felt as if a magician was juggling balls in her stomach.

After Joseph left, Grace asked Lorna, "What did you think?"

Lorna lowered her head and peered at Grace. "He's quite the charmer and you seem smitten. More so than with others. But I worry you're outmatched."

"Oh, Mother." Grace looked at herself in the mirror and adjusted her headband. "I hope I hear from him again. But with all the grilling you did, he might not want to come back."

"I think you took a fancy to him because he looks like that movie star you like. Could be an infatuation."

"No, mother. You couldn't be further from the truth."

It wasn't long before Joseph came to Everett nearly every other Sunday. They attended concerts, local baseball games, and the carnivals and fairs that came to town. Joseph always timed it so he caught the last Transit back to Tacoma. But one night they stayed too long at a dance hall, and he missed the train back.

"You'll have to spend the night with us," Grace said.

"What will your mother say?" Joseph asked.

"She'll sleep with one eye open."

Joseph laughed and squeezed Grace's hand. "And I probably won't sleep at all, knowing you're nearby."

When they arrived home, Lorna was waiting at the door. "Sheets and a blanket on the chair. You can make up the sofa for him."

After Grace readied the sofa, she and Joseph sat at the dining room table.

"Did you really mean it when you said you're looking for a new job?" Grace asked.

"I want to find something that pays better."

"Is money important?" Grace said.

"Sure. I've always told myself I won't get married until I have a house and a couple thousand dollars in the bank."

"Sounds like a good plan." Grace raised her eyebrows. "It could take a while though."

"I'm not in a rush. I'm only twenty-two. Got plenty of time."

Grace placed the tips of her fingers on her chin and looked down. It was not what she expected to hear from someone who regularly came to see her. Had she been misreading his intentions and fooling herself? And she'd assumed they were the same age—and here he was a year younger. She glanced at the clock. "It's two o'clock. We should say goodnight."

"You know how much I like you, Gracie. Can I call you Gracie?" Grace smiled and nodded. "I didn't think I'd be good enough for you."

"Mother said you told her you didn't believe you had a chance, and I wouldn't want to see you again. But I did."

"Can I have a kiss?" Grace shook her head. Joseph's face went slack and he bite his lip.

"I'll wake you early so you don't miss the train," she said.

Joseph wrote Grace regularly, not only the weeks he didn't come to Everett. After they'd been seeing each other for seven months, he wrote:

Did you tell your mother that I have no girl here? You are the only girl I have and the only girl I love.

Grace wrote back:

My dear Joseph,

I told her you said you have no one else. But I'm not certain she's convinced. You know the saying 'absence makes the heart grow fonder'? We'll have a chance to see if it's true. My sister, Ellen, is getting married in Sacramento and mother, Daniel and I are going to the wedding. I took vacation from work and we'll be there for two weeks. We're very excited and happy for Ellen.

Grace soon got a response from Joseph. After she read the letter, she told Lorna, "Joseph says since we have to pass through Tacoma on our way to California, he wants me to stop and meet his parents. You and Daniel are invited also."

Lorna explored Grace's face and harrumphed. "Go, if you want. We'll wait at the station."

"I don't know. Might be too rushed and I'll be rumpled from traveling. I wouldn't want to make a wrong impression."

"Why in God's name would you care what they think?"

"Mother, they're his parents and . . . it's important for me." She folded the letter and stuck it in her pocket. "If I do go, I'd really like you to come and give me your impressions."

Lorna shrugged her shoulders before pointing to the jars of tomatoes sitting on the kitchen counter. "Do me a favor and top off the rest of those and cork them."

Joseph met Grace at Union Station and they took the streetcar to his family's home, perched high on Tacoma Avenue. The three-story shingled house with sloped roof, had hipped dormers that kept watch on the street below. Grace stepped gingerly up the steep greenish-gray concrete stairs from the sidewalk to the front yard, and then up the wooden steps that led to the wide porch. A lone ladder-back rocking chair painted the color of roasted chestnuts sat near the railings.

Joseph's mother, Susanna, opened the door, the image of a kindly muffin-making grandmother in her long, Peter-Pan-collared gingham dress with puffed sleeves, her salt-and-pepper hair up in a topknot. "Come in. We've been waiting for you."

Susanna led them past the stairway and into the large parlor with its pale laurel-green walls. A somber aura emanated from the heavy wood molding and antique furniture that looked like it weighed a ton and no one had moved for years. Mingling with the staid air was the aroma of fresh-baked goods.

Grace looked around. It was a bastion of good housekeeping; nothing out of place, no clutter, no newspaper or idle eyeglasses in sight. A stark contrast from her home, where Lorna never bothered if there was dust on the windowsills, a pile of unfolded laundry on the table, or a few dirty dishes in the sink. She always said a house was to be lived in and not run like a military camp.

Her attention was averted when a tall, stately man came into the room. "My son has told us about you," said Joseph's father, Anton.

After a few pleasantries, Joseph directed Grace to a large clawfoot table, covered with a Turkish rug. On top was a silver tray with a tea serving and freshly made *vanillekipferl* cookies.

As Susanna handed Grace a white linen napkin trimmed with crocheted lace, she said, "I'm sorry your mother and brother didn't join us."

Grace looked down before looking up. "There's so little time, she thought it best I come alone."

"We would have liked to meet your family," Anton said.

I'm certain you would, Grace thought. *Better this way in case something was said, or insinuated, that mother didn't like and she became a bear with a sore head.*

"You're going to your sister's wedding," Anton said. "Have you met the man she's marrying?"

"No, but Ellen seems happy and that's the most important thing."

"What does the young man do," Anton asked.

"A variety of things, writing, photography."

"Her sister works in a law office, like Grace does," Joseph said.

"The same work as she did before in Everett and San Francisco." Grace's gaze bounced around the room. "You have a lovely home. Clara always said she wanted me to come down and meet you."

"Pity she couldn't change her shift at the hospital today," Susanna said. "And then Marta has school."

Grace fiddled with the top button on her dress as Jospeh's parents drilled her with more questions. She almost made the sign of the cross when Joseph took out his pocket watch, and said, "We'd better hurry. Their train leaves in an hour and her mother and brother might be getting nervous."

"Joseph, did you tell Grace that I did the decorative work on Union Station?" Anton asked before turning to Grace. "Look at the ceiling and vaults when you're there."

CHAPTER 10

♦

Marry in haste and be sorry at your leisure.

Lorna, Grace and Daniel arrived in Sacramento three days before Ellen's wedding to Edward at Sacred Heart Cathedral. It was a small affair with only the family and local friends in attendance. After the ceremony, the couple and guests celebrated with a luncheon at the Western Hotel.

After the nuptials, Lorna and Grace stayed on and toured the city, with visits to Sutter's Fort and walks along the waterfront. They also attended a musical performance at the Eagle Theatre.

"That Stanford Mansion was a right pretty building," Lorna said to Grace when they returned from visiting the State Park.

"You did well with all the walking. I notice you're doing much better here than in Everett. Must be the climate—no dampness."

Lorna nodded. "Arthritis is less painful."

"And you haven't taken as much codeine," Grace said. "You should stay longer."

"No. Don't want Ellen and her husband—" Lorna narrowed her eyes and walked over to the window. "Don't want to be beholden to anyone."

"You wouldn't be. Ellen would love to have you nearby. What if I stayed with you?"

"And jeopardize your job?"

Grace shifted her weight from one foot to the other. "I really like it here. Ellen says I can easily get a job at a law office or with the state government."

"You've discussed it?" Grace nodded. "What about your friends, Joseph—and Daniel? I don't want him to be alone."

"I mentioned it to him before he left, and he said he'll be fine, if I wanted to stay." Grace fingered the edge of the table. "Mother, I'm going to resign from my job."

Lorna's hand flew to her chest.

Grace wrote Joseph to tell him she would be staying in Sacramento. His reply came quickly.

Darling Gracie,

I was upset because you hadn't written every day, but not angry with you because I assumed you had good reason. But I did worry if everything was all right.

About staying there, it sounds like you'll find work that's satisfying, but will you be happy without me?

I'm a bit depressed without you nearby. I do love you and I want to make you happy, not by doing everything you want because I may not always be able to so, but by being honest in my love for you and giving myself to you. I'll figure out something soon.

Your loving, Joseph.

Lorna and Grace found a small place, near the State Capital, not far from the Crocker Museum. They'd been in their new abode less than a month when Jospeh wrote he was coming to Sacramento.

"He'll be here Sunday," Grace told Lorna, a bubbly cadence to her voice.

"Boy's more serious than he's been letting on."

"You think so? He always says he loves me, but he's never made a commitment."

"All that talk about a house and money." Lorna wiped biscuit crumbs from her mouth. "Humph. Fine words mean little."

When Joseph arrived, Grace asked him how long he planned to stay.

"As long as you're here, Gracie. What did you think?"

"What about your job, your parents?" Grace stopped and stepped back. "Wait. Did you quit your job?"

Joseph smiled. "I'll find something here. And my parents will get over it."

"Get over it? They're not happy, are they?"

"Same old stuff. I shouldn't be impetuous. I shouldn't quit my job. Why leave home when I've everything I need there." Joseph kissed Grace's hand. "But you weren't there."

She focused on a point in the distance and wondered if he really would stay. It was difficult to know how much sway his parents had over him. "I'm glad you came and I'm sure you'll easily find work. And you can help me decide which job to take. The one in the government has good benefits but it might be tedious. The law firm does a lot of work for—"

"Gracie, I did a lot of thinking on the trip down—and before, while you've been away . . . I don't want you to work. I'm going to find a good job and I'll make enough for us." He looked to the side for a moment. "This is not how I planned it, but . . . I think we should get married."

Words stuck in Grace's throat. "But . . . but you wanted a house—"

"See that little place over there?" he said, pointing to a shed alongside a Victorian house. "I could live in a shack like that or in a palace and be happy, as long as I'm with you."

She watched his lips and forgot everything for a moment. "I need to think about it."

"What's there to think about?" He held her tight around her waist; she leaned into him. "You know we're meant to be together."

When Grace told her mother she was going to accept Joseph's proposal, Lorna tossed aside a newspaper and didn't say anything as she stared with intensity at the back of a chair.

"Mother, you're worrying me with your silence."

After a long pause, Lorna said. "As I've been told, worrying is as useful as a hobby horse."

The headline on Grace's marriage announcement in the Everett newspaper read, "Belle of Everett Marries Tacoma Man." In the accompanying photo, she held two white roses and wore an off-the-shoulder white organza dress that draped gracefully at her neck. Her hair in a topknot, one long curl escaped and dangled alongside her right temple.

Joseph's family also announced the wedding in the Tacoma newspaper with a studio photo of him in his dark suit, high-collar shirt and white bow tie.

They married in the Cathedral of the Blessed Sacrament in downtown Sacramento, with Ellen and her husband as witnesses. On the marriage certificate Joseph listed his age as 22, and Grace listed hers as 21, determined to keep the truth from her new husband. After the ceremony the couple honeymooned in San Francisco, where they toured Fishermen's Wharf, visited the site of the World Fair and took a Red and White Fleet cruise on the Bay.

When they returned to Sacramento, Joseph started work at a railroad equipment supply company, near the former steamboat depot that took freight to San Francisco. He'd been on the job only two months when Grace thought she was pregnant. She told Lorna before Joseph.

"I never expected it would happen so quickly. We really haven't discussed children. I don't know what he'll say. He didn't even want to get married until he was financially established."

"Well, his reaction will tell you a lot."

After dinner the next evening, Grace joined Joseph on the sofa in the parlor. He put his newspaper aside and placed his arm around her. "Father told me about this Turn Verein Hall in town. Said it's the center of German-American life here. I was thinking we could go there this weekend and see what events are coming up. I heard they have a singing club—that's something you might like to do."

"I don't want to start anything right now." She smiled at him. "I may need to reorganize, do some things and make room for someone else."

"Who? Daniel? Wouldn't he stay with your mother? She has room."

Grace looked down at her stomach and patted it.

Joseph's eyes lit up. He bounded off the sofa and stood in front of Grace, taking her hands in his. "I've always hoped we'd have lots of kids." He kissed her on the forehead. "But I didn't want to bring it up and make you feel I was pressuring you. How are you feeling? Do you need me to get you anything?"

Grace placed her hand on his cheek. "I'm fine. No need to treat me like an invalid."

When Grace was in her fifth month, Joseph was offered a shipping clerk position with the Sierra Railway in Sonora, California. The hiring manager was impressed with his qualifications and experience, and stressed the post was a stepping stone to more important jobs within the company.

"It's only ninety miles south, Gracie. Site of the biggest gold rush in the country and the railroad's important there. It supports other railroads—brings lumber and mining ores out of the foothills and delivers goods to the mines, logging camps. Think of all the activity, darling, and we'll be a part of it. And I'll learn about another industry."

Grace saw how excited Joseph was about the new job, and she doubted she'd be able to persuade him not to take it. Still, it was worth a try. "I feel this is home . . . I want to be near my mother and sister, especially with the baby coming."

"We'll come back to visit and they can stay with us. What do you say?"

With her head down, she looked up at Joseph. "I prefer to stay here."

They discussed the potential relocation into the night. After Joseph assured Grace he'd do all possible to make her happy there, she said, "Since you're convinced it's best . . . if you'll be happy . . . but I want mother to come with us."

When she later asked her mother, Lorna said, "Newlyweds should be on their own to get to know each other. I'm staying here. Don't bother about me."

In Sonora, they moved into a flat not far from a carpenter's shop and the former Opera House, known as the "Jewel of the Mother Lode." Grace quickly warmed to the little town close to the Sierra Nevada foothills. When Joseph was not working, they attended plays and concerts, and picnicked in Columbia State Park under the giant Sequoias. One weekend, they drove to Yosemite, renting a cabin near a stream. Towards the end of that summer, she curtailed outdoor activities as she was nearing her ninth month of pregnancy.

Their daughter, Vivienne, was born mid-September. Soon after the child's birth, Joseph's parents started writing and calling Joseph at his office. They wanted them to come to Tacoma so they could meet their first grandchild.

"It's a long trip," Grace said, a sour tone to her voice. "It's too much for a young child. Invite them to come here."

"I did but mother said her doctor forbade her to travel. He said the water in California would make her sick."

"Ridiculous ruse. We have some of the finest water around."

"They're my parents, Gracie. I can't refuse them the one thing they want most."

When Grace told Lorna what Susanna said about the water, Lorna let out a knowing laugh. "Tell the old biddy you're wise to her tricks. *The old broom knows the dirty corners best.*"

Grace's patience was sorely tried by his parent's constant insistence, but she knew she couldn't continue to refuse. It was important for Joseph to have his family meet Vivienne. She agreed to go to Tacoma, but she wanted to wait until Vivienne was older.

"I know the perfect time," Joseph said. "When she turns one year old. We'll have the celebration there."

CHAPTER 11

◆

There's no need to fear the wind if your haystacks are tied down.

When Grace stepped off the train at Union Station, the Cascade Mountains "were out," as the locals say when a brisk north wind chases away the clouds. On the horizon, breezes ruffled the branches of the old-growth Douglas fir. Above, squawking gulls hovered momentarily on their way to the waterfront, their underbellies gleaming in the sunlight. As she breathed in the crisp air infused with briny sea smells, sudden gusts nearly toppled her forest-green felt hat. She held Vivienne closer and turned away. *The winds are angry. They know I regret leaving California.*

While waiting for someone to answer the bell at Joseph's home, Grace watched a ladybug creep up the glossy leaf of a begonia in the flower boxes on the porch railing. Remembering her mother's words about the *old broom knowing the dirty corners best,* she smiled.

"What are you thinking about?" Joseph asked, placing his hand on her back.

"Oh—this little creature." She stuck a finger next to the bug, willing it to hop on.

"We're going to have a wonderful time here, darling," Joseph said, stroking his bowtie.

Grace glanced across the way at the triangle roofs on the firehouse towers, and beyond at the view towards the water, marred with smoke spewing from the large sawmill and the coal-powered trains. *For your sake*, she told herself, *I'll try to make this a pleasant stay.*

The lace curtain on the front-door window slid back and Susanna peered out. Grace tugged down her belted jacket where it had ridden up and smiled as Joseph's mother opened the door. Susanna gave a quick nod as she said hello and offered her cheek to Joseph; he bent down and kissed her.

After wiping her hands on her long white linen apron, she clasped both of Grace's elbows. "I never imagined the next time I see you I'd greet you as my son's wife. We still wish you'd discussed it with us. You could have had the wedding here."

"Mother, we've been over that. What's important now is to meet your granddaughter."

Susanna tilted her head as she looked at the sleeping child. Her eyes lit up, accentuating her delicate features and temporarily masking her steely mien. "Porcelain complexion and your dark hair, Joseph." She stroked Vivienne's chubby cheek with her index finger and then hesitated, examining the child like a specimen. "What's this?" she asked, pointing to the slight bump in the center of her forehead.

"A birthmark," Joseph said. "You hardly notice it."

Susanna took a long look at her son, concern hovering above her brow.

Grace felt her neck get warm, but she kept her voice steady. "My mother says a birthmark is a kiss by an angel."

Susanna frowned briefly and then extended her hand. "Well, come in. Get the child out of the wind." The air in the unlit parlor had a faint musty smell, mingled with the scent of tobacco and cinnamon. "Your father's out back, Joseph. Go get him."

Susanna took a shawl from the piano bench and spread it on the wine-colored velvet sofa for Vivienne to lie on. The child woke up blurry eyed. She blinked a few times and stared at the unfamiliar face with an intense frown. "All's fine, *mein kleines Mádchen,* you're home."

Grace felt a pinch in her heart. *No, it's not your home. We're here to visit your grandparents and aunts so they can know you and then we're going back—to our home.*

Leery of the stranger, Vivienne whimpered and fussed while the older woman took off her hat and unbuttoned the powder-blue, A-line coat Grace made her for the trip. "There, that's better." Vivienne turned sideways and reached out for Grace. "All right, go to your mama and I'll put water on for tea."

Grace placed Vivienne on her lap. The child stood up and hugged her neck, her eyes following Susanna. After she left the room, the child squirmed down and stretched out her legs, trying to break free. Grace's gaze swept around the room. Vivienne had started walking a month ago and Grace realized she'd have to watch her every waking moment to ensure she didn't break any of the Dresden porcelain or Austrian crystal, or throw up on the patterned rug.

Grace jiggled her leg, bouncing the child up and down as she struggled to keep her on her lap. "That's Daddy's mother," she whispered. "Checking us out with her hidden motives."

Vivienne wiggled back and forth and fussed until another stranger entered the parlor. She reached back and grabbed Grace's jacket as she stared at the large man coming toward her.

Anton greeted Grace and held out his arms to take Vivienne. She went to him without so much as a whine. "What a beautiful granddaughter."

"Darling," Joseph said to Grace, "father tells me he's made an appointment for a studio portrait of Vivienne on her birthday."

"How nice." She cupped her hand around her mouth and leaned close to his ear. "Can you open the curtains? It's so dark in here."

In *sotto voce*, Joseph said, "Mother doesn't want the sun to fade the rug and sofa."

"Let's turn on the *schöne Lampe*," Anton said, "so I can see you better." He carried the child around the room, giving a running commentary. "Here's our Victrola. It makes beautiful music. And here there's a picture of your father when he graduated from college, and another with him and his baseball team."

Joseph picked up the framed photo and pointed to himself in the front row. "Who's that?"

"Dada," Vivienne said, reaching out to grab the shiny silver object.

Anton stroked Vivienne's outstretched arm and said with a chuckle, "What a smart little one." He directed her attention to another picture of a woman in a nurse's cap. "Here's Aunt Clara. You'll meet her and Aunt Marta later."

"She's in good hands," Joseph said, patting his father on the shoulder. "I'll see if Mother needs help."

Grace mused on the scene of Anton, cradling the child like a protective mother lion with her cub. He was the one who took to Vivienne, whereas she thought it would have been Susanna. The child was absorbed in everything he said and didn't shy away from him. She occasionally grasped his bow tie or tugged his bushy handlebar mustache to Anton's amusement.

Grace joined them and looked at the other photographs on the sideboard: a studio portrait of the entire family; another portrait of Clara in a dark dress with a V-shape flounce organza collar; Joseph in his three-button confirmation suit with a floral corsage on the lapel, holding a rosary and prayer book in one hand and a long, tapered candle in the other. Her eyes settled on a picture of a stoic black-clad couple. They stood in front of a quaint thatched-roof house with a fancifully curved central façade that bracketed the door. She didn't recall seeing it when she visited previously. But she'd been here only briefly on her way to Sacramento. And she was so nervous meeting Joseph's parents for the first time, much went unnoticed. She thought back to how at first, she hadn't wanted to stop. But Joseph had insisted. Like his parents insisted that they visit now. A thought flitted across her mind: *A family of insisters these Tschidas.*

"Is this a photo of your family?" Grace asked Anton.

"Susanna's parents in their village. They stayed in the old country. Mine came after I was naturalized. But they were here only a few years before they died." He looked to the corner where a gilt-rimmed icon of St. Stephen sat on an inlaid table; a small, unlit votive candle stood in front of it. "Family's important and I wanted my children to know them. Like I wanted to know Vivienne." Anton shifted Vivienne from one hip to the other and walked toward a window overlooking the side yard. He drew back the curtain and pointed. "See over there—my apple trees. Your grandmother will make us her good strudel." He handed the child to Grace. "I want to show her my garden. Put on her coat and hat. It's nippy out."

Plumes of smoke rose from the other side of the picket fence, scenting the air with the aroma of pine, and partially disguising the odor of burning garbage.

"What are you burning today, Mrs. Gartner?" Anton called out.

The head of a woman popped up over the wooden fence. Her frizzy gray hair formed a halo around her. "Old newspapers and stuff. Why, is that Joseph? Hello, son." She waved and laughed, jiggling the wattles of fat under her chin. "And she must be his charming bride and there's your grandchild."

"That's right," Anton said. "Isn't she a beauty?"

Joseph greeted the woman and introduced Grace.

"Now, you have a good day, Mrs. Gartner. Be careful not to let any sparks fly over. It's windy today." Anton turned to Grace and said, "She's also from the old country."

As Anton walked along the crushed grass at the edge of the garden, startled sparrows resting on the clipped hedges flew away. At the midway point of the vegetable plot, he stooped to pull out a few weeds from the tomato plants that grew in uniform rows.

Grace pointed to clusters of freckled toad lilies, hollyhocks and lavender-blue asters growing alongside the fence. "You have a wonderful garden. So many beautiful flowers."

"*Ja*, everyone says so. I love to work the land like I did when I was young. Look how many apples this year." He pointed to several trees heavy with fruit dangling from the branches, some glazed by sunshine filtering through the leaves.

Susanna came out the back door and waved her apron, beckoning them to come in. On their way into the house, Grace turned sideways and glanced back; the top of Mrs. Gartner's head was still visible over the fence.

Susanna had arranged the tea set and Linzer cookies on the dining room table. As they sat down, Grace offered to take Vivienne from Anton.

"She's fine with me. Aren't you, *mein kleiner Schatz?*" The child peered up at Anton and tugged on his ebony-colored silk sleeve garter.

"She has hazel eyes. Gets them from you," Susanna said to Grace. "I thought she'd have Joseph's dark eyes."

"Father has light blue eyes," Joseph said.

"Hmmm." Susanna gave a slight nod as she unfurled her napkin and placed it on her lap. "Now that you're here, you can tell us more about where you live," Susanna said with a touch of chill, as if doubting there'd be anything nice in such an outpost as Sonora.

"There's an interesting mix of people, weather's pleasant, and it's a good place to raise a family." Joseph squeezed Grace's hand. "And lots of history. They built the town with money from the famous Bonanza Gold Mine. Ever hear of it, Father, when you were hunting for gold?"

"Why would your father know anything about California? He went to the Yukon." Susanna titled her head toward Anton. "He came back soon enough when he found out how many mosquitoes there were."

Anton's face twitched.

Joseph laughed. "Is that true, Father? You never said much about your trip."

"No talk about that. We want to know about you." He sounded irritated.

Grace sensed an undercurrent of guilt or embarrassment. And hovering at the back of her mind, was what she remembered hearing about her father's time in the Yukon.

"And your place?" Susanna asked.

"It's in a central location, small, but large enough for us," Joseph said, smiling at Grace.

"There are many beautiful Victorian houses in town," Grace said, lacing her word with as much kindness as she could muster.

"She sketches them," Joseph said. "We framed some to hang on the walls." Joseph picked up a fallen leaf from the cluster of pale orange and yellow dahlias on the table. "Did I tell you about the swell New Year's Ball we went to?"

"Our neighbor lady offered to stay with Vivienne," Grace added. "But we didn't stay long as she was only a few months old."

"You can live in many houses, but there's only one home," Anton said.

Grace wondered what he was getting at, her senses on high alert.

"You really should come," Joseph said. "We're near the Sierra Nevada foothills and not far from Yosemite. We went there one weekend—I borrowed a co-worker's car. He has a Model T, like yours, Father."

"Good car. Mine was one of the first here," Anton said, nibbling on Vivienne's chubby fist. "I see you're enjoying yourselves, but now's the time to concentrate on your career, Joseph. You should have stayed longer at the import company to gain more experience."

Grace turned her head to the side and flicked her gaze upward.

"I learned as much as I could there." He squirmed and glanced to the side briefly. "I went to Sacramento, to be with Grace, and where I am now—well, the railroad's important and I'm getting diverse experience."

"I knew it was good for you to study business," Anton said.

"They also wanted someone who got on well with the workers. I deal with engineers, conductors and yardmasters, as well as people in the Sacramento office."

Grace watched as Joseph rubbed his palms against his knees. She placed a hand on top of one of his and said to Anton and Susanna. "We wanted to thank you again for the beautiful chest of silverware you gave us for our wedding. It's lovely."

Joseph smiled at Grace. "You must have known Grace's failing for silverware."

"And my friend Rose happened to send us a silver berry spoon that matches it," Grace said. "It was such a surprise."

There was a pause in the conversation and in the quiet, Grace heard the wail of a train whistle. As the pendulum grandfather clock ticked away the minutes, she fidgeted with her opal ring. *This may be harder than I thought. Two weeks to go and this is just day one.*

"I suppose, Grace," Anton said. "you're happy your mother and sister are close."

"Not for much longer. My sister and Edward are moving to Palo Alto and Mother's going back to live with my brother in Everett."

"Pity," Anton said. "You should be near family. They can help, should you need it." He swayed back and forth with the child, occasionally murmuring something in German.

As Anton continued to discuss Joseph's future, time moved slowly for Grace while her mind raced. She watched Susanna, a brittle smile on her lips, palms resting in her lap, one cradling the other, a nonchalant air about her, but with a keen eye and ear on the conversation. When she occasionally glanced at Vivienne, her lips relaxed, reinforcing Grace's impressions that in spite of her apparent rigidity, and what she'd gleaned from Joseph and Clara about Susanna's disdain for frivolity, she was at heart a kind woman. And one couldn't dismiss her mettle. As a young woman she'd left all behind to journey here.

"It would be good for you to see what opportunities are here," Anton said to Joseph.

Grace's teaspoon clattered against the edge of her saucer. She turned in time to see Joseph's jaw tighten.

"That's enough, Anton. They're worn out and have to unpack before dinner." Susanna scooted scattered cookie crumbs together in a pile with her napkin. "Your former room's ready, Joseph. I'll take you up."

Before they went upstairs, Susanna took Joseph aside and whispered something. He frowned, a bewildered look on his face as he took Vivienne from Anton.

Halfway up the stairs Susanna bent over the banister and called out, "The stair treads are creaking again, Anton."

A faint reply filtered up. "*Ja, ja.* I will fix."

"Fresh towels and a new bar of Ivory soap on the bed," Susanna said, opening the bedroom door. "A changing table for Vivienne against the window."

"The crib," Grace said, pointing to a baby bed with a hand-sewn coverlet embroidered with yellow daises and trimmed with scalloped edging lace. "It's beautiful."

"Clara made it. She wanted something special for Vivienne." Her hand on the doorknob, Susanna paused. "I'll call when dinner's ready."

After she left, Joseph placed Vivienne in the crib. The child put her thumb in her mouth and closed her eyes, occasionally cooing.

Joseph put his hand on the small of Grace's back and kissed the nape of her neck. "She's had a full day. And she's in for a treat. We'll eat well while we're here."

"Are you saying you haven't been eating well?"

"Darling, you're a good cook, but mother is better than the best." Grace pouted her lips and looked sideways at him. "I didn't marry you for your cooking. I married you because you are the sweetest, most beautiful and sensuous girl I ever met." He led her to the bed and cradled her in his arms.

"What did your mother say to you before we came upstairs?"

"Nothing," he said, adjusting the pillow behind his head.

"It was something. Why won't you tell me?"

"One of her silly superstitions. Something about her birthmark being like the ones Gypsy women have in the old country."

Grace felt blood rush to her face. She turned away and stared at the wall. *If she's implying Vivienne has gypsy blood, you can darn well tell her it isn't from my side of the family.* She was tempted to tell him and Susanna what her own mother said when she first saw Joseph. But it wasn't worth starting a row when they'd just arrived.

CHAPTER 12

♦

The man with the boots does not mind where he places his foot.

Susanna put all her culinary talents on display with her dinner. She radiated satisfaction as the family ooh-ed and ahh-ed over the garlic soup and stuffed boneless pork rib roast.

"Vivienne's a real charmer," Clara said, passing Joseph the cabbage strudel. Her pale blue chiffon blouse enhanced her dark eyes, giving them extra depth.

"Can I babysit?" Marta asked, spooning mashed potatoes on her plate in orderly mounds. Marta's long braid was tied in back with a large white bow that stood out on both sides of her head like dragonfly wings, drawing the eye to her aquiline nose with its slight hump.

"If you have time, I'd like that." Grace said. "I imagine you have a lot going on now that you're in your last year of high school. Have you decided what you're going to do after?"

Marta dipped her head down before glancing up at her father. "I'm going to St. Joseph's nursing school like Clara."

"Marta didn't want to study like Clara and Joseph," Anton said. "I told her a closed mind is like a closed book. A pile of paper."

"Grace didn't study," Marta said, in an accusatory tone.

"You know she did," Joseph said to Marta, his eyebrows pinched together. "I told you she went to business school."

"She was working at a law firm when I met her," Clara said, holding her billowing sleeve to keep it from touching the dish of peas and carrots as she served herself. "And also tinted photographs and sang at the cinema."

"My multi-talented artist." Joseph squeezed Grace's hand and winked; it was impossible to miss his affection.

Marta's eyes remained fixed on Grace, making her uncomfortable. She couldn't help but notice a coldness lurking in the young woman's eyes, a hint of a warning.

"Education is the best gift you give your children," Anton said. "I trust you'll send Vivienne to excellent schools and later give her a career."

Grace twisted one of her garnet earrings between her fingers and debated, but only for a moment. "I don't want expectations put on her. She'll decide when it's time. Parents shouldn't live their children's lives."

All eyes turned to Anton. His body remained rigid as he cleared his throat.

Grace sat motionless in the hush that fell over the room. "What I want to say is parents need to love their children, give them confidence and a moral bearing. With a good foundation, they'll make the right decisions. Don't you agree?"

No one spoke until Clara broke the impasse. "Look how well she uses a spoon." Paying no attention to her admirers, the child scooped up applesauce from her bowl. "Oops, spoke too soon," Clara said as Vivienne put down the spoon and began eating with her fingers.

"What's for dessert?" Joseph said.

"Linzer tort with *Schlag*," Marta said, her eyes crinkling with pleasure.

With Vivienne asleep in her crib, Joseph helped Grace take the pins out of her hair. "Father pays more attention to Vivienne than he ever did to us."

"Typical for grandparents. I like that he talks to her like a big girl," Grace said. "But I wish he wouldn't interfere in our raising her."

Unbuttoning the back of her dress, he said, "He's only trying to be helpful."

"Could call it meddling. He also meddles in your life. What did he want to talk to you about after dinner?"

He kissed the back of her head and then looked around the room. "Where are my trophies and books?"

"I'm certain your mother has them." She slipped off her dress and undid the hooks on her Ferris waist. She ran her hand over her unencumbered waist before sitting at the vanity. "You didn't answer."

"It was nothing." He rested his elbow on the dresser and watched as she slid off her garters and unrolled her white cotton stockings.

After slipping her cotton nightdress over her head, she stood on tiptoe to kiss him. "We promised each other we'd never keep secrets."

"He wants me to see about jobs here."

"You're not going to, are you?"

Joseph didn't answer and moved away. He lost his balance, taking off his pinstripe pants, and hopped over to the bed to sit down.

Grace went to the window and looked out at the dark night, towards the neighbor's house where a lone light glowed in a downstairs window. Against its panes, branches of a maple tree shadow-danced in the wind. Fiddling with the eyelets in the lace curtain, she said, "You said we'd stay two weeks and then go home. I agreed to come for two weeks." She let the curtain fall from her hand and faced him. "Don't change your mind."

On Sunday, Anton wanted the entire family together at Holy Rosary's nine-o'clock Mass. Susanna, as head of the church's Women's Guild, which she considered an honor, left early to lay out the priest's vestments, place flowers on the high altar, light the candles and ready the collection baskets. Before the rest left home, Anton said to Joseph and Grace, "We wanted you to baptize Vivienne here. You know how important our church is to me."

"Grace couldn't travel right away. You wouldn't want your granddaughter to live with original sin until we could visit."

A hint of dolefulness flashed in Anton's eyes. "No, I wouldn't."

"We baptized her at St. Patrick's," Grace said, resisting the urge to tell him to butt out. "The church looks similar to the photos of Holy Rosary Joseph showed me."

Joseph often told Grace how his father who, with other German-speaking Catholics, raised money to buy land and founded Holy Rosary in the Germantown section of city where they could worship in their own language. When they were searching for pastors, Anton recommended the Benedictines. He first came to know the Order in Europe, when he studied there, and later in Minnesota, where they presided over Assumption, the church he attended and where he and Susanna married. Joseph liked to say that if it hadn't been for his father, there wouldn't be Benedictines in Washington State.

Countless parishioners greeted Anton upon their arrival. He stopped to speak and shake hands with everyone, and introduce them to Grace and Vivienne. After the family was seated in the first pew facing the blue and white statue of the Virgin Mary, Susanna joined them. A metal container of flickering votive candles stood at the foot of the statue, and to the side a censer diffused incense throughout the sanctuary. Its sweet smell turned Grace's stomach; none of them had eaten breakfast as they were expected to take communion. A small choral group standing near the statue of St. Joseph sang a Gregorian chant *a cappella*.

Grace felt the parishioners' eyes on them as prayers whirled around. She touched her lapel, checking the placement of her pearl and green lacquer lily-the-valley brooch. She imagined everything was exactly as Anton wanted, assuming it important for him to portray himself as head of a prosperous, established, upright and growing family. With this in mind, she made certain to follow him and Susanna, kneeling when they did, bowing her head when they did, saying Amen when they did. And she didn't forget her mother's dictum to not slouch before God.

During the sermon, Grace tried to concentrate on the words. But her thoughts wandered back to the times she attended church with her family, when they were still a family. Her parents were both Catholics, but she never sensed religion was at the core of her family's life. Certainly not like it was with the Tschidas. Perhaps because tackling each day's challenges took all their reserves. Indeed, they pleaded with the Virgin Mary when someone was ill, wore St. Christopher medals and scapulas, gave the monsignor a coin or two for special blessings, and made certain they received the sacraments. But underneath was a skepticism, a wary eye for priests and religion in general. Her mother often said, *Many good people don't go to church and many not-so-good people do; don't be fooled by outward appearances.* They didn't always attend services—did you really need to go to church to pray? What was prayer but the concentration of your mind on something.

Thinking of prayer, a memory visited her of the story her mother told of the winter in Michigan when she was five years old and ill with diphtheria. Her mother wanted the bishop to come and pray over her. But her father fussed because a northern front was coming and he feared a snowdrift would bury her alive. In the end, he relented and said, "If that man comes for a wedding, he'll wait for the christening. We'll never get rid of him." Funny the things one remembers, Grace mused, as she eyed Anton place a crisp ten-dollar bill in the collection basket.

After Mass, the family went to Calvary Cemetery as was their custom, to visit Anton's parents in the family plot. A tall monument in the shape of an obelisk anchored it. Inscribed on it were only his parent's names and years of birth and death. No pithy sayings, no ornamental flower or angel, only an acknowledgment that they lived and died. Below was space for other names to be added. Grace surmised Anton and Susanna would one day rest beside these two peregrinators who spent only a few years here, denied their final resting place in the land that cultivated them. Flanking the headstone were three blank pillow stones for Joseph and his sisters and no one else.

Susanna set up a late breakfast in the dining room. The windows and curtains were open to air out the room. Swatches of sunlight streaked across one end of the table, casting the pumpernickel bread, butter and jam in a glow. On the other side were sweet peppers, cucumbers, tomatoes, and hard-boiled eggs. Coffee warmed in a carafe on the credenza. Center stage, on a silver platter, were Susanna's famous cinnamon buns she served only on Sundays. This is the breakfast, minus the buns, Grace would find every morning. She wondered how long before she craved one of her mother's baking-powder biscuits or a plate of French toast. Or fresh raspberries with a splash of cream, something her mother thought was also the perfect dessert. Here for such a short time and already she ached for the ease and comfort of being with your own. She told herself she could put up with anything for a short while, and it didn't require much to *ooh* and *ahh* like the others.

After Sunday dinner, that traditionally started with Susanna's chicken soup, the family gathered in the parlor. Anton crumpled newsprint as kindling and lit a fire, while they listened to the Victrola. Marta sat on the floor with Vivienne, rolling a ball back and forth and occasionally assuming the voice of her teddy bear and telling her what a good girl she was. Clara sat next to Grace on the sofa, crocheting a wool scarf in muted hues of green, lavender and gray.

"Clara, play a song Gracie knows," Joseph said, turning off the record, "so everyone can hear her lovely voice."

Grace glared at Joseph. "Oh, no, I couldn't. And Anton wants to listen to his music."

"It's fine," Clara said as she sat down at the piano. "Father pretends not to mind our music."

It bothered Grace she wanted to make a good impression. What was it her mother said? *Why do you care what they think?* She pointed to the sheet music. "Can I see what you have?" *If I don't live up to my billing, the hell with them.* She selected "Pretty Baby."

Clara started playing the melody and followed with "I Love you Truly" and "Broken Doll."

"You must sing at church next Sunday," Susanna said. "I'll speak to the choirmaster."

"I won't have time to practice. We're here for such a short time."

"If you lived here, you could sing with our theater group," Clara said. "We do musicals sometimes." She pulled a novel from the bookcase and took out a photo she'd used as a bookmark. She handed it to Joseph. "Remember this?"

Joseph stroked the photo. "That's the *Hard Times* Party after the play."

"The one where he looks like a gangster with a cigarette dangling from his mouth?" Susanna said. "Wish you'd get rid of it."

Joseph showed Grace the photo of some sixty partygoers. Half of them were dressed in turn-of-the-century period costumes. "That's me in the newsboy cap. My outfit for the play."

Grace was about to say she found it strange to have a party around a recession theme when Joseph said, "Let's talk about what we should do while we're here."

"We can go to the ocean, if it's not too cold," Clara said, "or to the Mountain. The trails are nice this time of year."

"A picnic at Point Defiance," Marta added.

"The Indian salmon bake is on before you go,' Clara said. She turned to Grace. "It's on an island in the Sound. You walk on a pathway of clamshells and gather around an open fire where they cook the salmon splayed on branches."

"Father, let's have my friends over for a game of cards like we used to," Joseph said. "It'll give me a chance to see them and we'll have some fun." He turned to Grace. "You don't mind, do you, darling?"

"Of course not." She picked up Vivienne, who kicked and resisted, not ready to stop playing "This Little Piggy" with Marta. "I think she needs changing. I'll take her upstairs."

As she was putting clean diapers on her daughter, she said, "Well, they're the ones, aren't they? Always asking their seemingly innocent questions and planning our lives away without considering us." Vivienne rolled over and tried to grab the edge of the changing table. "Here, take your dolly and let's sit on the bed." Vivienne pulled at the cloth doll's yarn hair and tried to yank off one of the button eyes. "Don't hurt her. Be nice." Vivienne looked up at Grace and patted the doll.

Be nice. Grace recalled the time her stepfather Max told her to be nice to the boys who came round to see her. Her mother piped up, "She doesn't have to be nice to anyone if she doesn't want to."

All the hardships her mother faced throughout life, and here she was upset because she had to contend with her in-laws for a while. She watched Vivienne rock her doll side to side. "Yes, sweet pea. We must think of the positive. You're getting to know daddy's family."

CHAPTER 13

♦

Joseph planned a game night for Wednesday, and Grace looked forward to meeting his friends. After dinner, he asked her to help him set up the table with the chips and cards. Susanna, who usually helped Marta and Clara take the platters and dishes to the kitchen, remained seated. She struggled to stand, using the table edge to push herself up. Grace tapped Joseph's arm. "Let's clear the table for your mother."

Susanna gave Grace a withering glare. "That's not a man's job."

Grace jerked back. She flinched when Joseph touched her arm.

"You meant well, darling," he whispered. "She didn't mean to snap at you. Help me get the cards. The guys will be here soon."

Grace tried to shake off the rebuke; she didn't want to appear upset when Joseph's friends arrived. But she had to say something. "Joseph helps me at home. My brother helps my mother. We help each other when we can."

Susanna looked away with a taut lip. As Joseph tugged at Grace's arm to lead her away, Susanna picked up the butter dish and silverware and marched into the kitchen.

Three of Joseph's friends came, all graduates of St. Martin's where they studied commerce and the classics. She wasn't disappointed when she met the well-dressed men in their suits and starched shirts, each toting either a felt derby or a bowler hat.

"We've heard so much about you, Grace," Frank said, with a slight bow of his head. "It's an honor to meet you."

"Could have used Joseph on the baseball team last season, but guess he had better things to do," Quincy said with a bit of swagger as he tried to tame his feral cowlick.

"Left for California without a word," Xavier said, giving her a two-hander shake. "Now I understand."

Grace sensed a tight friendship among the men, similar to the one she had with school and work friends in Everett. When she moved to California, she tried to keep her friendships alive with correspondence and the occasional phone call. But she never discounted the need for her and Joseph to make new friends in Sonora.

"Have you seen this?" Frank said, handing Grace a clipping of a newspaper photo and article. "It's one of our field days at St. Martin's." He pointed to the photo. "There's Joseph in the plaid cap, standing next to Father Lighthouse—he was the starter. It's yours to keep. I have other copies."

"Great fun those meets," Xavier said. "Lasted all day, from 8:30 am to 5:00 pm. All our friends and family came."

"Don't forget the grand feed after when they gave out the awards," Quincy said.

Joseph looked over Grace's shoulder. "That was the starting line for the hundred-yard dash." He scrutinized the clipping. "I think it was the Al Smith Derby. Do you remember who won?" All his friends shook their heads.

"It calls you JoeJoe Tschida here," Grace said, looking up at Joseph.

"That was our nickname for him," Xavier said.

"Those were the good years," Quincy said, as they headed to the dining room. "Baseball and cycling, acting club. How the other guys teased us, calling us hams."

"Not Joseph," Xavier said. "Father Jerome said he was good and should consider a life in the theater."

"He did," Joseph said. "That's why I joined the amateur theater here."

"He made me join with him," Quincy said to Grace. "I was envious of him though. Always got the best reviews—still does."

"You should go to Hollywood and get in pictures," Frank said. "You'd make it."

"You've got the looks," Quincy said, throwing several packs of Blackjack gum on the table. "Sort of the Francis X. Bushman type. And we know you have your Don Juan moves."

Xavier turned to Grace. "He's only joking."

But his words stuck in Grace's mind. Didn't her mother say she sensed Joseph knew his way around women?

"Go to Hollywood," Frank said, clapping Joseph on the shoulder. "You can get me a job writing scripts."

"And introduce us to the stars," Quincy said. "Of the female persuasion."

"I never saw you in a play," Grace said to Joseph, "but from what I'm hearing, you should think about it."

"Hollywood's no place to raise a child, darling. You read fan magazines. All those stories about what goes on in Hollywood." Joseph straightened out the ends of Frank's bowtie. "Hey, nice tie. But I think it would look better on me."

Frank took off his tie and gave it to Joseph.

"Does it all the time," Quincy said to Grace. "Can convince anyone of anything."

"Really?" Grace said. *I'd like to see him use that charm on his family.*

"Let's play," Joseph said, cutting the deck of cards.

As the game started, Marta placed bowls of assorted licorice, horehound candy, and Anton's favorite fruit pastilles on the table. Grace sat in the parlor chair with the clearest sightline into the dining room and pretended to read.

"Did you hear about baseball tryouts for the Tigers?" Quincy said.

"Frank should know all about it, that is, if he reads his own paper," Joseph said. "What's the pot tonight?"

"Five dollars," Anton said.

"Are you following the anti-war demonstrations in Europe?" Frank said. "At the paper we did a feature on the Stockholm Confer—"

"None of your work stories," Quincy said with mock gruffness.

"You should pay attention." Miffed, Frank spoke louder. "Hundreds of thousands dead. The Germans wiped out complete villages—remember Verdun?"

"Frank's right, "Xavier said. "What happens in Europe could affect us here. We're crazy to think it won't."

"It's helping the economy—opening new markets for us." Joseph said.

"Got to keep those military machines running," Quincy said. "But hey, we're playing now."

Joseph slapped his cards hard on the table and let out a holler. "Look at that hand."

"Another win," Xavier said to Joseph. "You're too good at numbers."

During a lull in the game, Quincy took out a pack of Pall Malls and said, "Let's go out on the porch and light up."

"Wait here, Joseph," Anton said, as the others stepped out. After his friends left, Grace overheard Anton say, "Think how nice it would be to stay here and have your friends nearby. You could study law like Xavier. It's a good career for you."

Joseph pursed his lips and shook his head. "I'd like to be near my friends, but I'm not interested in law and I have a job waiting for me."

"I'm not convinced that job has potential, Son. You can live here and I'll pay for school and your expenses."

Grace's throat tightened. The thought of living with his family, without the privacy and intimacy they'd known in California, made her stomach lurch. She unconsciously tapped her foot as she ran scenarios through her mind: she'd threaten to live with her mother in Everett or with her sister in Palo Alto; tell them the climate was unsuitable—if Susanna can claim the water in California is bad for her, well, the dampness here is not good for her and Vivienne.

She got up and stood behind Joseph's chair. "I don't think he wants to go back to school."

Anton swatted the air between them, as if giving her opinion a wallop. "You can work for my friend Charlie at the Bank of California."

"I don't want to be a teller—that's where he'd start me."

"Schaupp's store on 23rd and K. Only until something else comes up."

"No favors from your friends. Do you really think working at a grocery would be better than what I'm doing? Please, Father."

"I'm trying to make things easy for you, Son. Not like when I came and had to do hard labor at the lumber company. I didn't want that job, but I had to until I could do my work." A dark spittle from the licorice formed in the corner of his mouth.

"I appreciate your wanting to help but—" Joseph rested his elbows on the table and put his drooping head between his hands.

Grace squeezed his shoulder as if communicating in Morse code. *You're doing fine. Keep rebuffing the old buzzard.* When Joseph didn't say more, she blurted out, "I want . . ." She paused as she came up with wording that wouldn't offend. "It's important he does what he believes is best."

Anton opened his mouth to say something and stopped short. He crossed his arms over his chest.

Only ten more days, she thought, *and we can go home.*

The next few days Grace saw Anton corner Joseph and talk in conspiratorial tones. She had no doubt what it was about. He appeared to rebuff his father's suggestions, but she worried Anton would eventually convince him. And she feared he'd give in.

Before bed one evening she said, "I'm eager to get home. We can take Vivienne to the Sierras before it's too cold, or take a trip to visit Ellen."

"Aren't you enjoying yourself here?"

She dabbed a few drops of Coty perfume on her wrists to gain a second while she decided how dishonest she'd be. "I'm glad Vivienne met your family. They've been very hospitable. But it's not home."

A few nights later, Joseph's friends came over for another game night. Grace wanted to speak to them alone, to ask them to continue pressing the idea of Hollywood with Joseph. Or anything to get him to think of other possibilities that didn't include staying in Tacoma. They might have more sway over him than she or Anton did. But the night offered no opportunity, even though the subject of him trying an acting career briefly came up again.

After the men left, Anton stopped Joseph as he and Grace were about to go upstairs. "I don't want you listening to your friends. You already have too many roving interests. I want you to reconsider law school."

"*Roving interests?*" Joseph let go of Grace's hand.

Anton stroked his mustache. "I was too lenient. All that acting and sports. You need to create a good future."

"Say it—you're concerned I won't make a lot of money."

"I've taken pride in my work and if it brought me a good living, you and the family benefitted. How many young men your age have had the opportunities you've had? Live in a nice house, study at college? Huh? Answer me."

"Did you ever think I have my own dreams and goals?"

"You can't live on dreams. Education, a good job and hard work will make you successful."

"Successful? Say what you really mean, Father." Joseph pulled Grace toward the stairs.

"We'll have this conversation again," Anton called after him.

With Vivienne asleep, Grace combed her hair and gazed into the mirror, catching Joseph's reflection as he lay on the bed, his spirits dashed.

"It makes me angry he thinks I'm a dilettante, a dabbler." Joseph stroked the corners of his mouth with his thumb and index finger.

Grace pulled up her nightgown where it had slipped off her shoulder and joined him. "Don't let him force you into something you don't want to do."

"He's done a lot for me and there are expectations." He rubbed the back of his neck with both hands. "I'm his only son—I don't want to disappoint him."

"I understand that. But he left his family and did what he wanted. One could say he was a dilettante." She picked at a thread in the comforter. "As my mother says, *A fox smells its own hole*."

"I love you, Gracie." He nuzzled her neck. "No *roving interest* there. I'm constant in my love for you. Do you remember how I hesitated before talking to you about love? I wasn't sure if you'd laugh or shrug it away." He pushed aside the hair that had slipped over her face. "I'm glad you can tell me these things. I know I'm selfish and want my way, but I hope you'll always love me." He scooted over. "Here, lie down."

She snuggled close to him and he pressed his nose against her head.

"I know you think of Vivienne and me. . . and I know you say Hollywood is no place to raise a family, but couldn't you try it and see if it's something you might like? It'd be terrible to wonder later if it would have worked out."

"Father thinks I'm a dreamer. If I said I was going to try acting, it'd convince him."

"I see no any harm in being a dreamer. Dreamers create."

He placed his finger on her lips. "I may be good for amateur theater here, but not in competition with others who really know acting."

Grace winced as thunder from an approaching storm crashed.

"Reminds me of the time I came to Everett during that rainstorm," he said. "We got so wet—it was like the clouds were being squeezed of their last drops."

Gazing at the domed-lead crystal boudoir lamp, Grace thought back to other small, meaningful moments they shared. She longed for those easier times and wished she could tell Joseph how much she disliked being here. But as he found it difficult to say no to his father, she couldn't tell her husband the truth.

CHAPTER 14

♦

He is scant of news that speaks ill of his mother.

Foghorn moans drifted in from the Sound and greeted Grace as she woke from a sleepy haze. Her eyes gently opened as a delicate light of sunrise streamed through a crack in the curtains. The room smelled of dirty socks and baby diapers.

Sounds rose from downstairs: furniture scooting around; a tin lid clanging on the floor until it found equilibrium; wisps of a cloth or rag moving back and forth. It was Wednesday, Susanna's day to polish, according to her weekly household ritual Clara told Grace about: Monday, mend and wash clothes; Tuesday, iron and dust; Wednesday, polish floors and furniture; Thursday, shop and clean kitchen; Friday, cook for the weekend; Saturday, the women's auxiliary meeting and prepare church for evening rosary services; Sunday, attend Mass and rest.

"Joseph, what happens if your mother doesn't keep to her schedule?" Grace asked, still half asleep under a twisted sheet, the aroma of coffee wafting up from the kitchen.

"Hmm?" said Joseph, turning and rubbing sleep out of his eyes. "What'd you say?"

"Nothing." She got up and stood barefoot by the window, gazing at the mist surrounding the shrubs on the lawn. A dusty purple and pale pink halo of haze surrounded the rising sun. A cock crowed. "Another day, Mr. Rooster. The hens are waiting," she murmured. *And another day fending off the onslaught of Anton's manipulation.* A hushed sigh escaped her lips and vaporized into the air.

That afternoon, as Grace walked downstairs after putting Vivienne down for a nap, she heard Anton and Joseph talking. Muffling her steps, she stood behind the parlor doorframe and eavesdropped.

"Have you thought about asking Xavier if there's an opening at Alber's?"

"The grain mills? No. Xavier's only there until he has his law degree."

"It could be something temporary, until something better comes along. Or what about Quincy helping you get a job at that new company he's working at on the way to Seattle? What's it called—Boeing?"

Grace peered in and saw Joseph pacing in front of the fireplace, his shoulders raised. He turned and faced his father. "All right. I'll see if there's something here."

Grace squeezed her eyes shut. She shook her head from side to side.

A short time later, she found Joseph on the front porch, slouched in the rocking chair, his head titled back. One arm dangled over the side as blue smoke from his cigarette swirled upward. "I heard what you told your father. You promised we'd stay two weeks and go home."

Gazing across the street, he continued rocking, his eyes averted. "I know, but maybe the railroad job isn't the best for me—for us."

"We don't have to return to Sonora. We can go to Sacramento, or wherever you want. You'll find a job. You're more qualified than most. Why are you giving in? Is this what you really want?"

"It doesn't hurt to see what opportunities there are here, darling." He pulled her onto his lap and embraced her. "I'll always take care of you, Gracie. And as long as we're together, that's all that really matters. Isn't that what we told each other? That we could live in a shack or a big palace and be happy as long as we're together."

She punched his arm. "I love it there. I don't want to live here."

"Think how nice it would be for Vivienne to grow up around family, and you'll be closer to your mother and brother. It'll be easier for us."

"We can come back for holidays—"

"The trip's long. And visits are not the same. Plus, my friends are here and I could rejoin my theater group—so could you. You could sing in the productions. Gracie, you'd be swell."

"I don't want to be in your theater group. I don't want to live in one room with a small child. I don't want you catering to your family's whims." Her chin fell to her chest.

"You'll do this for me, won't you, darling?"

It took her a few moments to respond. "This was their plan all along, wasn't it, JoeJoe? The old connivers knew if they got you here, they'd manipulate you to stay. I don't think I can forgive you." She got up and eyed him with a potent stare. "You mismatched your socks."

Two days later, on the day Grace previously thought would mark the beginning of the end of their stay in Tacoma, she dressed Vivienne in the white dress she'd made for her first birthday. She'd taken special care to make the perfect dress, adorning the hem and sleeves with crocheted eyelets, and stitching delicate shirring on the bodice.

"Hold still, sweetie," she said as she clasped the gold chain and cross around the child's neck, a gift from Anton and Susanna at birth. She struggled to mask her glumness, not wanting her low spirits to take away from her daughter's day. On Vivienne's middle finger, she placed the gold ring her friend Genevieve sent. Then she combed her bangs, taking care to make them straight. "Now the pretty hat Aunt Clara made you," she said, picking up the white crocheted bonnet embellished with large rosettes on each side.

"Are you ready?" Anton called out from behind the closed bedroom door.

"Come in." She straightened the cross around Vivienne's neck. "I only have to put on her shoes and socks."

He entered with a small blue box and watched as Grace finished dressing the child. "She has the Greek toe. We studied it in sculpture." Grace looked at Anton with a bemused expression. "The second toe is longer than the first. A sign of beauty. And such cute dimples in her knees." Anton took Vivienne's hand. "I have something for you." On her other middle finger, he slid on a tiny silver ring set with a blue oval gemstone. "Sapphire for September. Clara told me." As he held her hand, she sat without moving, her eyes fixed on her grandfather. "Now we hurry, so we aren't late for the photographer."

On his way out the door, he added, "When we get home, Joseph can take pictures of Vivienne and me with my Brownie camera. And tonight, we have your grandmother's apple cake with whipped cream—and one large candle in the middle."

When the photograph of the one-year-old roly-poly-cheeked, wide-eyed little girl with a serene and beguiling look in her eyes came back from the studio, Anton placed it on his bedroom dresser. He kept it there for the rest of his life, only hers and no one else's.

Joseph thought it best for Grace and Vivienne to stay with his family while he returned to Sonora to resign from his job and clean out the apartment. Grace wanted to accompany him to get away from his parents, but she had to agree it wasn't practical. And so, her life with the Tschidas continued, with its daily hassles and bewilderments. One mid-morning, when she returned from taking Vivienne for a walk in the new Lloyd Loom wicker pram Anton bought, she found Susanna with a dozen plastic replicas of the saints on the dining room table. When she asked what they were for, Susanna said, "I've plans for them."

Later in the day, she saw Susanna dig holes in the ground with a trowel. When she finished, she came inside and folded her apron into a makeshift pouch to carry the saints into the backyard. One by one, she put a saint upside down in a hole, and marked each one's location with a numbered stick. Taking a hand-drawn map from her apron pocket, she scribbled down each one's spot. Grace joined her outside and asked, "Why did you put them in the ground?"

"If they want to get out, they have to get Joseph a job." Susanna gave a sharp nod.

Grace didn't know whether to laugh or cry. The following days, she eavesdropped when Susanna talked to the saints.

"St. Cajetan, I need you to work hard. St. Paschal, my son needs your help. St. Jude, make it happen. St. Xenia, I know your specialty, so get at it. St. Joseph, if you don't like it down there, you know what you have to do to get out."

Unable to quell her curiosity, she said to Susanna, "I heard you talking to St. Xenia. Never heard of her."

"Russian saint Father Gerhard told me about. She helps find jobs."

Grace thought about getting her own St. Rita, the saint of impossible causes, and putting her in the ground, with prayers for the saint to reverse the headwinds and send them back to California. On the days Susanna was at her guild meetings or out shopping, Grace wandered among the saints, giving them her own instructions. "St. Jude, wherever you are, listen to me. You're not going to get Joseph a job here, but you're going to get him to California. And St. Xenia, you can work with St. Jude and do the same—no, I'll make your jobs easier. Get Joseph anywhere out of Tacoma."

The railroad manager in Sonora asked Joseph to stay on to train the employee taking over his position. He agreed, as he might need a good recommendation for future jobs. He wrote Grace he'd be back in a week or two, saying he didn't want to stay longer because he missed her and Vivienne. But the next letter Grace received, he'd taken ill, which he attributed to working long hours and not getting enough sleep. And he was having more of his fatiguing headaches. He'd have to stay in Sonora longer. Crestfallen, her mood became as dark as a moonless night as she read on.

My Darling, without you, I'm feeling lonesome. Wish you were with me. I always feel good when I'm with you. Do you still love me, Gracie? Don't be stingy when you tell me, please.

Of course, I do. Although, you've put my love to the test with your decision to stay here.

Quincy tells me that on February 22nd they're giving a play called Those Dreadful Twins. *I might join the cast. I don't think it'll be good, but there's one part I'd like—a detective, no villain this time. Clara is going to play an old maid.*

Clara asked if I'd like to join the production back stage. I don't think I will. Vivienne is still young and I prefer to be with her and not away for rehearsals. Maybe if you act in the play, it'll make you think about Hollywood.

Once I get better, I'll be busy finishing up at the office, but will try to write to you every day. I'm afraid they won't be long letters, but you won't mind, will you, dear? Do you remember you are the only girl I have ever loved?

Quincy's words flitted through her mind: *a Don Juan.*

Are you taking more photos? Send me some if you have. Oh, I left the gold watch you gave me on top of the dresser. Please see nothing happens to it.

I already put it inside the bureau.

Father wants me to start night school to study advanced bookkeeping when I return. If you have any suggestions, tell me because I know you only tell me things that help.

I've tried, but I'm no match for your family.

With lots and lots of love, as ever, Joseph.

Grace wrote Joseph back, saying she hoped he wouldn't mind, but since he was delayed, she was taking Vivienne to stay at her mother's until he returned from California, not mentioning she also longed to see her friends.

But mind, he did.

I know you're upset—and I'm certain you're counting up my faults while waiting for me to return. But I must tell you, I don't like you going to Everett, in spite of your sensing I may not like it.

Why else would you have said you hoped I wouldn't mind? I wanted you and Vivienne to spend time with my family while I'm gone, so you can form a bond.

When you said those things about being selfish, I thought it chatter. But now I see you're telling the truth—you're damn selfish, Joseph Tschida.

The day before she planned to tell the Tschidas of her trip to Everett, she received another of his letters.

Darling, Gracie,

I don't know where to start. I'm so tired and there are so many things I'd like to say to you. It's nearly midnight, and I just finished packing up boxes. You do realize I have all this work to do after I get out of my job.

I wish I could have gone with you and helped, even if I am peeved at you.

I didn't intend to upset you, but I was disappointed and thought it was natural to let you know. I can't conceive of not telling you how I feel anymore. Darling, I realize you know your own mind. Before, you only had yourself to think about, and now you take me into consideration. I feel this is the way it should be, as I consider you.

True. I consider some of my actions—because of you. But how in heaven's name can you say you consider me? Did you consider what I wanted when you agreed to stay here? Did you consider how cramped we'd be living in one room? Did you consider you may have to do a job you don't like? Did you consider you may be giving up a promising career elsewhere?

Darling, in a true union, you give up a certain degree of independence, but it's compensated by sharing everything. This doesn't mean you'll lose your individuality. Sorry, I don't mean to get carried away. It's the way I see things.

Your loving, Joseph.

Grace re-read the letter several times, pacing back and forth in the parlor, each step striking the floor harder and harder. She wanted to be considerate—isn't that why she wrote to tell him she was going to Everett? But it was never a question of whether to go or not—she was going. She never imagined he'd think anything besides it being a good chance for her to see her mother and brother and have them spend time with Vivienne. Instead, he rambled on about considering his desires. *Heavens, I'm visiting my mother, not booking passage to Africa.*

While Susanna was making bread the following morning, Grace watched the daylight stream through the window, bathing the cupboards in a glow the color of coconut cake. She casually mentioned she planned to leave the next day.

"Tomorrow?" Susanna's eyes narrowed with suspicion as she sprinkled flour into a mound and smashed the top with her fist, creating a cavity.

"Just while Joseph's away." Grace avoided eye contact and fidgeted with the silver bangle on her bracelet.

Susanna separated an egg yolk with her fingers and mixed it with the flour.

"He wants me to spend time with my family." As soon as she said it, she wondered if Joseph told his mother he wasn't keen on her leaving and asked Susanna to see they stayed in Tacoma. "Like you, my mother would love to spend time with her first grandchild." Inside, she silently yelled, *I'm aching to get away and share my true feelings with my mother and friends.*

Susanna's mood shifted as she took warm milk from the stove and poured it into the flour. "*Ja, ja,* families want to be with their children." Susanna's head bobbed as she kneaded the dough.

CHAPTER 15

♦

The day after Grace arrived in Everett, Lorna watched her toy with the gold beaded fringe around the light shade, a faraway look in her eyes. "I know you never want to say anything bad about people, but you're not fooling me. What's wrong?"

"Joseph promised we'd return to California." She let out a humph. "I should have known. He said it in that half voice of his, without conviction."

"Don't go back. Stay here."

"No. He's a good husband and father and we love each other." Grace clasped her hands together under her chin. "His family does a lot . . . but I feel someone's always watching me."

"Sugarcoating it, aren't you? Let me tell you: only son, of course they're judging you. Like I did him." Lorna fluffed the faded sofa pillow, embroidered with multi-colored autumn leaves. "A woman doesn't need to be loved. Any woman who needs it will do anything to get it."

"Didn't you need love? Didn't you want father to love you?"

Lorna stared at the missing chip in the corner of the wood-base mantel clock. "I needed to love you children and him. And I did in spades." She motioned for Grace to sit next to her at the table. "He was a smooth talker, and you were smitten the moment you saw him." Lorna stretched out her legs and leaned back. "Didn't I say you had a lot to learn? You marry the man, you marry the family. Does he know yet you're older?"

"No. I don't want him to find out. His family may—"

"Ah, the family again," Lorna scoffed. "Clara may be nice, but I didn't like the way she doted on you, either. *You're so petite and dainty with your size four shoes. Oh, the clothes you make are so beautiful.*"

"Mother, please."

"Don't you *please* me, Lady Jane. I'm your mother and I've every right to be concerned. The lot of them are schemers. And don't think I wasn't worried when I heard his parents picked out a lass that they wanted him to marry."

"Olga. A friend of his sisters."

Lorna flung a hand up and uttered a loud *Tabanak*.

"Shh. Don't wake Vivienne." Grace glanced at the sleeping child. "Joseph told me many times he was never interested in her. He always says I'm the only one he's ever loved."

"Lying like a pig in lavender, yes siree, showing himself in the best light." Lorna waggled her head. "That matchmaking mother should've given you misgivings a long time ago." She straightened the black velvet ribbon around Grace's neck, making certain the cameo was in the center. "You're too kind for that kind of folk. Do me a favor and stay here. You've plenty of people who love you."

"Manage alone with a child?"

"Daniel and I are here." She placed her hands on Grace's shoulders. "I had the four of you when your father went to hospital. If I could do it, you can, too. Never feel trapped. If you do, you'll put up with things you shouldn't put up with."

"He always says he's worried I'll leave him."

"Good. Let him keep worrying." Lorna gave a kick to the Collier's magazine peeking out from under the table. "Going to tell you something, there's one in a relationship who loves more than the other. It's better if it's the man—I never saw one refuse something offered to him."

"Oh, mother. The things you say sometimes." Grace got down on her haunches and fished out the magazine. "There's dust under here . . . and crumbs."

"Dust and dirt never hurt anyone." She tugged on Grace's arm. "I made a pot of chicken fricot we can warm up for dinner.

Now go have fun with your friends. Vivienne and I will have a grand old time."

Grace met Rose and Genevieve at a tea shoppe on Hewitt Avenue. Tables and banquettes filled the spacious room and vintage floral prints covered the walls. Keeping with the botanical motif, a navy rug with large yellow hibiscus flowers screamed for attention.

"Remember Yvonne, the steno for Vandenberg and Nelson?" Rose asked Grace, as she pointed to the black pekoe on the tea wagon. "She had her appendix out. Oh, I love how you wear your brooch *a La Valiere*. Did your husband give it to you?"

"Ellen did," Grace said, fingering the beige and ivory pendant, "for my birthday." She turned to the server. "I'll have the Ceylon, please."

"Same for me," Genevieve said, "and we'll all have raisin scones." After the waitress gathered the menus and left, she asked Grace, "Did you bring new photos? I want to see how Vivienne's grown."

"And your dear hubby," Rose said, her close-set, doe-like eyes lighting up. "I want to cast my optics on his countenance again."

Grace handed a photo to Genevieve. "Before I forget, mother wants you both to come for lunch Saturday, a simple affair, homemade cabbage and sausage soup, and her soda bread."

"Honey, she's more adorable than ever," Genevieve said, handing the photo to Rose. "Did you bring one of Joseph?"

Grace smiled as she looked at the next picture. "Here's one of my favorites with him sitting near the boxwood hedges."

"Nice striped pants and striped shirt. Does he always wear a bowtie?" Genevieve asked, leaning toward Rose so she could also see the photo.

"Both him and his father."

"He's handsome," Rose said. "Has that come hither look in his eyes. I can see why you'd be taken by him. I would be, too." Rose flushed as if she felt she made a mistake.

"Know what mother said when she first saw him?" Grace said. Both friends shook their heads. "You're the only ones I've told this to and don't tell anyone else—she thought he looked like a refined gypsy, like he had 'mixed blood.'"

Rose fingered the Venetian lace on her jewel neckline. "His exotic sultry looks, that's why. Say, how do you pronounce your new name?"

"Think of the cheetah cat. It sounds like that," Grace said.

The server returned and placed a cup and saucer and small tea pots in front of each of the friends. In the middle of the table, she plopped the cream and sugar and a three-tier stand with the scones and little containers of strawberry jam, clotted cream and lemon curd.

"Don't you love how they use these gorgeous antique chinaware patterns?" Rose said.

"So, honey, how is it living there with his family?" Genevieve said.

Grace bowed her head and paused.

"Don't be a Griselda," Genevieve said. "Get everything off your chest."

"His father tries to control his life. And his mother, she's always cleaning or cooking or praying."

"A bit tight-laced," Rose said, raising her eyebrows.

"The two of them often speak German." Grace flicked her gaze upward. "I can only imagine what they're saying."

"Honey," Genevieve said, raising the teapot lid to check if her tea had steeped enough, "families can be messy and people from the old country have their ways. Have to hope your love gets you through the emotional torture. Are you sure, you can't go back to California?"

Grace ran her finger around the rim of her water glass. "I didn't realize how much I liked living there. Something you learn when you no longer have it."

"If you can't go back, have Joseph look for a job here and you'll be near us," Rose said.

"His family would prevent it," Grace said. "I'm caught between wanting to be nice—his family's important to him—

and wanting to tell them to keep out of our lives." She took a deep breath. "I hate to admit it, but I go along."

"I've never seen you be mean," Rose said. "It would be hard for you to be nasty to them."

"You go along to make it work." Genevieve put her hand on top of Grace's. "If you could isolate yourself from his family, Tacoma might be nice."

"We liked Clara," Rose said. "What about the other one?"

"Marta. I feel sorry for her. She gets more criticism from her parents—I think it makes her insecure.'

"Could also be because she's not as attractive as Clara," Rose said

Grace winced. "I shouldn't have said that." She continued in a hushed voice, "There are reasons to like her—to like anyone, really. She helps me with Vivienne. She's good at playing games with her."

"I nearly forgot," Genevieve said, pulling the book *Of Human Bondage* from her bag and handing it to Grace.

"Did you like it?"

Genevieve nodded. "Everyone's reading it. Hard in places, but good."

"Did you read *Parisienne* this month?" Rose said, looking around to see where the faint music was coming from.

Grace shook her head and remembered how they'd search for the latest copies of *La Vie Parisienne* to get fashion tips, veiled gossip and short stories about love. Such innocent divertissements and such innocent days.

Rose slipped her hand into her coat pocket and frowned. Her mouth flew open as she pulled out a five-dollar bill. "Haven't worn this coat since spring. Ladies, tea today is on me."

On their way out of the tea shoppe, Genevieve said. "Tell your mother I'll bring one of my gooseberry pies for our lunch."

"Oh, gosh, what should I bring?" Rose asked.

"How about the Jello you make with Coca Cola," Genevieve said. "It's really tasty."

When Grace arrived back at her mother's apartment, she found a gift from Joseph. It was a silver German Jitney purse along with a note, saying how much he missed her and Vivienne.

"It's beautiful, isn't it?" she said to Lorna.

"Beauty is as beauty does. Careful now, he wants something."

"He wants us ho—back at his parents." As she gazed at the purse, she thought of her mother and friends, realizing all she missed and had given up for Joseph. For now, her dream of returning to California had faded and folded like a paper flower in the rain.

CHAPTER 16

♦

There is no fireside like your own fireside.

Grace returned to Tacoma the day before Joseph arrived and took advantage of a quiet moment while Vivienne napped. Sitting on the velvet-padded window seat, she rested her arm on the windowsill and felt cool air seeping through a crack. She absentmindedly watched girls play hopscotch across the street. *Life's a mosaic,* she thought. *All these little unimagined events come together—meeting Clara, Clara introducing me to Joseph, Joseph following me to California, and now Tacoma—and you hope in the end it was all meant to be and worth it.*

Her eye caught sight of the entryway table and its pile of unopened mail. She riffled through it; bills in Anton's name, a circular from Holy Rosary, a Montgomery Ward catalog page, and a letter for her. Seeing the curlicue script, she knew it was from Genevieve. As she opened it, dried rose petals slipped from the letter onto her dress.

Chere Grace,

I wish I could've seen you more when you were here, but I'm a working gal. I must tell you, honey, Vivienne is a lovely baby. She'll soon outgrow the ring I gave her and I'll get her an honest-to-goodness one. There's little choice in tiny rings.

Genevieve, always so thoughtful.

Bien, I hope you teach Vivienne to speak French as soon as she takes up her ABC's. Baby lips learn to form the words easily, and after this war, French will be much used and a wonderful accomplishment for anyone. If I were older, I'd join the Hello Girls in the Signal Corps to use my French to help the allies at the front lines.

The war. When would it ever end? Grace's mind wandered to the latest news bulletins; the German assaults in Belgium and France, American soldiers going to Europe to train and fight, the firing-squad execution of the German spy, Mata Hari.

I've been doing a lot of thinking since you left and I want you to know you have a good friend in me. I'm always here to listen and help.

With love from your friend, Genevieve.

Friends understand, Grace thought. Even though they couldn't fully fathom what living with the Tschidas was really like.

Her gaze swept over to the credenza. She paused and glanced around as if to make certain no one was nearby. With one of her hairpins, she picked the lock on the middle drawer. *If I have to live here, let's see what secrets you hide.* She found various papers she assumed were in German. There was a flyer with an image of a woman holding a yellow banner, and written below was something with 'bank,' and a small red and white flag with a crown. Among the foreign coins was a small box that contained a medal with an enamel centerpiece of a double-headed eagle. And there was a photo of Susanna sitting on the porch. Behind her were her daughters and another woman Grace did not recognize. She wondered why she'd lock away a seemingly innocent photo. She placed everything back where it was and tried to re-lock the drawer. After multiple tries, she gave up and hoped they wouldn't notice.

A few days later, as she was preparing Vivienne's breakfast, Grace overheard Susanna in the parlor. "Anton, you forgot to lock the drawer."

"I did not. Why are you accusing me?"

"I haven't opened it, so it had to be you."

A sly smile inched up Grace's face as she took Vivienne's porridge off the stove.

In November, two days of heavy rain caused a leak on the roof that seeped between the walls on the west side of the house. Anton had Joseph put tarps on the roof. It was another unplanned chore Anton added to the list of tasks he wanted Joseph to tend to since he hadn't secured a job. Grace worried he wasn't experienced enough for some things he was expected to do and could injure himself, or flare up the back injury he got playing baseball. But Joseph did all he was asked. It was only at night when they were alone that he grumbled and groused.

"My bones ache. Cold hits them and can't get the chill out."

With a touch of bitters, Grace said, "This cold and dampness is not good for any of us. Your parents rarely light a fire or turn on the furnace." She gave her head an abrupt jerk and tsked. "I bet it bothers your allergies and gives you those terrible sinus headaches." Joseph didn't answer and finished taking off his shoes and socks. Softening her tone, she said, "You know, darling, it's not too late to go back to California where it's warmer."

He titled his head to one side. "We've decided to stay."

"I don't know you can say *we* decided. It was more like *your family* decided."

Joseph got up and put his arms around her. "One day we'll have our own place and you can keep it as warm as you like."

Once the rain subsided in late November, Anton replanted his flower boxes with camellias, pansies, and hellebore. And the family started preparations for the holidays. Little did Grace know the festivities, which replicated the ones they had back in the old county, would go on until early January. It started with Susanna's Advent wreath of evergreen twigs, decorated with red ribbons and four candles. There was one for each of the Sundays in Advent when the family would gather to light one.

About the time the second candle was lit, Germany resumed submarine attacks on passenger and merchant ships. The United States had declared war on Germany in April after Germany had instructed Mexico to invade the county, and now it added its ally, Austria-Hungary, to the declaration. Until then, most people, including the Tschidas, thought the country should stay out of the war. But gradually opinion changed and people of German heritage fell out of favor and were shunned. Holy Rosary stopped holding Mass in German, as it was seen as unpatriotic. None of this was lost on the Tschidas, although it was never talked about, until one night at dinner.

"Today they brought in a German man who was nearly killed down by the docks," Clara said. "People at the hospital are saying German-Americans should be in prison camps."

"Frank told me they took German books out of the library," Joseph said, jamming his hands under his armpits. "And they set fire to that German family's house."

"What if your job's affected, Father? Or I lose mine?" Clara turned to Jospeh. "You might not get one."

"It *could* prevent me from getting a job," Joseph said, looking askance at his father.

Grace froze at the thought; they'd be stuck here longer at the mercy of his family.

"At school they say terrible things about Germans—they call them Huns," Marta said, rubbing her wrist. "One girl said no one should say anything around me because I might be a spy. I wanted to spit in their faces."

Anton shifted in his chair. "Don't listen to them.".

During a pause in the conversation, Anton looked at Susanna for a moment too long, as if struggling with his thoughts.

"What is it, Father?" Clara asked. "Should we take precautions?"

"It's necessary you know." A twitch as the corner of his mouth hinted at a mind at work.

Susanna kept her gaze on Anton, one hand pressed against her breast.

Grace was nibbling on a forkful of cucumber and onion salad when Anton said, "We're not German, we're Czech."

Grace inhaled sharply and nearly choked.

"Czech?" Marta looked around with imploring eyes. "What are they like? Do people like them?"

"Why did you always say we were German?" Joseph asked.

"Yes," added Clara, wanting to suss out the truth. "Why did you lie to us?"

"We're from a part of the Empire, the Sudetenland, where they speak German. People assumed we were German," Anton said, rubbing below his nose. "I saw no need to explain and correct them."

"Is that true, Mother?" Joseph said.

Susanna nodded, but didn't utter a word.

Grace's mind whirred. She didn't like it when she became petty. But she was a tad pleased this family was uprooting themselves from a history they had invented to make themselves "desirable." She'd heard their innuendos about the Germans being a more desirable émigré, one more educated and skilled than those from other countries. But more than that, they were liars.

A telltale silence descended over the room. There was palpable tension as each of family contemplated their new identity.

"Now I say we're not German?" Marta asked. "Will they believe me?"

After they put Vivienne to bed, Grace asked Joseph how he felt about the revelation.

"Don't know." His mood clouded over as he took off his bowtie. "I always felt they had secrets."

"Why did you think that?" Grace said, suddenly suspicious.

"Things I overheard." He flung his tie on the chair and helped Grace undo the last button on the back of her dress. "I never understood how Father knew people in the military. And I vaguely remember someone talking about smuggling people." He put his hand on Grace's shoulder. "It was long ago. I may be mistaken."

"What other lies have they told?"

"Don't torment yourself. We'll be fine."

"But secrets have a nasty habit of rearing their ugly heads at the wrong time."

Late autumn striped the leaf-bearing trees, turning them into stick figures. The evening the family attended the annual Christmas boat parade, the outlines of the trees contrasted against the smeared streaks of red, orange and yellow in the buttermilk sky. From the Tacoma Yacht Club to Dock Street Marina, and continuing down the City Waterway, there was a party ambiance with musicians roving through the crowds. On the water, they anchored dozens of lighted boats, all gaily decorated with wreathes and paper-mâché figures of snowmen and reindeer. On a pier, a string of boys sat, legs dangling, fishing rods bobbing in the water, their bait buckets glued to their sides. A small brass band played on the dock near the Yacht Club. Further down, off a side street, a man played a jangling tune on his musical washboard, a contraption he'd concocted with two washboards bolted together, a frying pan, some pot lids, a wood block, a cowbell and an old car horn with a rubber bulb.

"Pack up your troubles in your old kit bag and smile, smile, smile," Joseph sang as he danced with Vivienne in tune to the lively music. The air, scented with cinnamon sticks stewing in the hot cider stands, gave hints of the holidays. Joseph turned to Grace. "Let's get some cookies and cider."

No sooner had he suggested it, a squall came up and catapulted uncollected trash into the air. Signs flapped against the buildings like four-rigger sails in a gale. Grace tightened her paisley shawl around her neck and Joseph wrapped his overcoat around Vivienne. Several young soldiers from Fort Lewis walked by; their gruff voices carrying with the wind and rebounding off the wooden storehouses on the pier. One nodded and touched the edge of his hat as he passed by. Following them were young women in a flurry of giggles, sashaying their hips and calling out to the men.

Susanna frowned as they went by. "We have Schnapps and my apple-walnut cake at home," she said, rubbing her arms as if sanding off her goose bumps.

Grace pulled Joseph aside and said, "Let's linger longer. Vivienne's enjoying it."

"We all go home now," Anton said, his eyes on Grace.

"Mother's shivering, darling," Joseph said as a blast from a ferry pierced the air.

Grace's lips tightened. "For once, JoeJoe," she said in a half-whisper, "I wish you'd stick up for me and do what I want. Is that too much to ask?"

Arriving home, Grace bumped into Anton when he abruptly stopped before walking up on the porch. Then she heard Susanna gasp, and Marta say, "Who did this?"

Fragments and bits of egg shells lay on the porch. An unsightly mess of sticky egg whites and yolks dripped across the façade, and streaks of egg slid down the windows. Not even the plant leaves in the flowerboxes were saved from the onslaught. And written in chalk across the front door was, *Get Out Traitors.*

Grace grabbed Joseph's hand and moved closer to him.

"We forget this." Anton's neck muscles contracted. "Ignorant people do things like this."

"Clara, Marta," Susanna said, "fill the pails with soapy water. We're cleaning this tonight."

In their room later, Grace said, "What if they do more than pelt eggs? And I'm worried you might not be able to find a job."

Joseph stroked the back of his head. "Remember what Father said. And look how the neighbors offered to help clean the mess. We'll get by with this kind of solidarity."

She tried to forget but the incident lingered; she dreamt about it for several nights.

Two days after the boat parade, Susanna was not feeling well and stayed in bed, certain she had caught a cold or a bug at the festival. Grace was the only one home and asked if she needed anything.

Propped up in bed by pillows and surrounded in a mist of lavender-scented talcum, Susanna said, "You can make me some tea and toast." Grace started to leave. "Wait. Take a slice from the middle of the loaf. Put it on a plate and leave it there three and a half minutes on one side, and then three minutes on the other side. Put it in the oven for two and a half minutes, and after you take it out, let it sit for one and a half minutes. Spread the butter from right to left. Then cut diagonal strips."

Grace nodded. *Wait till I tell Rose and Genevieve this.*

As she was leaving, Susanna called out, "I'll be timing you."

Grace dashed to the credenza in the dining room and opened the leather desk pad, cracked dry from time. She jotted down the instructions. It did not escape her that even if she followed them to perfection, Susanna might not be satisfied. As she set the water to boil, she muttered, "Oh, Lord, what a cross you've given me to bear. "Rankled by all the instructions, she paced the room. *Joseph thinks it's so wonderful we're with his family. But he's out all day, seeing friends, doing chores, looking for a job, while I, I'm the one who has to stay in and put up with all this tomfoolery.*

She put the bread on the plate and left it there only one minute each side. "This is crazy. She won't notice the difference."

"Shall I put the tray on the bedside table, or do you want to sit in the chair?"

"On the table."

As Grace poured the tea, she glanced at the photo next to the lamp. It was Joseph's first-year picture. Dressed in a long white christening dress with a wide lace hem, he sat on a furry rug, holding a small chrysanthemum, his fingers touching a petal as if about to pluck it. The prim expression on his face contrasted with a tuff of hair standing on end in the middle of his head. Around his neck was a gold St. Stephen medal. Yes, Grace thought, he's her son, and she's not letting him get far away from her.

She handed Susanna a napkin and placed a spoonful of sugar and a few drops of cream in the tea, the way she knew her mother-in-law liked it.

"It's not right," Susanna bellowed, scrunching up her face and taking a piece of chewed toast out of her mouth. "You didn't leave it out long enough."

Grace's posture stiffened. "Do you want me to make you another?"

"This is not a wasteful house. Next time, do better." She looked at Grace with a gaze that could puncture.

"If there's nothing else, I'll see if Vivienne's awake from her nap."

Susanna waved her out of the room. Back in the kitchen, Grace clutched her stomach with one hand and covered her mouth with the other to muffle her laughter. She wanted so much to tell Susanna she didn't follow her directions.

CHAPTER 17

♦

If Candlemas is wet or foul, half the winter has gone at Yule.
If Candlemas is fine and fair, half the winter is to come and more.

After her bout with gripe, Susanna was in fine shape and in a frenzy, decorating the house with plumb red candles for the tables and fireplace mantel. She placed brass containers with seven green tapers in a row on the windowsills. On the Douglas fir Anton had had Joseph pick up from a lot outside town, she strung tinsel and dangled garlands made of popcorn, dried cranberries and cherries that swayed whenever someone touched the soft, shiny bough needles. Under the tree was a finely carved wooden crèche with figures of the Holy Family and Wise Men, along with a donkey and sheep. When Grace asked Susanna about it, she replied, "It was my grandmother's. One of the few things I brought from home."

"Tell me about your grandmother."

"A saint. Always stood up for me, protected me. She used the little money she had to buy me nice things. She died when I was twelve. I was heartbroken. I still cry when I think about her."

An image formed in Grace's mind of a young Susanna, clinging to a grandmother she adored. She felt the urge to reach out and comfort Susanna. But before she could make the gesture, Susanna spun around and said, "Get the girls. Time to shell the almonds."

Marta placed chairs around the kitchen table, while Clara put little bowls and nutcrackers out. When they were assembled,

Susanna set a large pail of almonds in the middle. "Keep the shells for my compost."

"Mother makes us do this each Christmas," Marta told Grace, grimacing.

"For her almond strudel," Clara said, "so don't complain." She nudged Grace with her elbow. "It's hard on the hands. My nails are always a mess."

Marta scanned the room as if looking for something. Then in a half voice, said, "I met a man at the soda fountain by the library."

"Really?" Clara said. "Tell us about him."

"His name's David and he's from Los Angeles." With a coy closed-mouth smile, Marta continued, "A real gentleman. He works for Richmond Oil and he asked me out."

"He's older, isn't he?" Clara said. "Father may not like that. You'll have to get his approval."

"I'm not going to tell them yet." She turned to Grace. "And don't tell Joseph. I don't want him to tell them before I do."

"When are you going to say something?" Clara asked.

"After the holidays."

The Tschidas celebrated Christmas Eve, and throughout the living and dining rooms were bowls of red and white ribbon candies and fresh Navel oranges covered with cloves. Their spicy fragrance mixed with the earthy scents of the mini pine-bough wreathes hanging over the framed paintings and windows. Dinner featured roasted goose on a bed of rosemary and parsley, and accompanying it were dishes of applesauce, fried carp, roasted potatoes, pumpkin soup with a dollop of cream and grated nutmeg, and traditional pear bread. Completing the meal was almond strudel and *Sachertort*, a specialty Susanna made at Christmas. Afterwards, Anton lit the Christmas tree, and the family opened their presents.

"It was Anton's idea to give Vivienne dolls," Susanna said, referring to the two porcelain dolls with real hair, one dressed in a white sailor dress with navy trimmings, and the other in a floral cream brocade dress with pink satin waistband. "I said she was too young, but he insisted. Would've been better to give her day frocks."

Grace was glad Anton prevailed. The dolls were beautiful. But she wondered if it wasn't better to keep them until Vivienne was older and would treat them better. But seeing the delight in her daughter's eyes as she held her new toys, it was impossible to take them away.

Marta unwrapped a crocheted bag from Clara. "For your croquet ball," Clara said, "so it won't roll all over the floor."

Anton handed Marta a cardboard box with a lithograph of a woman on the top. Inside was a garnet necklace. As she tried on the necklace, Susanna handed a small box to Grace. Inside was a green-colored stone brooch. "It's made of Edelserpentin. Comes from my village."

Before bed that evening, Grace held the brooch against her shoulder for Joseph to see. "I'm happy your mother gave me this. It's nice to have something with meaning." She put it aside and picked up the pearl pendant necklace Joseph gave her. "I love this. It's perfect and will go with all my outfits."

"I wanted to get you more, and I will, once I start working."

"I wish you would've taken one of those jobs they offered you—at least temporarily, so we could get our own place."

"They weren't right. And around the holidays is no time to start." His laugh lines crinkled around his eyes. "Don't worry, we'll get a nice place for the three of us."

"Or the four of us?"

He sat up in bed and clutched his knees. "Are you saying—"

"I believe we're going to have another baby." She sat next to him and put a hand on her stomach. "If I'm right, in June or July."

He pulled her close and kissed her on her temple. "I still may get that large family."

"It'll be nice for Vivienne to have a sibling close in age. But don't say anything yet to your family. I want to be certain the pregnancy goes well." Joseph nodded. "We can't continue to live in this one room with another child. I want to look for places now so we know where we want to move as soon as you get a job."

"Don't tell Mother and Father you're looking. I don't want them to think we don't want to be here."

Grace stomped her foot. "I don't care what they think. What we need and want is more important."

"I wish you wouldn't get riled up whenever I say something about my parents. Give them a chance. They're really caring." He caught her eye and smiled.

Grace crossed her arms and glared at Joseph. This was always going to be an uphill battle she'd have to wage alone.

"Wait, I forgot. I had to register for Selective Service." He stroked his eyebrow. "What if I get called up?" He looked to the side. "But I'd get a salary. It might be enough for you to get a place, if I'm gone."

"They won't take you with your bad back."

"Is that your wishful thinking?" He tipped his head back and looked at the ceiling. "But you might be right."

After High Mass at Holy Rosary on Christmas Day, Susanna brought Father Francis a basket of food left over from the previous night's dinner to give to the less fortunate. She explained to Grace that St. Stephen's Day is always for the poor. Then there was a lull and a delicious somnolence in the house until New Year's Eve. At the stroke of midnight, the Tschidas called out *Guten Rutsch* and rang a bell in honor of the Pummerin in Vienna's St. Stephen's Cathedral. Anton played the Blue Danube Waltz on the Victrola. And Susanna served a red wine punch, flavored with cinnamon and sugar, along with pepper cookies and marzipan *Glücksbringer*, little good-luck charms in the shape of pigs.

Grace was happy to create memories for Vivienne with these holiday traditions. But it was tiresome to feign high spirits with the never-ending customs. "How much longer does this go on?" Grace asked Joseph one evening.

"A few more days," he said.

"What rigamarole should I expect?"

He grinned and gave Grace a playful nudge. "It's our heritage. Don't tell me you haven't enjoyed them."

She drew a breath in and released it. "They're interesting."

"Interesting? Well, you'll be relieved to know Mother makes a sign for over the door, and while the clock strikes midnight, we eat stollen and drink mulled wine—or hot chocolate with strips of orange rind. That's all."

"What's the sign for?"

"To protect the house for the new year. It'll say 19CMB18 and reminds us of the Wise Men's visit. The initials are for the names of the three men and the numbers for this year."

When Grace later saw the sign in gothic-like calligraphy over the front door, she muttered to it, "Wish you'd protect me from all the folderal here."

A few days after Epiphany, Marta told her parents about David.

"He's not from here," Anton said. "You know nothing about him or his past. No friends to tell you about his reputation."

"I know he's kind and generous, Father, and seems to do well in business."

"You're young, Marta," Anton continued. "You don't know how to judge what's important. And most important is his character. I want to meet him before you see him."

Marta arranged for David to come for late afternoon tea the following Sunday. Using the fruit she canned over the summer, Susanna prepared poppy-seed and apricot dumplings, and served them on her white porcelain plates trimmed with gold.

Grace's first impression was that David was an amiable man with a ready smile. He was about the same height as Marta and well dressed. You couldn't help notice his ears stuck out like saucers, and his voice was thin, but he was attentive to Marta, his eyes implying fondness. Anton and Susanna scrutinized him, pinning him like a butterfly to velvet.

After speaking with him, Grace agreed with Marta's assessment, and seeing he had a good job, she was certain the family would approve. When he had gone, she was taken aback when Susanna said, "I don't think you should see him."

"You hardly met him," Marta said. "What didn't you like?"

"He's too old for you and he told us little of his past."

"He's a salesman," Anton said. "They know how to talk. He could tell you stories."

"Marta knows him better," Joseph said. "It's her life."

Grace swung her head around. *How ironic. You could have said the same to your father—it's my life.* She turned back to the others and said, "I found him congenial."

Anton twisted his mouth to one side and looked at Grace.

Pitted again, she thought, *between Joseph wanting me to be a part of the family and the family setting a boundary as to when and how I can be involved. I wonder what Olga was like—probably a docile simpleton they could manipulate.*

"You must finish nursing school," Anton said, "and we don't want anything, or anyone, to distract you."

"I can still go to school and see David."

"You're only nineteen, Marta," Susanna said. "You haven't dated much."

"What about Larry from Seattle? He stayed with us many Saturdays till Monday."

"That beautiful dress I made when you went with him to that dance," Clara said. She turned to Grace. "Yellow satin with an overlay of thin organza—lampshade style—with a big blue rose in front."

"She wore tango slippers," said Joseph. "She looked classy."

"See, Mother, they remember. I don't see how you can forget."

"He wasn't a beau. He was Charlotte's brother. That's different."

Marta crossed her arms. "When you met Father, did people say you knew nothing of him?" Her speech was halting, with barely contained fury. "But you knew he was right and I also know David's right."

"I didn't like the way he fawned over you." Susanna pulled her shoulders back. "I don't think he's good enough to be part of our family."

Grace felt an outpouring of protective instinct toward her sister-in-law as Marta paused to get her voice under control. "I'm going out with him. If you try to stop me, I'll find a way."

"She should see him," Anton said to Susanna, "but not now." He turned to Marta. "You wait a month or two, so you can learn more about him."

"A month or two?" Marta trembled with annoyance.

"If he's a good man, he'll respect my wishes and see that you're from a fine family." Anton brought his hands together, his fingertips touching, signaling finality.

Grace wanted to give a rousing shout to Marta for standing up to her parents. She'd never seen any of them oppose the parents so forcefully. It was going to be interesting to see how Marta maneuvered.

Later, Grace asked Clara to take a walk with her around the dimly lit streets, leaving Joseph to care for Vivienne. The golden glow of lights appeared in windows, casting warmth against the night winds whipping in from the Sound. When they were a few houses away, Grace said, "I couldn't believe how they disparaged David. If they talk that way about him, what do they say about me behind my back?"

"Grace, you make Joseph so happy, and we all think you're lovely and wonderful—we're fortunate to have you in our family."

Grace put her head down. "It doesn't seem that way. Some of the things Marta says makes me think they still wish Joseph had married Olga."

"Not true. I shouldn't have told you about her. But it was before you met him and I had no idea how things would turn out." Clara touched Grace's arm. "Marta's envious. Joseph could only think about you after you two met."

The wind picked up, blowing Grace's hair into her eyes and catching a curl in her eyelashes.

"We want you to be happy," Clara said. "Try and think of it this way. You have a roof over your head and you're eating, so you have nothing to worry about."

Grace was momentarily indignant. *How condescending. But she doesn't mean it the way you take it.* "I wish it were my own roof."

CHAPTER 18

♦

A handful of skill is better than a bagful of gold.

After taking Vivienne to the park one day, Grace found Susanna in the kitchen, buffing a copper pot. She asked if she could help with anything.

"Take care of my granddaughter, and help Joseph."

"I wish I could help him more. Hopefully he'll soon find a job he likes."

"Likes?" Susanna huffed. "One takes a job that's available and that's what Joseph should do." Susanna put her rag down. "Do you know what Anton had to do when he first came to St. Paul? Had to work for his sister and her husband in a store." Susanna closed the tin of polish. "Think he liked it? Not really, but he was lucky. Most new immigrants had to chip ice off the lakes and rivers."

It's different now, she wanted to say. *But let it go.* "How did you meet Anton?"

"We went to the same church, not that far from where we lived in Frogtown—I guess it once had frogs."

"Joseph told me you were young when you came, about eighteen."

Susanna put the tin under the sink. "I wasn't one of those flamboyant, happy-go-lucky girls that went around with men. Anton wanted a nice girl from home and one from his own class. We were both *coloni*. We had our own lands and didn't work for others."

There it was again—thrown up to her, making her feel she was of a lower class, no land owned, although her mother once owned a stable in Butte. But she doubted it would count much with the Tschidas. She held back a snipe. Since *you were so prosperous, why did you leave?* But she couldn't help herself and not-quite-so-innocently asked, "How much land did you have? Hundreds of acres? Thousands?"

Susanna bristled. "All our people had a strong faith and two hard-working hands."

"What did you like about Anton?"

"He was a serious man and had a good reputation. He knew important people and he'd studied, so I knew he'd make a good living."

"When did you know you were in love with him?"

"All this talk of love from young people. We did not think that way. I was expected to marry, be a good wife and mother."

Grace was still for a few moments. "But you've been happy, right?"

"A woman's duty is to help her husband. God will reward me in heaven."

"You deserve to be happy now." How different from her experience; she married for love, as had her mother—at least with her first husband, Grace's father—and she wouldn't have had it any other way. When Susanna didn't respond, she asked, "Did you come alone or with family?"

"With my older brother, Stephen." Susanna ran her hands under the faucet.

"You never mention him. Where is he?" Grace was baffled. She'd met Anton's sister Ilona, who had a large farm and dairy outside Tacoma, but she'd never heard anything about Susanna having a sibling.

"In Seattle." Susanna pressed her lips together as she dried her hands.

"Does he ever come to visit?"

Susanna jerked her head ever so slightly. "I've been meaning to tell you—you're not cleaning Vivienne's diapers correctly."

Grace gave Susanna a quizzical look. She always took extra care. The diapers were free of residue and Vivienne never had any irritation or rashes. Her eyes darted around the room. *Time to play their game.* With false cheeriness, she said, "I hadn't realized. I can watch you clean them next time, so I learn."

Susanna looked sideways at Grace, her mouth tightly set. She never brought it up again.

The next day, when everyone was out, Grace rang up her mother. "I have to put up with so much nonsense. It's maddening."

"Aching for sympathy, eh? It isn't necessary to drown yourself in a glass of water."

"The skullduggery, the secrets, living in a cramped room, eating all this heavy food—"

"Ah, it's the food now, too. Well, many a woman has found being a wife is hard."

"And Susanna has a brother in Seattle. The mention of him set her off. There's something fishy."

"What did Joseph say?"

"He's her half-brother—her mother's first husband died. But why doesn't she want to talk about him? Strange, especially when they say family's all important."

"You have more important things to concern yourself with," Lorna said.

"And Rose and Genevieve say they're going to come visit and they never do. They say they have to work all week and then there are the parties and outings."

"Distance makes the heart grow fonder—for someone else. And my dear girl, that applies not only to lovers but also to friends."

By the end of January, Joseph had not been called up for military service and he took a job on the waterfront, working in the administrative offices of Pacific Steel and Boiler. He showed Grace a wallet-size card with his name, his photo and the name of the company. "Gives me admittance to the wharf."

"How's this different from working in the office in Sonora?" Grace said, trying to hide her resentment.

Joseph threw down his beret. "You'll never forget and you won't let me either."

No, I won't, she said to herself. *You promised.*

Joseph knelt beside her and stroked her arm. "Sorry, darling. Look, there are seven shipbuilding companies in town and they make fifty ships a year. It's interesting to learn a new industry and see how everything's done." He kissed her on the forehead. "Things will get better."

She wanted to say the only thing that would make it better was getting out from under his parents. "I'm going to look for a place. I want to get settled before the baby is born."

Grace's pregnancy was going well with no morning sickness, heartburn or out-of-the ordinary fatigue. Her belly was beginning to protrude, so they'd have to tell the family soon. But she wanted to postpone it as long as possible. She didn't know how they'd react to another child, especially when Vivienne was still young. And what if they weren't able to move before the birth and the child had colic or a temper and cried at all hours? She turned sideways and stroked her stomach as she looked at her reflection in Clara's free-standing oval mirror. Vivienne waddled over and tugged at her skirt. "Yes, sweetie, we're going downstairs. Get the Cupie doll Auntie Genevieve sent you."

On the parlor floor, Grace sat beside Vivienne, helping her stack blocks and singing "Row, Row, Row Your Boat" when Marta came in and plopped down on the sofa.

"You're home early," Grace said.

"Upset stomach." She bent over and watched Vivienne with a smile that reached her eyes. "She'll be building castles before long."

"How's David?"

She sneered and cast her eyes upward. "Joseph was smart to run away and marry you. Serves them right."

"You're still wearing my opal ring." Grace said, in a lighthearted voice, trying to hide her annoyance. 'It's a nice ring, isn't it?"

A flush crept across Marta's cheeks. She covered the ring with her other hand.

"When you have a chance, I'd like my coat back," Grace said. "I want to wear it on Sunday."

"You know, Grace," Marta said, "Father's been supporting you and Joseph. You're taking advantage and eating too much. You're getting fat." She looked briefly at Vivienne before stomping out of the room.

Vivienne started whimpering.

"I know, sweet pea. She's taking out her frustrations on me."

Marta's blistering comment stung and stayed with Grace during dinner. She felt Marta watching each mouthful she took; she started limiting what she ate.

After the meal, Grace brought the salt and pepper shakers and the cut-glass container of toothpicks into the kitchen where Susanna and her daughters were washing the dishes.

"I don't think father should give Grace money to buy new outfits," Marta said.

There she is again, rattling her sharpened scythe, Grace thought, tilting the glass and spilling the toothpicks on the floor. Joseph appeared next to her and picked them up.

Susanna took hold of Marta's arm and yanked her away from the sink. "He isn't. Why do you say that?"

"She brought them all with her," Clara said. "She accessorizes in different ways and makes them look new."

Marta looked over and saw Grace at the entryway to the kitchen. Susanna followed her gaze and then turned to Marta. "Apologize to Grace."

"Yes, apologize," Joseph said. "She's always borrowing Grace's things and never gives them back."

"Is that true?" Susanna asked. Marta stared at the floor and said nothing.

"I would like my coat back before Sunday Mass," Grace said.

"How long have you had it?" Susanna asked. Marta shrugged. "Return everything. I didn't raise a thief."

Back in their room, Joseph said to Grace, "You mustn't lend her any of your things."

"What do you want me to do, JoeJoe? We're living under your family's roof and I should say, no, I won't let you borrow anything?" Grace splayed her hands wide. "Your parents are strict. They won't let her buy new things." Her lips tightened. "I'm trying hard to make life pleasant—bearable."

"Marta's spiteful because she envies you."

"You and Clara say that, but what's to envy?" Grace crammed her underpinnings in the drawer without folding them. "At least your mother stood up for me—a first."

After a few days of house hunting, Grace leaned against the bathroom door frame as Joseph frothed-up lather in the mug. "I like to watch you shave."

"You do?" He slathered the soap on his face and ran the blade over the razor strop.

"I wanted to talk to you last night about the places I saw near Stadium High."

"Sorry. I was so tired. Couldn't help falling asleep." He tested the blade for sharpness on his thumb. "What about the one you liked on Proctor?"

"The ones by Stadium have a view of the water and there's one that has three bedrooms that I really like." She ran her finger over the ivory water knob, marked *Hot*.

He glanced sideways at her. "Sounds expensive. I'm not head of the company yet." He winked and slid the razor across his face.

"I'd like you to see it Sunday."

Whiskers dotted the foam as it disappeared down the sink. "Darling, I want you to be happy, but I'd like to save up before getting a large place." He patted lotion on his face; wisps of sandalwood wafted through the air.

"The extra room will be handy, if my mother comes to stay with us."

"Have you mentioned it to her?" The scent of bay rum mixed with the lingering sandalwood as he brushed talcum on his face.

"Not yet but she's getting older and may need help later." She bent over to gather up the specks of talcum dotting the floor.

"I think your mother will never need—or want—help."

The following week, Grace and Joseph told the family she was expecting. Anton, as Joseph predicted, said he hoped the child was a boy to carry on the Tschida name.

"How many do you plan to have?" Marta asked.

Grace looked squarely at her sister-in-law. "As many as come my way."

The color left Susanna's face and Anton reprimanded Marta, "One does not ask such questions."

Smarting from the admonishment, the corners of Marta's mouth turned down. "I was only making conversation."

"Well, I, for one, hope we have many more," Joseph said. He stroked Grace's arm. "As long as you agree, darling."

It tempted Grace to quip Marta should realize what she mistook as getting fat was pregnancy. But what good would it do? She didn't want to make more of an enemy of Marta. She tried to feel sorry for her, rationalizing that she had plenty to tend to with her studies and David. But it still rankled her Marta returned only her coat and not her ring.

In April, World War I was in its third year when the United States entered the conflict. Grace's brother, Daniel, who recently turned twenty, believed it his duty to serve. He enlisted in the Navy, the first enlistee from Washington State. At five feet nine inches tall and one hundred and thirty pounds, he cut a handsome figure in his uniform. Lorna had him take a studio photograph in it before he shipped out to his base in San Francisco. She sent a copy to Grace, which she kept tucked into the frame of the mirror in their room. His leaving meant Lorna would be alone for the first time and her afflictions made it impossible for her to work. She had no pension from either of her husbands or from the State. Daniel had given Lorna most of his paycheck all these years, and

Grace knew he would continue to do so with his military pay. With her limited savings, Lorna decided to give up the two-bedroom apartment, and take a room in a boarding house on Rockefeller Avenue. She gave friends many of her belongings, and kept only the furniture and household goods that would fit in her new dwelling, along with two suitcases of clothing and a box of photographs.

"She's got the morbs," Grace told Ellen. "It's not like her to be melancholic."

"She has many friends she can visit and do things with," Ellen said.

"It's hard for her to get around. I was thinking she could live with you."

"Los Angeles is too far." Ellen hesitated. "Things are difficult. My husband—" When Ellen didn't say more, Grace asked, "Is anything wrong? You sound upset."

"I send her money as often as I can. I have to hide it from Edward. When you move into your own place, couldn't you take her?"

"I found several I like but Joseph always has an excuse. He thinks we should wait until he saves for furniture and who knows what else." Vivienne whimpered with outstretched arms; Grace patted her on the head. "I have to go. Try to think of something."

As she picked Vivienne up, she cursed her luck. "Why couldn't we already have our own place? There's nothing like a grandmother's love for her grandchildren."

The day after her conversation with Ellen, Grace saw a flurry of activity in the side yard. As clouds zipped past on the current of a strong northwest breeze, several workmen in overalls walked around, assessing the area with measuring sticks and showing Anton drawings.

At dinner that night, Anton said, "Son, I had a few of my friends see about building you a house next to ours. There's plenty of room on the west side."

A spoonful of mushroom soup went down the wrong way, and Grace started coughing.

Joseph turned to Grace. "Why, that's swell. Isn't it, darling?"

Grace found it difficult to think. But she had to. She forced a smile. "That's generous, Anton. But it's too much. The noise would be disruptive, and you'd lose some of your beautiful yard. I've found some nice places to rent."

"I'll still have plenty for my garden. I've already signed the contracts."

Unable to change the winds of fate, Grace's mood darkened. *Why didn't I pressure Joseph to sign a lease for one of the houses?*

"It'll be smaller than ours, but big enough for the four of you," Anton said. "You need your own place with the baby coming. I'll have them put in an extra room in case you need it later. We might add a sitooerie—it'd be nice for Grace to have in pleasant weather."

Later, Grace ate only one of the *husarenkrapfen* cookies filled with raspberry jam and excused herself. "Vivienne didn't nap. Before she gets cranky, I'll take her upstairs."

She shut their bedroom door and laid down next to the child on the bed. Tears welling, she tossed a pillow off and let out an *Osti*, one of her mother's favorite swear words. Vivienne patted her face and garbled something to comfort her. "I know, dear heart, but I had dreams of another house. You're happy here, aren't you? And your father is." She sighed. "Well, no use crying over spilled milk, as they say. I guess we'll have to cobble together some kind of life. I see no way out." *Doesn't Joseph always say that as long as they're together, they could endure anything? Well, it's about to be tested.*

CHAPTER 19

◆

He who has water and peat on his own farm has the world his own way.

Soon it was May and the weather turned balmy. One Sunday afternoon Grace and Joseph sat with Anton in the backyard. There was an air of lazy calm as a warm wind wove across the yard. Two high-pitched birds resting on a branch made their presence known. Mrs. Gartner interrupted their chirps when she waved and called out, "I'm keeping an eye on the new house. They're doing mighty fine work."

"That's good of you," Anton said, pulling down the front of his vest.

"Did you know a man took some lumber with him when he left for the day?"

"I'm sure they were scraps they didn't need, and the supervisor approved it. Don't be telling him how to do his job now."

"She doesn't miss much," Joseph said.

"Not bad to have a neighbor who watches out for us," Anton said.

Noisy old bitty, Grace muttered to herself.

"Son, there's something I want to discuss."

Grace fought rising panic as she wondered what scheme he was cooking up to take over more of their lives.

"Soon you'll have your own place. I'm paying extra so they finish before the new baby comes." He allowed himself a moment. "Now that your home is settled, I want to talk to you about your career."

Joseph looked up at his father under hooded eyes. "I have a job and I'll—"

"You can't work for someone else and make real money. The business has to be you or revolve around you." He extended his legs, putting one ankle on top of the other.

Grace nearly stopped breathing as she waited for him to continue.

"I want to set you up in your own business. There's a vacant store in a good location at 11th and K Street. I checked the area and there are no fish or meat markets around." Anton arched his back. "You could do well if you established one there."

Grace knew K Street. It was a fashionable part of town with a lively commercial district; a good place to open a new business. If Anton was again dictating their lives, at least it would be in a nice neighborhood.

Joseph turned his palms up and shrugged. "I know nothing about meat and fish."

"You have your commerce studies and experience running offices. You can get meat from Aunt Ilona and she and her husband can teach you what you need to know about that part of the business. Most important are quality, price and flavor. Ilona will ensure you have the best. So can the fishermen. You only have to ask. I have my connections."

Joseph rubbed his forehead. "I don't know."

"I thought Quincy could come into the business with you. His job doesn't seem to hold a lot of promise."

"Why do you say that?"

"Boeing's a new company and who knows how it'll go. Regardless, promotions don't come along often and who's to say they'll tap him to rise in the organization? Think of it—your own business and with your friend." He touched his steepled hands to his lips and waited.

Joseph's face clouded with thought as he stared at the trampled grass. Then his expression changed. "It would be better to have my own place and be my own boss." He glanced at Grace. "I can take a salary and profits, and it would be swell if Quincy joins me."

Anton tilted his head up and nodded. "Think about it, Son."

Kismet laid out a new path and this time Grace didn't try to figure out how to stray from its path. It might be better for Joseph to have his own business. He'd make more money and Quincy might have influence over him, making him less willing to abide by his father's every dictate. Yes, it might work out better, although he'd be more beholden to his father in another way.

The following Sunday, the family had lunch at Aunt Ilona's farm to discuss her supplying beef, chicken and veal for the market.

"My friend Quincy's coming in with me. He met with father and me the other day at Swiss Hall to discuss a partnership," Joseph told Ilona and her husband. "He thinks it's a great proposition."

"I said I'd finance the startup," Anton said.

"I already prepared a preliminary business plan, and I'm calling it Crescent Market," Joseph said. "A good symbol for growth, wouldn't you say?"

Grace noticed the misgivings Joseph had at the beginning were gone, replaced by optimism. She hoped it would turn out well for him and for the family. At least there'd be no more talk of his career.

"I signed a five-year lease for the property," Anton said. "My building-trade friends will help refurbish the space and locate equipment."

"Many professional people live in the area," Joseph said.

"They can offer high quality local items," Anton said, "with good profit margins."

"I haven't been this excited since I married Gracie," Joseph said, giving her a wink.

Everyone looked at Grace. She met their eyes with a smile.

A few days later, after he took off a day from work to meet the owner of the K-Street property, Joseph came home from the shipyard office in a black mood.

"My boss was wild eyed. Said I didn't have permission to take time off. If he's thinking of discounting a day's salary, he—"

"You should've met him on the weekend."

"Nothing will happen. I'm his best employee—I do more than what's called for." He finger-traced the worn outlines of raised flowers on Grace's silver hand mirror, lost in thought. "He's impulsive. Forgets he isn't head of the department."

"Don't jeopardize your job until you're certain the market will work out."

"If it weren't for your love, I'm certain I'd have gone mad by now." A smile crept up his face. "I'm egotistical, aren't I—wanting you to reassure me? I always thought I wasn't good enough for you. I want to prove to you I am."

And prove it to your father. He's the ghost hanging over everything you do.

The evening before the official opening of the market, Joseph and Quincy invited family and friends to the store for a party. They parked the used delivery truck Anton bought in front of the store and decorated it with balloons. Its newly painted side panels announced the name of the market in large letters with a scroll underneath. Further down, it advertised *Homemade Sausage, Hams, Bacon and Lard.*

"Here are our cure pump and cast-iron ring-de-hairer. That's the grinder in the corner," Quincy said, as he pointed to equipment they bought from an industrial supply store.

"This is the newest in slicing machines," Joseph said, pointing to a heavy metal machine with a crank.

Anton glanced at the paperwork next to it. "Why did you buy something so expensive? And from England? You could've got one made here."

"The supplier said it's the best. Built to British specifications."

Anton scoffed. "So was the Titanic." A flicker of irritation flashed in his eyes. "No more overspending before you have profits."

"When are you going to trust my judgment?" he said in a low voice. But everyone heard.

Grace saw the pride in Joseph's eyes turn to embarrassment. She moved next to him and placed her hand on his back. *He never should've said such a thing in front of everyone.*

Rains that spring were light, and two weeks before the birth of their second child, the workmen finished the new house. As Grace watched the workmen paint its façade a medium taupe, the same color as the big house, a delivery van arrived. She turned to Susanna and said, "Joseph didn't mention furniture coming. We were going to shop for it next week."

Susanna stopped stirring her pot of apricot preserves. "Anton ordered it. His friend gave him a good price."

Grace bristled. "This is too much. He builds us a house, decides the color of paint and now decides what furniture we should have. That sofa is big and fussy."

Susanna froze, stark astonishment on her face. "You should be thanking the Lord for all he's done for you."

Vivienne rocked on the kitchen chair and babbled, "Go by-bye, wagon."

"He could've asked our opinion," Grace stuttered.

"Another thing he did," Susanna said, pointing to the wagon. She unscrewed the Mason-jar lids and lined them up on the counter. "She was too big for the pram and too heavy for you to carry. He didn't want anything to happen to the new baby."

"I appreciate the wagon." Grace helped Vivienne down from the chair and took her hand.

"You should see how others live," Susanna said. "You'll realize how much you have to be thankful for."

Grace was silent. She might've been a bit harsh. There was some truth in what Susanna said.

"We've talked about you joining St. Anne's Society and helping needy families with education and spiritual matters. It would be good for you and allow you to serve the Lord."

"Vivienne's still young and with the baby, I won't have time." *If you want to spend half the week with your religious organizations, that's your business.* "She's fussing. I have to go."

Grace fumed as she pulled Vivienne in the wagon up the sidewalk, muttering to no one, "Yes, I should be grateful. But in this blasted family, I can't have a say in anything."

As she crossed the street, a woman stepped out on her porch and yelled to a scrappy youngster. "Otis, go to the store. Get three pounds of smelt."

Starting up an incline, Grace saw a young woman in a V-neck dress with tiered hemline; her dark curly hair formed a halo around her head. As she approached, the woman smiled and said, "You must be Joseph's wife."

Grace nodded. "Do you know him?"

"Everyone knows everyone around here. I went to Holy Rosary with Joseph and Clara but I haven't seen them in a while." she said in her willowy voice. "I'm Betty. Elizabeth really, but I prefer Betty."

After Grace introduced herself and Vivienne, Betty got down eye level to Vivienne and patted her hand. "Aren't you the little beauty."

"You live close by?" Grace said.

"Over there with my mother." She pointed to a green-trimmed white house with a tall monkey tree. "You and Joseph should come out with me and my beau. Clara, too. It would be nice to see them again."

"Joseph wants to rest after work and—" Grace placed her hand on her stomach. "I'm expecting."

"You can still go out. We can meet at the Tacoma Hotel."

Grace knew about the Tacoma hotel, built by Stanford White and reputed to be the height of luxury for Tacoma and the finest west of the Mississippi. But she had never so much as stepped inside.

"Tell him Betty wants to see him. Better say Elizabeth."

At dinner that evening, Grace mentioned she'd met Elizabeth. "Very friendly. I liked her. She works at Tacoma Biscuit and Candy Company." She turned to Joseph. "She wants us and Clara to go out with her and her boyfriend."

"That Campbell woman?" Anton said. "Absolutely not. She's not our kind of people."

"She doesn't have a good reputation." Susanna made soft clicking noises of disapproval with her tongue against her teeth. "Even wears nail polish."

"Darling, if you want to go out," Joseph said, "we can go with my friends."

"You shouldn't be going out in your condition," Susanna said.

The roast pork turned dry as dust in Grace's mouth. She didn't say more. But she wasn't about to let them tell her who she could make friends with. She began going past Betty's house on her daily walks, and the two women established a routine.

Every evening Joseph arrived home, he placed a brown-paper package wrapped with twine on the kitchen counter.

"Some thick pork chops and oysters," he said to Grace as she opened the package.

What he brought each night depended on the season and day of the week. Sometimes there was Alaskan sockeye salmon, halibut, scallops, sirloin strips, or big fat hot dogs. And occasionally Grace found her favorite Dungeness Crab they'd eat out of the shell.

"Another customer said ours is 'the best market in town.' It'll please father when I tell him."

"He said you'd be successful. Of course, he said it with total vindication."

"I bet he did," Joseph said. "I've made friends with some of the other merchants on the block, Mr. Carp with the tobacco shop and Mr. Allen with the candy store across the street. Had coffee with him and his wife today. He told me Tacoma's mild weather is perfect for making candy and keeping it fresh. Chocolate's cool enough to not melt, yet warm enough not to become brittle in the cold. That's why more candy manufacturers are moving into the city—Mars, Baskin-Robbins, Brown and Haley."

"Hope you're not thinking of starting your own."

"You needn't fear. I have my hands full." He pinched her cheek. "But one day, after the market exceeds our expectations, we could think about a mercantile empire."

On the first Tuesday in July, Erika was born, a child with large blue eyes and light-auburn hair. True to the nursery rhyme, she'd prove to be gracious, agreeable and refined. She looked frail, which Grace attributed to her not eating enough to nourish a growing child. Joseph gifted Grace a silver rosary for giving him another lovely child.

The day after Grace came home from hospital, Anton visited. "All's arranged for her baptism. She'll be a Christian on Saturday, with all the honors that come with the religion."

Grace glanced sideways at Joseph. *They could be construed as burdens.*

"I was thinking," Anton said, "her name should be grand like Victoria, or another Queen."

Disbelief flashed across Grace's face. "I read Erika means 'eternal ruler,' as *grand* a name as Victoria, wouldn't you say?"

Anton raised up his suspenders with his thumbs. "That *is* a nice meaning,"

Her eyes bore into him. "I didn't think you were a monarchist. Didn't you have to renounce nobility and allegiance to your home country when you were naturalized?"

After he left, she barked at Joseph, "Now he takes over our daughter's name?"

Joseph knelt beside her. "I know it's frustrating, but he doesn't know any other way, Gracie. That's how he was raised. His father was the decider—for everything." He stroked her hair. "It's natural you're emotional now."

"Emotional? You think I'm emotional? No, JoeJoe, I'm angry your family always has to put in their two cents. It's one cockamamie thing after another."

Thoughts of the buried saints popped into Grace's mind and she wondered if there hadn't been something to it after all—she should have talked to them more.

A week after Grace gave birth, Betty came to visit. "I heard you had a girl." From her boxy tooled leather bag, she took out a gift wrapped in French envelope liner. "I made her something."

Grace opened the pink floral pattern on white and found a pair of knit booties and a crocheted bib with embroidered flowers along the edge. "They're lovely. More so because you made them. Come meet her."

Betty looked down at the sleeping child and gently stroked her closed fist. "She's the most beautiful baby."

"She'll be waking soon and you can hold her," Grace said.

"I'd love to but I have to run some errands before work." She rummaged in her bag and handed Grace some wafers from work.

As Grace saw Betty off, the kitchen curtain in the big house moved. *Spying on me, are you? I'm not turning away a nice woman because you believe neighborhood gossip.*

CHAPTER 20

♦

*A whistling woman and a crowing hen will bring
no luck to the house they are in.*

S hortly after Erika's christening, Holy Rosary made plans to
build a new church; the walls of the wooden structure were
not strong enough to withstand a renovation after sixteen inches
of snow caved in its roof. They selected Anton to spearhead the
construction committee.

"We've decided on a brick revival Gothic structure," Anton
told the family one evening. "We'll build it to last a century or
longer. The steeple will be two-hundred and sixteen-feet-high.
I took inspiration from the one atop St. Stephen's in Vienna."

"Your work, your garden and now the new church are taking
up too much of your time," Suzanna said. "Hire someone to
tend the garden, or give up one of your organizations—like the
Catholic Order of Foresters."

"I imagine yardwork's relaxing for him," Grace said. "I hear
his friends and passersby admiring his work. They call him a
master gardener."

The corners of Susanna's mouth hardened.

"*Ja*, they ask for advice, and I'm happy to help."

"He's not checking up much on me now," Joseph said, taking
Grace's hand. "So he has time to do everything."

In early October, as the Hundred Days Offensive raged on the
Western Front, Clara came over in the evening to speak to Grace
and Joseph.

"The Spanish flu we've been hearing about back East has come to our area. We knew city officials were delusional when they thought it would miraculously skip the Northwest. There are reports of over one hundred cases at Camp Lewis, and more at the Seattle and Bremerton naval training stations. Camp Lewis is under quarantine."

"Frank says millions have died and over fifty thousand got infected in one day in San Francisco," Joseph said. "It's that contagious?"

Clara nodded. "They're going to pass laws if anyone is outside without a mask, they'll fine them up to ten dollars and possible imprisonment."

"What are they doing to stop it?" Joseph said.

"The health department wants to isolate cases quickly. And they're experimenting with several remedies, like the new aspirin. But they don't know if it's working—several died after taking it and they don't know if the doses were too high or they succumbed to the flu."

"What should we do?" Grace asked.

"Isolate and wear masks—it's the only way," Clara said. "Soon they'll close movie houses, theaters, poolrooms, all places of amusement. Your girls are young and you must keep a strict individual voluntary quarantine and avoid all gatherings."

"Does that include Mass?" Grace asked, trying not to appear elated.

"The city may halt church services. Until then, it's best you don't attend for a while. I'll tell Mother I advised you to stay home to protect the girls."

"I have to work," Joseph said.

"Wear a mask, and keep the doors open, if you can. It'll help." Clara glanced at her lapel-pin watch. "It's good you're no longer at the shipyard. Perfect breeding ground, if it gets infected."

No one in the family contracted the flu, not even Lorna. She was now fifty-two years old and her chronic arthritis made it difficult for her to get around. Grace sent her more money each month, but not as much as she would have liked. It took most of her allowance for the upkeep of the house and family. Joseph wanted to plow profits back into the business and repay his father. He considered Anton's startup infusion of funds a loan, despite Anton never having him sign a promissory note. What Grace sent, along with what Ellen and Daniel contributed, was enough to pay for her room, food, and necessities, with some left for amusement. But she depended on her friends and neighbors for help with daily tasks.

After finishing duty in the Philippines, Daniel had military and diplomatic duties with the American expedition force in Russia on the U.S.S. Brooklyn in Siberia.

"Did he tell you he saved lives when an explosion blew eighteen men overboard?" Lorna asked Grace.

"He did. And he told me how much he likes the Navy."

"It's been two years since he enlisted," Lorna said. "I was told he can petition his Commanding Officer for his honorable discharge. I need him home to help me."

"Don't interrupt his career. Come live with us."

"No, siree. I'd rather spend the day plowing a field than sit and listen to the stories that bunch of scallywags tell."

"I hope you are not lumping in Joseph with them."

"You know I care for the boy. Anyway, I already filled out and signed the petition, and six of my friends signed an affidavit, saying I'm in need of his help. Daniel's fine with it. The war's over."

Daniel was discharged in San Francisco, his naval training station. He returned to Everett where he found work at the port and he and Lorna settled into a larger apartment in town.

When Erika turned one-year-old, Grace learned she was pregnant again. Certain she would carry this child as well as she had the two girls, she and Joseph didn't hesitate to tell Anton and Susanna.

"If it's a son," Anton said. "I'd like you to call him Benedict. In honor of the Benedictine fathers at Holy Rosary."

Oh, no, here we go again. "We were thinking of Leo for a boy," Grace said.

"If there's another, he can be Leo. I hope you'll grant me this request."

"Your father's done a lot for you and you can do this for him," Susanna said.

After they put the girls to bed that night, Grace said to Joseph, "We tell him no. We're the parents, not him."

"It's a name. It won't change who the baby is." Joseph sat next to Grace and took her hand. "Why must everything be a fight? These petty arguments are not worth squabbling over."

"Petty? I think naming a child is important." Resentment flooded her like a breached dam. "Benedict can be his middle name."

"I don't think that'll satisfy father," he said, jingling the coins in his pocket.

She turned away. "I can't do this any longer." A few moments later, she whipped back around and pointed her finger at Joseph. "Benedict was the pope who sold the papacy for money. I'm certain. Tell your father and see if he still wants to call him Benedict."

At seven months pregnant, Grace still took the girls on daily walks in the neighborhood. One day she watched as Betty raced up and down the street, her dark eyes red and watery, her long legs snapping back and forth. She nearly tumbled when her shoe tangled with a crack in the sidewalk. But she caught herself and stopped when she saw Grace.

"You must think I'm mad." Betty's voice was shallow, her eyes downcast.

"Why are you running in good clothes?"

"It's not exercise." Betty left out a long *aargh*. "Probably won't do any good."

"What won't?" Grace's moment of realization lasted a split second.

A door opened in the house above them. An elderly lady, her eyes staring straight ahead, held onto the door frame for a moment. Then she searched with her hand for the arm of the rocking chair on her porch.

"How are you today, Mrs. Aiken?" Betty called out.

"Doing wonderful. Such a beautiful day."

"It certainly is. Nice to see you."

Betty turned to Grace. "Everything's always beautiful with her—lucky woman." She touched Grace's arm. "I'll come see you tomorrow."

As they sat in Grace's kitchen, Betty tugged on her earlobe and said, "He wants nothing to do with it, so that's not possible. Tells me I'm on my own."

"Could you go away?"

"I have to work. My mother depends on me since father died." Betty's voice went limp. "She can't know. It would break her heart. Besides, I have nowhere to go."

"You don't know what she'll say. Maybe she'll say—does she think it's . . ."

"A sin?" Betty's expression dissolved. "I'm going to find one of those women."

Grace grasped Betty's hand. "No, you mustn't. You could die."

"Doesn't seem so bad, considering how I'll be ostracized."

Time crawled as Grace escaped into her thoughts. "I see you're determined . . . we'll figure out something."

"I've thought of all the options. Are there others you know of?

Grace smoothed out the corner of the tablecloth. "Onions, vinegar, lemon juice."

"A recipe?"

Grace nodded. "I used to overhear my mother talking to women in the mining camps. Women with little means who were certain they would die." She crossed her arms and tilted her head up for a few moments before redirecting her gaze at Betty. "I'll speak to her."

The following week, Grace gave Betty a small mesh bag. "My mother sent these herbs. You make a tea with them. Sip it slowly and see how you tolerate it."

"Do you know what's in it?" Betty asked.

"One thing is pennyroyal. She said it's been used since the beginning of time."

"Should I take it right after the vinegar and lemon juice?"

"I don't know." Grace pressed her lips together. "Try one and wait, then try another. Are you sure your mother will be home in case you need help?"

Betty gave a hesitant smile. "I'll be OK."

"What will you tell her?"

"I have a stomachache—ate something bad."

After a week passed, Betty met Grace and the girls for lunch at a restaurant on Pacific Avenue.

"Did your mother suspect anything?"

"She was comforting. Made me toast and tea and fussed over me."

"Have you heard from him?"

Betty dug in her bag for a handkerchief. "I had a lot of time to think." She dabbed the corners of her eyes. "He was as slick and polished as the Bank of California floors. Showed himself to be a real spiv. I don't know how he fooled me for so long."

"People fool people every day."

"We're fortunate, we women. We have a special connection, a spiritual one—we can confide in each other and share." Betty gave Grace's hand a quick squeeze. "You've helped me so much."

"You also help me. Always listening to my tales of woe." Grace reached down and picked up the napkin that had slipped from her lap. "Your friendship means so much to me . . . especially now." Her thoughts drifted to her former classmates; Rose had married and moved across the mountains to Yakima, and Genevieve now lived in San Francisco's French Quarter where she worked for an importer of French goods.

That March, Grace gave birth to their third child, a boy they named Benedict. It'd been a battle royal for months as Grace refused to give in, saying if she had no other say in life, she wanted the right to name her own child. Joseph kept reminding her it was his child also, and he was as determined to give his father his wish. It was Lorna who tipped the scales.

"Child, St. Benedict came to me in a dream. It's an omen. If it's a son, you should name him Benedict."

"When have the saints ever come to you in a dream?" Grace said.

"When have I ever told you a lie? This is the sign you've been waiting for."

"How do you know it was St. Benedict? It could have been St. Peter or St. Anthony."

"I saw Benedict's name on the book he was holding."

"He's pulling one on you, Mother." Grace was silent for a few moments. "Are you in cahoots with Joseph and his parents behind my back?"

"If there was ever a case of being in cahoots, it would be against those rapscallions."

It nagged at Grace that it really might be a sign. Now she was wrangling not only against her husband and in-laws, but also her mother. And then, a funny thing happened. She started to like the name Benedict.

"Finally, a son, to carry on the Tschida name," Anton said. "Good he wasn't as big as Joseph. Weighed nearly nine pounds when he was born."

Susanna gazed down at the baby. "Dark hair like Joseph and Vivienne. And born with the veil. Means he's special and will be lucky with special abilities."

Grace later asked Clara about Susanna's remark.

"I don't know about special powers—that's something women in mother's village said when a child was born *en caul*. It's not common, but makes an easier delivery."

This was the most logical to Grace and *en caul* or not, he was special to her.

Anton and Susanna finally agreed Marta could marry David, but after the dedication for the new Holy Rosary Church, so her wedding could be performed in the cavernous structure with its crème-colored arches and aquamarine ceiling dotted with gold stars. Marta asked Clara to be her maid of honor and she wanted four-year-old Vivienne to be the flower girl. Clara made all three silk dresses; tea-length for her and Marta, and a short one with delicate ruffles for Vivienne. The white-and-pink silk rosettes around the crown of Marta's three-foot long veil matched those sewn on the garters of Vivienne's knee-length white silk stockings.

On the day of the wedding, Marta and Clara carried lavish bouquets of ivory roses, calla lilies, orange blossoms, and myrtle; their long silk streamers reached the hems of their dresses. Vivienne carried a hoop-handle basket with the same flowers.

After the ceremony, Anton and Susanna held a reception at home, decorating the parlor and dining room with the same florals as in the bridal bouquets. A white linen tablecloth edged in lace covered the dining room table with its seven tapered white candles in holders of different heights. In the center was the wedding cake; Marta's favorite—chocolate cake with ganache filling, covered with a thin marzipan layer and dotted with silver candy pearls.

"You didn't see it," Clara said to Grace and Joseph, "but Vivienne held up the procession on the way up the steps to the church."

"She did so well in rehearsal," Joseph said.

"One of her stockings fell down." Clara laughed. "I prodded her on, but she said, 'No, Auntie, I have to fix it.' When I asked if she needed help, she shook her head, tugged it up and continued on."

"That's my girl," Joseph said. "She won't let you tell her what to do, Clara." He held Grace tightly around the waist and she leaned into him.

"The embroidery you did on Marta's dress panels was beautiful," Grace said.

"It did come out nicely," Clara said.

"A bit extravagant they're staying at the Tacoma Hotel tonight," Joseph said.

Grace remembered when Betty wanted them to meet her and her beau at the Hotel. She always thought of it each time she passed the landmark with its tall totem pole in front.

"If you don't treat yourself well, who will?" Clara said.

"Mother's not happy they're moving to Los Angeles," Joseph said. "But the company's giving him a promotion, so it's better he accepts."

"Hopefully she'll find a good hospital for her year of practice," Clara said.

Yes, Grace thought. *In the land of hope, there's never winter.*

CHAPTER 21

♦

*May you get all your wishes but one, so, you always
have something to strive for.*

Three months after Benedict's fourth birthday, Grace had another son, Leo, born the same year Marta gave birth to a girl she named Pauline. As they'd done with Joseph and Grace, Anton and Susanna wanted to meet their newest grandchild and they pressured Marta to visit.

"Wait and see," Grace told Lorna. "They'll pull the same tricks and rope them into moving back."

"Does she like Los Angeles?"

"How could she not like California?"

"Phonus-balonus, Daniel tells me it's different. Not as nice as up north where we were. Don't tell me you're still pining away for Sonora. Your destiny was set when you met Joseph."

Grace rolled her mother's words around in her mind. She wondered if there was a moment she might have been able to change directions, or if there was something she could've done differently. Could she have refused to stay in Tacoma, or adamant they not live next door? How does one know how much to protest and how much to give in to get along?

When Pauline was two years old, Marta and David came to Tacoma for a visit. A cupid-face girl with twinkling eyes and an engaging smile, Pauline charmed the entire family. David was as pleasant as always, but Grace thought Marta nervous and on edge. She surmised Anton and Susanna were as overbearing and coercive as ever. To her surprise, Marta visited her daily and was genuinely nice. *Using me as a respite from the tyranny.*

"Looks like he was crying," Marta said one afternoon as Grace rocked Leo on the porch.

"Benedict squashed his finger in a drawer. Needs some attention." She kissed the top of Leo's head. "He and Erika are my sensitive ones."

"Pauline's helping mother dust." Marta glanced at the side of the house where Benedict played with die-cast cars and airplanes on a flat spot of concrete. "It's good she's getting to know her family."

"Do you have nice neighbors there?"

"The ones near us are in the business, as they say. If you aren't, they aren't interested in you." Marta waved away a fly, buzzing around her head.

Grace briefly imagined what would have happened if she and Joseph had lived near *people in the business.*

"He's on sales calls all day and we're stuck at home." She picked up a nearby flyswatter and squashed the bug, leaving a red stain on the railing. "I work private duty two days a week. I'd like to work full time, but it's difficult to get babysitters."

"Your new bob haircut is flattering," Grace said.

Marta stroked a spit curl. "Mother associates it with immorality—smoking, drinking. She was horrified when David told her we went to a Black and Tan club to hear jazz. Didn't think we should mix with others."

"Did you enjoy it?"

"We did. Good music. Lots of fun." She picked a begonia leaf from the flower box on the porch ledge and rubbed it between her fingers.

"They weren't keen on Clara entering the Charleston Jam and Lindy Hop contests, but she did anyway. I'm missing out."

"Well, four children."

Grace stared at the sprigs of grass sprouting through the cracks in the concrete and recalled the time she overheard Marta tell Susanna she wouldn't breed like a rabbit—a thinly veiled reference Grace couldn't ignore.

"Father asked David if his company can transfer him here again. He thinks it would be good for Pauline to be near family and go to Holy Rosary."

Grace concealed a knowing smile. "What did David say?"

"He's not keen on the idea. He likes his job . . . I'd be happier here and we have to think about Pauline's future."

"There must be good schools there."

Marta looked away. "Mother still doesn't think he's up to snuff. They both think he drinks too much when he entertains clients."

"But it's illegal now."

"Anyone can find hooch. You only have to know where to go. Well, I'd better not *dawdle*, as Mother says. She wants me to make the *spätzle* for dinner." Marta jumped as Benedict leapt from behind a bush, let out a whoop and fired his cap pistol. "Don't do that again. Hate those darn things."

As Marta crossed the yard, Grace pondered if she married David to get out from under her parents, or if she was truly in love. It was easy to understand how his attention bowled her over. Had she ever before received such care? She had a hunch they'd move back to Tacoma because, as Grace learned, the parents were formidable.

The next morning Grace visited Betty with the two boys while the girls played at home with Pauline.

"Sorry to trouble you with the goings on at home."

"Heavens, with the clan Tschida, you need a battalion of sounding boards." The hint of a smile appeared on Betty's face. "Watch. The bullies will chase David away. Like they tried to do to me."

Later, Grace told Joseph what Marta said about the parents wanting them to return to Tacoma.

"I know. But David told me he wants to stay in Los Angeles. He's moving up in the company." Joseph undid his onyx and gold cuff links and placed them on the dresser. "But my parents are right about one thing—he does drink a bit too much."

"We all have your father's plum brandy."

"Not talking about home brew. He wanted me to go with him to some speakeasies in town. Knows them all."

Grace understood Marta missing friends and family and being stuck at home, but why would she want to be back with her overbearing parents? And if she returned, would she revert to her malevolence?

Following their departure, Clara told Grace and Joseph, "Marta and David are moving back to Tacoma."

They did it, Grace thought to herself. *They finagled them into moving back.*

"David agreed?" Joseph asked.

"He was reluctant at first," Clara said. "He asked the company to transfer him back here, but they already have someone in the job. So, he's resigning and he'll look for something after they return."

"It may be better in the long run," Joseph said. "Marta didn't like it there."

"And David wants to make her happy," Clara added.

"Oh, the Model T I ordered will be here next week," Joseph said. Got one like Father's with a rumble seat. We should go to the ocean and dig for razor clams and geoducks."

"Business must be good," Clara said.

"It is. I already paid back Father's original investment."

While Clara and Joseph talked, Grace thought back to when David courted Marta. He was considerate and respected Anton's wishes that Marta wait before they dated. He was outmatched then and still was. The parents did well to foster all their obeisance.

Two months later, David and Marta settled in Joseph's old room, and Pauline in Marta's former bedroom. David found temporary work with the owner of several gas stations, and Marta started working at St. Joseph's. While she worked, Susanna took care of Pauline, a giggling, happy child with puffy cheeks and free run of the house, doted upon and pampered beyond measure.

She gave new life to her grandparents. Her pictures filled the house, although none appeared on Anton's dresser. It still held only Vivienne's.

They'd been living in the big house six months when Marta told Grace, "Father wants to build a house for me next to yours."

Grace's gaze ping ponged between the big house and the garden as Marta's words sank in.

"I told him I didn't want him to build anything for us," Marta said.

Grace felt relief wash over her. She was certain it was because Marta didn't want to be closer to them. She often complained about the noise Grace's children made.

Marta ran a thumb against the ends of her fingernails. "David's leaving."

"Back to Los Angeles?"

"He'll stay here for Pauline and find a place in town." Marta looked squarely at Grace. "We're separating. Father won't allow a divorce. It's against the Church."

The matter-of-fact way Marta told her gave Grace a chill. "I'm so sorry."

"My parents were right. He's a nice man, but . . . well, it's better."

Later, Grace told Joseph about the separation. "They persuaded Marta, I know it." She titled her head and paused. "They're always talking about how important family is. So, why didn't they want to keep them together? It'd be better for Pauline."

"She can't stand up to them. Nor can he."

Grace looked hard at Joseph. *Nor could you, my dear. Nor could you. And Betty was right—they chased David away.*

The following April, when the rhododendrons in Anton's garden were at peak bloom, Grace found Susanna baking a batch of *punschkrapfen*. It was Joseph's thirty-third birthday, and they planned a party that evening in the big house. She had last made the delicacies for Thanksgiving, and seeing how her grandchildren loved the chocolate, nut and jam-filled cakes covered with cotton-candy pink icing, she wanted to treat them again. Anton was outside pruning the winter-killed branches on the trees, and cutting back the spent perennials.

"That man and his garden," Susanna muttered to Grace as she took the dough out of the oven and set it aside. When it was cool enough, she took out her biscuit cutter and began cutting out circles. As she was finishing the last one, she collapsed on the floor.

Grace shuffled back a step, dazed. A moment later, she ran outside and called for Anton to come in.

"Finishing up the pruning." He ran his finger over the pickets on the fence. "Paint buckled. Need to scrape it off so I can repaint it."

Grace waved both her hands in the air. "Anton. Now. Come. Susanna fell."

He rushed in. Seeing Susanna, he dropped his shears and gardening gloves and knelt next to her. He cradled her head in his arms and swayed back and forth, muttering things in German and stroking her hair.

Grace heard a sob and turned to see Pauline in the kitchen doorway. Her hair was matted on one side and her Dolly Dingle doll dangled from her hand.

"Did you wake up from your nap?" Grace led Pauline into the parlor and nestled her on her lap as she telephoned Clara. Anton's moans grew louder, and the toddler whimpered and pointed to the kitchen. "Yes, Grandfather's upset. It will be OK."

Clara said she'd tell Marta and have the doctor come to the house. She asked Grace to tell Joseph. He arrived home first and after Clara and Marta came, they helped him place Susanna on her bed.

"With her hypertension, it's possible she had a stroke," Clara said before asking Grace what happened.

"I came to talk to her about Joseph's party—she was baking. Then she crumpled to the floor. She made no sound and if I hadn't been there, your father wouldn't have heard." Grace thought back to the cacophony of sounds in the yard—chirping birds, hammering from a neighboring yard, a mother calling children home.

The doctor determined Susanna died of a cerebral hemorrhage. Grace had Vivienne and Erika take Pauline to their house while the family decided on funeral arrangements.

Marta leaned against the wall, each hand gripping the opposite elbow. "Who's going to watch Pauline?" she said, with a catch in her breath.

"Father can't take care of her," Clara said. "You'll have to stay home until we figure something out."

"I have to work."

Anton moaned. "I don't want to live."

Joseph looked to Clara, his eyes wide.

"It's the shock talking." Clara looked up at the ceiling and drew a long breath.

"Can Grace take her?" Marta said.

A spreading puddle of silence fell as everyone looked at Grace.

"You're asking a bit much. She's got four to look after," Joseph said in a tone that did not hide his displeasure.

"She loves children, or so she says," Marta said.

Clara narrowed her eyes. "And you expect her to care for Pauline, too?"

"I'll be happy to take her until you find a solution," Grace said. "Her cousins will love to have her with them."

"Are you certain, darling?" Joseph said. Grace closed her eyes and nodded.

"Thank you," Marta said.

"We could ask cousin Sára to come," Clara said.

"Father's niece in St. Paul, his sister Julia's daughter," Joseph explained to Grace. "She's about eighteen now."

Clara sat down next to Anton and put her hand on his shoulder. "Father, why don't we ask Sára to come live with us?" Anton didn't respond as he gazed through the window. "When she visited, she told me she'd like to live here. She'd be perfect to care for Pauline and help us with the house."

"It's not up to him any longer," Marta said.

Joseph sprang out of his chair. "This is his house, Marta. He has every right to decide if someone comes to live here."

Marta crossed her arms tightly. "He can't decide anything right now. We must."

Joseph strode in front of Marta and leaned in. "Stop it right now."

"We're all stunned," Clara said, "but let's try to work out something together."

"I need some water," Marta said. She went into the kitchen and returned a few minutes later. "Mother's *punschkrapfen* are still there. Someone should put the icing on them."

"I'll do it," Clara said before turning to Joseph. "We'll have to forget your birthday party. I don't think any of us feel like celebrating."

Only two weeks before, they'd celebrated Susanna's sixty-second birthday.

CHAPTER 22

◆

The women from Susanna's church auxiliaries helped arrange the funeral services, along with the rosary vigil held the night before the High Mass. Outside, the wind shrieked, and the rain fell in thick sheets as Father Gerhard led the vigil. Friends, parishioners and the family, including the children, were in attendance. Susanna lay on the four-poster bed, wearing her dotted-swiss dress trimmed with navy grosgrain ribbon. She wore her gold cross and in her hands was a bouquet of her favorite pink roses Anton had collected from his garden. Near the bed was a large lit ivory-colored candle on a pillar that cast an eerie spell in the darkened room and gave off a faint lavender scent. She looked serene and beautiful, the roses complementing her pale skin.

Each mourner took a turn standing near Susanna. Some made the sign of the cross, others touched her hand, or kissed her on the forehead. Grace listened to the sobs muffled by handkerchiefs and the hushed tones around her. She overhead one of the auxiliary ladies say, "She killed herself working for the church."

There's much truth to that statement, Grace thought. Susanna held onto an upward vision, believing people were on earth to struggle and receive spiritual rewards in the next life. *Hopefully now she'll get the rewards she dreamed of.*

After the service, Grace walked out with Mrs. Gartner, who whispered to her, "I suppose no one ever told you Susanna was illegitimate?"

Grace stopped, a stunned look on her face.

"Her mother was a widow when she was born. But she knew her father. People say he was part Jewish and hid it. If you weren't Catholic, you couldn't get far." Mrs. Gartner clicked her tongue. "One of her relatives was hanged for stealing a horse."

Grace's gaze drilled into the ground. "Could be rumors. Anyway, now's not the time to talk about such things."

Mrs. Gartner chuckled. "That woman made the best cinnamon rolls."

The following day, Grace called Lorna to tell her what Mrs. Gartner said. "Maybe that's why she was so secretive and placed so much importance on religion."

"You never really know someone," Lorna said. "Anyway, sometimes in those villages, the priest came only twice a year. Can't expect people to wait." Lorna's throaty laugh rang out. "Seems they're always saying way back there's a horse thief in a family—don't give it much thought."

Grace reflected on the day before Susanna died. She had watched as her mother-in-law took a loaf of black pumpernickel bread out of the oven, using her apron as a potholder. She touched the large crack atop the loaf before placing it on the table next to a can of lard. As they discussed the upcoming potluck dinner at church, Susanna stirred the goulash simmering in the iron kettle; its pungent garlic and paprika assailed Grace's nostrils. After tasting the stew, she grumbled that the potatoes still had a crunch and needed another ten minutes. No one could match her culinary skills.

A few days after the funeral, on a day when only a few cirrus clouds drifted around the azure sky, Grace hung the laundry outdoors. She draped items on the bushes and shrubs when she ran out of clothesline.

Mrs. Gartner popped her head over the fence. "Mighty nice of you taking Marta's little one."

"The more you have, the easier it is. They take care of each other." Grace brushed off a leaf that had fallen on a sheet. "Anton's niece's coming in a few weeks to care for her. Until she gets here, Anton hired a lady three days a week to give me a break. She's the aunt of parishioners from St. Nicholas Greek church, a Miss Thea."

"That old maid? She's at least fifty. She can't run after a child."

"It was difficult to find someone on short notice."

"Came from Thessalonica with her brother and his wife about twenty-five years ago." Mrs. Gartner picked a hollyhock growing on Anton's side of the fence and twirled it in her hand.

Miss Thea arrived the following Monday, a portly woman dressed all in black. She brought her own lunch, preferring her fare of lamb stew, stuffed grape leaves and Daktyla bread. While Pauline took her afternoon naps, Grace would see her light a candle in the backyard and intone something in what she supposed was Greek. She waved her hands over the smoke trailing from the wick and swirled it around. Grace thought it had to be a traditional custom and she didn't mention it to anyone.

One afternoon, Grace saw Miss Thea taking Pauline toward the front of the house.

"If you're going for a walk, wait until Leo's up and take him with you."

"We go now. I come back." After she tightened her black headscarf, she yanked Pauline's hand and led her down the steps.

A few minutes later, Grace heard a child screaming. It was coming from the street. She ran to see what was happening. On the sidewalk, near the bottom of the steps, Grace saw Miss Thea with her hands around Pauline's neck, strangling her. The child kicked and wailed, trying to pry herself away. Her screams pierced the air. Miss Thea held her grip, a wild look in her eyes.

Grace yelled out, "Stop. Stop right now." Her heart pounding, she ran down and grabbed Miss Thea by the arm. The woman jabbed at Grace with her elbow and rammed her body into her, pushing her away. Grace staggered back. Regaining her balance, she lunged at the woman and grabbed hold of one of her arms, prying it away from Pauline. With her other arm, she pushed Pauline away from Miss Thea. The child fell down; her screams turned to sobs.

Grace twisted Miss Thea's arm as hard as she could. "You could have killed her."

Miss Thea spit on the ground and pointed to Pauline. "Her mother does black magic. Now that she's baptized, if she dies, she'll go straight to heaven."

"Nonsense." Grace held onto the woman's arm, wrenching it while shoving her farther away. "Go away. Now."

Miss Thea gave her a piercing look and spit on the ground again. Grace gave her one last thrust and pointed down the street. "Never come back."

Grace took Pauline home with her. She cuddled the child in the rocking chair, stroking her hair and humming a lullaby. They stayed this way until Leo woke from his nap. Pauline stopped sucking her thumb and sat up. "You're feeling better, aren't you?" Grace said. "Do you want to play with Leo?"

Pauline nodded. She scrambled down and took Leo's hand.

After Grace told the family what happened, Marta confronted Anton. "You hired an insane woman. Didn't you check her out?"

"They told me she loved children." Anton's eyes darted to the side. "They thought it would be good for her to do."

"If she needed something to do," Joseph said, "she could've weeded gardens."

After Susanna's death, Anton found it difficult to work and he cut back on jobs he took. He started visiting Grace during the day while Joseph was at the market and the girls at school.

"How are the girls doing?"

"Busy with dance and painting classes after school. They'll both be in the school play next month. They're talented. Take after their father. You'll come, won't you?"

"I will. But encourage them to develop more practical things."

My daughters are going to do what they love. I refuse to dictate their lives like you did your children. She finished cleaning tarnish off the silverware and put away the polish. "Sit down. I'll put some tea on."

"What's that big pile in the corner?"

"Joseph's always bringing the boys new toys—a train set, Lincoln Logs, Erector Set."

"They don't need so much. Shouldn't spoil them." He shook his head. "My parents were strict. There was much work. We had little time for fun."

"It makes Joseph happy to do it."

Anton cleared his throat. "Sára comes next week—all the way by train from St. Paul."

Grace put a plate of sugar cookies on the table. "Freshly made this morning." She lit the fire under the kettle and placed black pekoe tea leaves in a strainer.

"Ilona was the first to come to America," Anton said. "Worked for a family until she married Karl. He had a tavern and store that sold groceries, flour, feed. I worked for them until they moved here." He looked down and stroked one of his hands. "Their dairy's the largest in the area now. The kids drive the wagons around town to deliver milk. Silke, she's the middle daughter, drives the horse and buggy to Tacoma to do the shopping." He twirled one end of his mustache. "The kids aren't happy going to Holy Rosary. The others students make fun of them and call them country bumpkins."

"Their lives in the country are probably nicer than half the kids in the city."

"*Ja*, Silke tells those kids not to think they're any smarter than the next one."

"You grew up in the country—I remember you saying you helped your family with their farmlands and vineyards."

"Our land was in the countryside, but our house was in town—directly across from the church." Anton drew an imaginary diagram with his hands. "It had a big courtyard with a pergola. Mother hung laundry there." He chuckled. "The rooster and chickens would run around her, pecking at her wicker basket." He gestured to the right. "At the other end, the root cellar and a wine cellar were next to the barn where we kept our animals."

He swept his hand upward. "On top of our chimney a stork built its nest with sticks from the marsh. There were many storks in the village. We had a saying: 'A stork that builds a nest on the roof of a house, brings good luck to that house and to the entire village.' But no one had much luck."

"What happened?" As Grace poured the tea, she sensed Anton's need to talk about his life and the past, as one often does when one feels one's mortality.

"There was a drought and the Swine Flu. We'd hoped for a plentiful harvest, but an insect or louse devastated the vines and the yield was small. No one could depend on the Esterházys to provide extra work. Their lands were mainly vineyards and were also affected."

He took the lid off the beige and brown earthenware bowl and scooped out a teaspoon of sugar. "Many men left the village. Immigration fever, they called it."

Anton went on to tell how the Northern Pacific ads said they wanted people in Minnesota. And the priests who went there wrote back telling of the high wages, economic opportunity and the good soil in a healthy climate, in the center of America. They said newcomers would benefit from social, religious and business contacts. But only good Catholics should come and no free thinkers, red republicans, atheists or agitators.

"The steamship passage was inexpensive, included railroad tickets in the price."

"What else do you remember about your home?

"We had apricot and apple trees. Mother made the best homemade *kuchen* and apricot ice cream." Anton nodded as he recalled a distant memory. "At the end of the season, around late September, the old fruit-grinder came around to save the fallen apples from rotting. He'd crush them up into cider with this contraption he built out of old metal parts. It traveled at a snail's pace down the narrow lanes. Made an awful commotion, but nothing like the noise it made when he ground up the apples."

"It must have been a wonderful place to grow up. You still hear those sounds, don't you?"

Anton nodded and smiled. "And the tingling of the cow bells when they returned after grazing on the hillside pastures. The button box accordions and double-neck guitars that played at festivals." He rubbed his forearm; the hairs on it were turning white. "The wooden oxen carts as they lumbered down the paths. Many had drawings and sayings stenciled on the wooden yokes."

Grace noticed a faraway look in his eyes as if he was seeing long forgotten images.

"Sureau trees with their white flowers." Anton smiled. "At Epiphany, we dressed like the Three Kings and serenaded house to house to collect donations for charity." He brushed crumbs off his vest. "But that's the past."

He stood up and looked at the window. "Best trim the hedge around the house before the kids get home. Tomorrow, I'll tend the flower beds. The tulips are coming in nicely. Wish Susanna could have seen them."

He scooted his chair in. "I heard Richard Byrd flew over the North Pole."

"I'll tell the children to look it up on the atlas." She stacked his cup and saucer on top of hers. "I hope you'll tell them your stories one day. It's important to know where one comes from."

Anton took one of his favorite chocolate-covered mint patties from his vest pocket and gave it to Grace; it was one of the candies Marta hid around the house for him to find, replenishing them when he'd eaten all. He patted the top of Grace's head. "You're a nice woman."

CHAPTER 23

◆

*It's better to spend money like there's no tomorrow than
to spend tonight like there's no money.*

In mid-September the Western Washington Fair was taking place in Puyallup. The weather was still pleasantly warm and Grace and Joseph thought it would be a nice family outing. They insisted Anton join them. It'd been five months since Susanna's death and he was lost without her, especially on weekends.

Arriving at the fairgrounds, Joseph and Anton took the three oldest children to see the agricultural and pastoral displays. Grace took Leo on the carousel. After he rode the tiger and zebra, they stayed under the tent near the bandstand, watching various musical revues, jugglers, acrobats, and trained animals. When Joseph and the others returned, a band was playing *Clap Hands! Here Comes Charley!,* with Leo clapping in unison with the music.

"Mommy, we went on the Ferris Wheel," Erika said, handing her a flaky Fisher scone, oozing with melted butter and raspberry jam. "We got this from a nice lady in a white dress and hat."

"We saw livestock, like the ones on Aunt Ilona's farm," Benedict said. "And new automobiles and a map of the States made from different colored beans."

"There were baby contests," Erika said, tapping Grace on the arm, "for the prettiest, the one with the reddest hair, the most teeth."

"And the heaviest," Vivienne added with a grin. She handed Grace a roll filled with sweet onions, pickles, and mayonnaise. "Daddy got us all onion sandwiches."

"Sounds like you had a good time," she said, putting the scone aside and giving Leo a bite of the sandwich.

"We should head home," Joseph said. "You have school tomorrow." A bevy of moans rose up.

A woman Grace didn't know walked by and greeted Joseph and Anton.

"Olga, nice to see you."

When Grace heard the woman's name, she twisted around to get a better look. Olga's face was partially hidden by a lacy parasol. When she lowered it, it took but a few moments for Grace to realize she was the woman in the photo locked away in the credenza, the woman the family wanted to claim for Joseph. She was pleasant enough, nicely dressed in a sheer floral print, cloche hat and a long multi-strand pendant necklace. As Joseph introduced her to Grace and the children, Olga scanned Grace from head to toe.

"Come visit," Anton said. "The girls would love to see you."

Did Anton also want Olga? Why invite her? I don't need her compiling her secret agenda. There's always a secret agenda.

"I will," Olga said. "Would love to stay and chat, but I'm seeing *Son of the Sheik* at the Music Box—in honor of Valentino." The silent screen star was one of Grace's favorites and she had also hoped to see the film, especially after his untimely death.

Grace watched Joseph keep his narrow gaze on her as they talked, as if she was the only person who existed. He could be charming and draw people to him, which made it difficult to tell if he was being nice or if he was more than pleasantly surprised to see her. He waved as Olga walked away and stood watching her for a few moments before turning to the family. "Time to go."

"Well, fiddle-dee-dee," Vivienne said with a pout that turned into a smile. "But we had a swell day."

Ten days after their excursion to the Fair, Joseph came home from work early. His face was flushed, and he had chills. When Grace asked what was wrong, he waved her away with a vacant stare. "I'm going to lie down." He looked around, disoriented. "Where's the bedroom?"

Grace knew something bad was happening. She took his arm and led him into their room. He plopped down on the bed, fully clothed, and fell asleep at once. She covered him with a patchwork quilt and he lay scrunched up and inert for some time. Clara was unavailable at the hospital but she reached Marta. "He's delirious and running a fever."

"Probably the flu," Marta said. "Give him aspirin and plenty of liquids. Let him sleep."

"You'd think she'd show more interest in her brother's wellbeing," Grace muttered to the wall. She decided she'd speak to Clara when she returned from work. But later, when Joseph started vomiting, she called their family doctor.

After his examination, he confirmed the worst. "It's smallpox. He's contagious. He'll have to go to the Pest House."

"I'll never let him go there," Grace said. "Tell me what to do."

"It's hard to care for someone with this illness. And it could last three to four weeks."

"I can do it."

The doctor shook his head as he put his stethoscope in his bag. "You could get it, Grace. The diphtheria you had as a child could have weakened you."

"He can't go there. I refuse to let him go."

"All right. We'll have to quarantine the house. I'll put up a sign that says smallpox is in the house and the children will have to stay somewhere else. Keep an eye on them. One of them could have picked it up when he did."

When Anton heard of Joseph's smallpox, he told Grace the girls must stay in the big house and the boys could go to Ilona's farm. "How are you going to take care of him by yourself? I'll ask Clara to stay home from work."

"I can do it, Anton. The doctor told me what to do and if Clara or Marta can come over in the evening to check on him, I'd feel better."

Word about Joseph's illness spread like a rash throughout the neighborhood and in church. The family, along with friends and fellow parishioners, arranged a daily schedule to leave food and supplies. Wearing cotton masks, they'd approach the house hesitantly, put the groceries and cooked meals on the porch and run off. Anton left bottles of Lysol and arranged for a local laundry to collect the washing Grace left on the porch in a large white laundry bag.

Anton still visited Grace while Joseph was ill. He'd ask her to come out on the porch and sit, not wanting to come inside. "Come, Grace, you need a break," he said one night as sunset streaked the autumn sky with the colors of salmon, fire coral and alabaster. She kept the door open and sat next to it so she could hear if Joseph needed anything.

"Clara says he's strong and has a good chance of beating it," Anton said.

"The doctor says it should be over in two weeks."

Anton took a waded-up handkerchief from his vest pocket and blew his nose. He whisked the cloth back and forth under his nose after finishing. "I asked the priests and nuns at Holy Rosary to say novenas."

Grace scooted her chair nearer the porch railing. The leaves of the apple trees gave off a faint susurrus as a light breeze wafted over. They carried the fragrant clove-like scent of the buttercream and burgundy carnations Anton planted at the side of the house.

"It's nice having Sára here," Anton said. "Makes me think of her mother. She died years ago and now it's Ilona and me. We were six."

"What happened to the others?" Grace said, noting the scratches on his chin where he'd cut himself shaving.

"Georg was the oldest." Anton lowered the tone of his voice. "He fell off the roof and died. Twenty-eight years old. Left three children; the daughter was blind." He took out his pocket watch and twisted the winding knob. "We'd already lost my younger brother Martin. He drowned in the river near town when he was thirteen. Marta's named after him."

Grace shook her head. "It's nice you honored his memory."

"Baby Gisella died before her first birthday, when I was four." He raised himself up and sat back down, adjusting his posture.

"It was hard for my parents—children dying or leaving. I left, too. The parish priest thought I had artistic ability. He arranged a sculpture apprenticeship in Vienna." Anton gazed across the yard. "We visited France and Italy to study the masters."

"And you brought your skills here."

"Ilona and Julia wanted me to come and Mother said it was better for me to leave, too." He cocked his head to the side. "I sailed from Hamburg to New York on a ship named Gallard. I can still see that ship after all these years."

Listening to the far-off laments of a foghorn, Grace said, "And you're glad you came."

He was silent for a few moments, as if he'd never before considered what might have been lost or gained. "We made a nice life here."

"You've left a legacy with your work."

"*Ja, ja.* The children can see the things I built."

Anton pushed himself out of the chair. "I've taken up too much of your time. Tell Joseph I'm praying for him."

After he left, she thought about all his talk of death. The only surviving son, he must have felt obligated to help the family. And losing a sibling, one with whom you share memories and a past, alters your life. She knew. She lost her brother, Andrew. And now, after losing Susanna, Anton had to be distraught about Joseph.

Joseph's fever dropped three days later. A rash appeared on his skin and his face grew three times its normal size. Soon, yellow pustules formed. When the doctor next examined him, he confirmed it was not the regular smallpox but the rare black smallpox. "There's bleeding under the skin. It'll look charred and black. You must watch him. This kind is dangerous."

Joseph's malaise made him too weak to get up, and though he was confined to bed, Grace kept the mirrors covered with black velvet and their bedroom dark so he wouldn't see his swollen face and the scabs. She sat at his bedside throughout the night to guard against his picking his scabs for fear they would scar him.

His fever never returned and one evening when he was feeling better, he wanted to talk.

Taking Grace's hand, he said, "You're a saint, caring for me all these days. But it wasn't only the caring, I could sense your love. You know what I thought about?" Grace shook her head. "When I missed the train in Everett and we talked till two in the morning."

"You had to sleep on our couch."

"I didn't sleep. Walked the floor, thinking about you. I was afraid you or your mother would hear me."

"I heard you. I couldn't sleep either, knowing you were in the next room."

"When I asked you for a kiss and you said no, I was worried I'd offended you. You wouldn't even let me hold your hand." Joseph squeezed Grace's hand. "But I thought more of you because you said no."

"That's when you told me you didn't want to get married until you had a house and a couple thousand dollars in the bank."

"But the heart rules all.' He squeezed Grace's hand again. His smile was tender.

Joseph recovered and once he regained his stamina, he wanted to return to work.

"Stay home a few more days," Grace said as he looked over the receipts for the last month.

"Can't. The Armour salesman is coming in to put up a display of their line—hams, bacon, lard. We have to get booklets and letters out to customers. It'll mean good volume. Father will be pleased to see how we're growing the business."

"I hope you're not pushing yourself just to please him."

"No. It's for us—for the store. I want. . .I want to give you all I promised."

"Then promise you'll come home early."

His first week back, he put in full days, often staying late for customers, or delivering packages on his way home. But he had no relapse and the doctor gave him an excellent prognosis.

CHAPTER 24

◆

Wisdom is the comb given to a man after he has lost his hair.

Grace felt she'd made peace with staying in Tacoma, and she'd look back at the years since Joseph opened the market as some of their happiest as a family. The market grew more successful, and Joseph hired additional staff to service and deliver to customers. The children were busy with school and extracurricular activities. Grace made most of their clothes, along with costumes for school plays and Halloween; one year she sewed bumblebee costumes for all of them after they complained the tails on the black cat ones made it too hard to sit. Vivienne and Erika began cooking—Erika's specialty was fudge and Vivienne's was sugar cookies made with a cookie press. Benedict, about to turn eight, took up baseball and roller derby and started collecting baseball cards. Leo, a budding artist, would start first grade in the fall.

There was only one incident during this time that elicited veiled comments from the Tschidas—Benedict's First Communion. After he reached the age of reason, he attended a year-long class to prepare for receiving Christ in the Eucharist.

The day of the service, Benedict wore the white suit Anton bought him. On his arm was a white armband, embroidered with a chalice in gold thread.

At the service, Grace accompanied Benedict to the altar railing where they knelt alongside other children and parents. Father Gerhard made his way down the row, administering a Communion wafer on each child's outstretched tongue. After Benedict received the Body of Christ, he spit it out. Grace caught it. She held out her hand and softly called to Father Gerard. After the priest stepped back and took it, Grace whispered in Benedict's ear with a harshness he'd never heard from her. "Swallow it. Don't you dare spit it out again."

As Benedict squinted and chewed the wafer, Grace felt her neck get warm. *I can already hear what they'll say.*

After the ceremony, the family met in the back of the church, under a painting of St. Ignatius in the lion's den. Benedict stood close to Grace and clenched her hand. When Anton started to say something, Joseph put his hand on his father's arm. "Grace and I will speak to him later."

Back at the big house, a sheet cake with a large cross and the names of saints written on it took center stage on the dining room table. Red Jell-O cups, representing chalice wine, surrounded it.

Anton handed Benedict a small box. "I hope this guides you to be a better soldier of Christ." It was a gold St. Benedict medal, the patron saint of Europe and students.

When they were back at their house, Joseph asked him why he spit it out. "You knew it was the Body of Christ."

"It tasted funny."

"You were taught how important this day is," Grace said. "Not liking the taste is not an excuse."

Benedict hung his head, his hands clasped behind his back. "I don't know, Mommy. I don't like all this religion stuff."

"Don't ever let your grandfather hear you say that," Joseph said.

Grace found herself sympathizing with Benedict. She wondered if she wouldn't have rebelled, had she been reared in a home where religion cast a shadow over everything and demanded complete fealty. It should be Benedict's choice how he wanted to engage with religion. But this was the Tschida family.

Anton didn't let Joseph and Grace forget the incident for weeks. Grace's surprise shifted the conversation—she was pregnant again. Joseph thought it wonderful news and when Grace mentioned that with five children, they'd need a larger house, he said, "Let's think about it."

"We've been here nearly ten years—I've had plenty of time to think."

"Our house is fine and I like living near the family," Joseph said. "Didn't you say once you never wanted to move, you'd moved enough in your life?"

"That was in Sonora."

Ain't She Sweet came on the radio and Erika tugged on Joseph's sleeve. "Daddy, let's dance." Joseph held the girl's hands as she poised her feet on top of his.

As he whirled Erika around, Grace looked on in a sullen stew of annoyance. She knew living next to the Tschidas was never easy, but was it entering the realm of the impossible?

One day when Grace had morning sickness, Vivienne asked her what was wrong and she said, "Virus #5.

Vivienne wrinkled up her nose. "What disease is that?"

Grace smiled and it didn't take long for Vivienne's eyes to widen. "Another one?"

A few days later, Marta came to see Grace, when she knew Joseph was at work. Rocking back and forth on her heels, she said. "I thought you were finished. Honestly, what will people think?"

"People or you, Marta?"

"If you think I'd want a bunch of bratty kids like yours, you're out of your mind. I don't like my daughter playing with them."

"Then you haven't noticed Pauline asks to play with them. Poor thing, she doesn't have any friends because you chase them away."

"I do not and she's not a *poor thing*." Marta stared at Grace for a few moments before tromping down the porch steps.

Grace watched Marta storm across the yard. *I should stop telling them to play with her to teach Marta a lesson—but it wouldn't be fair to Pauline.*

When Joseph came home, Leo told him, "Aunt Marta called us dirty brats, and she yelled at Mommy."

"It was nothing." Grace said without turning around.

"Tell me what she said, Gracie."

"Let it go," she said in a strained voice.

"I'll find out myself." Joseph left and walked to big house.

"Is Father going to talk to Aunt Marta?" Leo asked.

Grace pulled Leo close to her. "Did what Aunt Marta said bother you?"

"No, she's always crabby. We don't pay attention to her."

"She doesn't mean to yell. She has a lot on her mind."

Leo put his arms around Grace. "You're the best mother."

Joseph returned, a fierce look on his face. "She won't be saying anything to you again." He pushed aside a schoolbook primer and sat down on the sofa.

"I don't need a knight to rush off and defend me," Grace said. "I can do it myself. Heaven knows I've had plenty of practice in this nest of wasps."

On a Sunday in July, when Grace was in her eighth month, she and Joseph rested at home while Vivienne and Erika took their brothers to a nearby park; Vivienne and Benedict had promised to help Leo learn to skate, and Erika wanted to collect flowers and leaves for botanical pressing.

As Joseph napped on the sofa, Grace mended socks, placing a light bulb inside each, opening its hole wide as she surrounded it with tiny stitches. She looked up when Anton knocked on the door.

"Joseph, I need you to remove that boulder on the side of the yard."

"The big one?" Grace said. "That's too heavy for one person." She turned to Joseph as he stirred and stretched out his arms.

"It's not that big," Anton said. "Get the wheelbarrow from the shed."

"Let me change my pants," Joseph said.

Grace stuck her needle in the spool of thread and followed him into the bedroom. "Wait until someone can help you."

"If I don't do it now, he won't stop badgering."

"Let him. He can get someone to do it later." She saw he was not paying attention to her, and it vexed her.

Joseph patted Grace on the cheek. "It'll only take a few minutes."

Joseph got the wheelbarrow and joined Anton. As Grace watched him struggle to pick up the stone, she groused aloud, "Damn you, Anton. Help him."

After dropping it several times, Joseph got the stone in the wheelbarrow and took it to the back of the house. When he came back in with an odor of sweat lingering, Grace fussed with cleaning the pantry and ignored him.

"See, it's done. Better to do it and get it over with." She continued wiping down shelves and rearranging the dry goods. "What? You're not speaking to me?"

"You're not your father's slave."

"There's no sense in arguing. I moved a stone. That's all." Joseph went to change clothes again.

Grace stood at the kitchen sink, her chin trembling. *Why did I make such a fuss? All I've done is upset him. And I didn't prove anything.*

Later, Joseph held his side and swayed, exhaling soft puffs. "I must have pulled a muscle."

"Let me get some ointment for it." Grace rummaged through her medical kit: plasters, boric acid, iodoform, zinc oxide, arnica, belladonna, mercurochrome, morphine, Dr. Hostetter's Stomach Bitters. She spread arnica over the area where he held his hand and she moistened a washcloth with vinegar to place on the back of his neck.

In bed that night, the pain got worse. He moaned and turned from side to side, and then sat up, knees to his chest, head dropped between his knees.

"I'm calling Clara. You're in too much pain."

"Wait till morning. She worked all day. It may go away."

"You need to be looked at."

Marta answered the phone and came over. After examining Joseph, she said, "Probably an inflamed or strained muscle. It'll be better in the morning."

"He's in a lot of pain for a strained muscle."

"You asked for my opinion and I gave it to you."

Early the next morning, Joseph held his stomach. "It hurts so much." Grace felt his forehead, and it was warm. Then he started vomiting. She again called over to the big house and got Marta.

"Put cold washcloths on him to relieve the fever and keep him in bed. Try to get him to drink fluids so he doesn't dehydrate. I'll check on him when I get home."

Grace made bouillon, thinking it was something easy for him to digest and would give him nutrients. When Vivienne and Erika came into the kitchen with their school books, she said, "You'll have to fix your breakfasts today.' She pointed to the breadbox and peach jam next to the Toastmaster. "Fix it for the boys, too."

"What's wrong with daddy?" Erika asked.

"He hurt himself when he moved that rock. Hurry, you don't have much time. Make certain you get to school on time."

Grace brought the bouillon into the bedroom and saw Joseph sitting up in bed, looking around without focusing. "I have to get to the market."

"You're sick, darling. You can't. I'll tell them you'll be out today."

Joseph stumbled out of bed and went to the cupboard. He stopped before opening it. "Who's that man standing there?"

Grace looked around the room. "There's no one here but us."

"The one with the wool cap. What's he doing here?" He searched through the clothes. "Where's my smock? I need it today." He wobbled and grabbed hold of the bureau. "I have to go to Aunt Ilona's. We need more pork. Where's Mother? She wants to come with me."

Grace stood motionless in the quietness that comes from fear. As soon as the children left for school, she called Quincy. Her voice crackling with alarm, she said, "Something's wrong with Joseph. He's been in a lot of pain and now he's delirious."

Quincy agreed to come and take him to hospital.

Grace felt a tug on her skirt. "Is Daddy going to die?" Leo asked.

"No, darling. He's not feeling well."

"I don't want Daddy to die."

"Please play with your train while I help Daddy."

But the boy followed Grace into the bedroom, where Joseph was looking around the room. "Where's the key? I have to open the market."

Grace led Joseph back to bed. He was still warm. He threw his head back and moaned. In a moment of lucidity, he said, "Something's not right."

Leo stood in the doorway and watched. "Go listen for Uncle Quincy," Grace said, motioning him out of the room. "Open the door for him when he comes."

A short time later, she heard Quincy greet Leo; he came in the bedroom and led Joseph out. "I'll stay with him at the hospital. The staff will manage without us today."

Leo hid in Grace's skirt, gripping her legs; she put her hand on his shoulder. "Let me know how he is as soon as you learn something."

Leo started whimpering. "Daddy's not coming home."

"Of course, he is. But he needs the doctors to check him. Get your Raggedy Andy book and we'll read." As Grace read the words, her mind was elsewhere. Difficult as it was, she told herself not to imagine the worst and to wait until she heard from Quincy.

The doctor who examined Joseph in the emergency room admitted him immediately. "He thinks he may have burst his appendix and they have to check for gangrene," Quincy told Grace over the phone from the hospital.

"His smallpox," Grace said. "It may have weakened him. And Quincy, please find Clara and tell her. I'll tell Anton."

On the way to the big house, she debated how to tell Anton without alarming him. She tossed aside that thought as animus poured out of her. "This is your fault, you wretched man. You had him move that heavy stone. See what you've done."

The next day, Sára took care of Leo so Grace could spend the day at the hospital. As Joseph was on heavy medication, he flitted in and out of consciousness. There was little she could do besides hold his hand and talk to him. "You're strong, Joseph. Look at how you pulled through your bout with smallpox. You'll get through this, too, and be back home with us soon, darling."

Anton came for an hour and Clara and Marta stopped by several times during their shifts.

"The doctor says the infection needs to be cleaned out," Clara told Grace. "He's scheduled surgery for tomorrow."

"Will he be all right?" Grace asked, sensing that something worse may be skulking around.

"They have to find out what it is. He isn't responding to the medicine." Clara massaged her temple; dark circles were forming under her eyes.

With labored breath, Joseph asked Grace to stay with him as long as possible the night before the operation; he needed to talk to her. Torn between wanting to be with him and sensing the children needed her comfort and assurance, she said, "I'll stay as long as they let me." A bird that had been resting on the windowsill flew away.

"Please don't think I wasn't paying attention to what you said yesterday, Gracie." His smile wavered as he continued, "But I was so miserable and upset at the thought of not being with you and the children that my mind was in a daze. But I understood everything. It was beautiful." Joseph touched her cheek. "The best thing I did was marry you. I felt we were meant to be together the moment I met you. And our wonderful kids. I wanted them to be near my family and you gave me that. You've given up much for our happiness. You give so much of yourself. I've always loved you."

Grace thought she saw a flickering of panic in his eyes. "And I've always loved you. And the children love and adore you. We miss you more than words can say."

A tear formed, and Joseph dabbed at it with the back of his hand. "Tears are more eloquent than words, aren't they?"

After the operation to remove what they could from the infection and the necrosis in his intestine, Joseph died. He was thirty-five years old.

CHAPTER 25

♦

May neighbors respect you, trouble neglect you,
angels protect you, and Heaven accept you.

The hospital performed an autopsy. Joseph died of venous thrombosis; a blood clot had formed in one of the major veins in the intestines. Anton could not accept that his only son died. He railed at the doctors, and also at Clara and Marta. And Grace couldn't stop herself; she lashed out at Anton, "You caused his injury. You made him move that stone. I told you it was too heavy."

Anton reared back, shaking his head. "How can you say such a thing? No one can say with certainty what caused it."

But Grace knew, and she was not about to forget.

Something else she would never forget haunted her after Joseph's death—the memory of the day she entered the orphanage. She'd slipped away from Sister Stephanie to run back and hug her mother one more time. But she remained at the top of the stairs when she saw her mother doubled over, sobbing in a recess under the stairs. The tangle of emotions she felt those many years ago flooded back; the bewilderment, the fear, the burning urge to comfort, and the feeling of being powerless.

Grace held on to hope she'd never have to face a similar decision. Shattered as they were by Joseph's death, she'd do everything to keep the family together. She tried to help the children make sense of their father's death.

"It's hard to understand why someone dies. We're sad, but we mustn't be afraid because your father wouldn't want that. Never forget, he loved you very much. His spirit will always be with you." Grace forced a smile to reassure them, as well as herself. "Talk to him, tell him what you feel, what you think, what you're doing."

"How'll he know what we're saying?" Benedict said.

"Don't the nuns at school tell you about miracles?"

"Yes," Benedict said, his voice fainter than usual. "Jesus changed the water into wine and made the dead man come alive."

"Can he make Daddy come alive?" Leo asked. Grace shook her head.

Benedict looked up and said, "Hey, Daddy, are you here? Can you hear me?"

"He may not answer you in words. Ask for signs. He'll send them to you."

"How do you do that?" Benedict said.

"Think about something you'd like to tell him"

Benedict scrunched up his face and looked around. "The race car Tommy and I are building. He didn't see it."

"Ask him what color to paint it," Vivienne said.

"Good idea," Grace said. "Watch, he'll point you to a color and you'll know that's the one."

"That's crazy," Benedict said, crinkling up his nose.

"No, it's not," Erika chimed in. "Listen to mother."

There was a knock at the door and Erika answered it, letting a stream of honey-colored light into the parlor. Anton put his hand on Ericka's shoulder and said, "Marta and I need to talk to your mother."

"It's best we talk alone, Grace." Marta said, looking at her nieces and nephews with a grave expression.

Vivienne took Leo's hand and motioned for the others to follow her.

"Joseph left an insurance policy for you and the children," Anton said to Grace. "You're the beneficiary."

Grace nodded. "He said it was to take care of me and the children."

"We need to discuss the funeral. Of course, it'll be at Holy Rosary," Anton said.

"We realize you're in no condition to think about these things," Marta said. "You have the children to care for, and the new baby coming. We'll do the planning."

"Some of the insurance money can be used for it," Anton said. "We want him to have a memorable one."

"It's to care for us. Can't you pay for the funeral?" *You're responsible for his death*, she screamed inside.

"Insurance money always covers funerals," Anton said. "This is your house. You have a place to live. And I'll pay the children's school fees." He gazed at Grace with unwavering intensity. "After the funeral expenses, you can put the rest of the money in the stock market. That way, it'll grow and you'll have income."

Grace looked at the splotches Leo had decorated on the wall. She'd never discussed the insurance money in depth with Joseph; neither of them ever imagined he'd die so young. Anton knew more about business and investments, but she was wary. "I'd feel better if I kept the money in a savings account."

"That won't yield good returns. You can put some in a savings account for daily expenses, and my friend Charlie at the bank will take care of investing the rest." Anton glanced at Marta before returning his gaze to Grace. "We want the best for you and the children, and we believe this is the best. Now about the funeral."

"I want Joseph to have a nice funeral . . ." Tears ran down Grace's face. She didn't wipe them away. *Let them see my pain.* "But I can't think right now."

"We'll take care of everything," Marta said.

Anton and Marta didn't tell her what they planned, and Grace was taken aback when she saw the elaborate arrangements of flowers—triple the amount of those at Susanna's funeral—two priests and a solid mahogany wood casket. Anton also arranged for a parade of cars to arrive at the church together. A week after the services, Anton presented her with the bills for the funeral and burial.

"How could you have spent so much? Joseph would never have wanted such a display." Grace stared at Anton in disbelief. "Yes, I wanted something nice, but this takes too much of the insurance money. You've taken what we need."

"You gave him a lovely tribute to show how much he meant to all of us. So many people came. Not everyone could fit in the church. You needed that."

"You made those decisions; you should pay it. It's not like you can't."

Her mind emptied while she felt roiling turmoil inside. She pointed to a paper on a side table. "A notice for my widow's pension from the State. Thirty-five dollars per month. It won't be enough."

"This is your house," Anton said, "and I said I'll pay Holy Rosary expenses."

"They're growing and need many other things, not only school fees." She stroked her forehead. "I don't want them to give up their activities."

"We're investing in the stock market for you. You'll get good returns."

"Someone took an interest in you, Anton, when you were young. Can't you do the same with your grandchildren?"

"Everything I've done has been for them. Putting Joseph in business was for them."

"The lies you tell yourself. You did all those things for yourself. To keep Joseph here."

At eight and a half months pregnant, Grace stayed home and her mind filled with thoughts of Joseph; how he never had the patience to stir his coffee long enough to dissolve all the sugar at the bottom of the cup; how he'd pretend to be the boogeyman or a wild chimpanzee and chase the children around the house; how he'd come up behind her and kiss the nape of her neck. Memory can be a cruel curse.

Betty often visited mornings and Clara came most nights to keep Grace company, spend time with the children and help with household tasks.

"You mustn't always cook for us, especially after you work all day," Grace said one day when Clara brought over a pan of meatloaf. "But I appreciate it."

"It's no trouble. I have the day off tomorrow. Do you want me to take Leo so you have some time for yourself?"

"No, he's good company. Helps me forget for a few moments." Grace paused. "I keep thinking my mother must have also felt this emptiness and loneliness when my father died."

"We're here for you." Clara embraced Grace. "You once wanted to return to California. Would you consider it now?"

Grace stared into space, lost for a few seconds. "Perhaps there was a moment it was possible—when we first arrived." She turned to Clara. "But that moment is gone."

"I suppose it's not realistic. A place you haven't lived for many years and four—soon five—children and no friends or family there to help."

"My sister's still in Long Beach." Grace absentmindedly fiddled with some crayons Leo had left on the table.

"We'd be devasted if you left, especially father. I sense he needs the grandchildren more than ever. But he'll never admit it."

"Joseph wanted the children to be near the family . . . before he died, he thanked me for staying here."

Grace wondered if she could get a place near Ellen. But this is where the children had lived their entire lives. It would mean uprooting them from school, their friends and all they'd known—and she'd have to pay rent and school fees, not to mention relocation costs. She didn't see how she could make it work. Like she said, the moment had passed.

Grace put off going through Joseph's things, as it would mean she'd have to acknowledge he was gone. But with the baby coming, she could postpone no longer. As her fingers stroked the carved rosettes and garlands on the bedroom dresser, she longed to see him again inserting his initialed cufflinks with a tilt of his head, to see him raise his chin when he put on his bowtie, and see him bite his lower lip as he evenly coated the pomade on his head with his tortoise comb.

Leo came into the room and broke her reverie. He clambered onto the bed and asked what she was doing.

"I'm going to cut down daddy's shirts for Benedict." She took the white cotton shirts she had starched and ironed the other week and placed them on the bed. "We can give his suits to his friends. Did you put your train set away?" He shook his head. "Finish, and then we'll read a book."

After Leo left, she took the suits out of the closet. She went through the pockets, pulling out a handkerchief with his initials in blue, a few stubs from the grocery store, nickels and dimes, and in one pocket, she found a note. She sat on the bed and unfolded it. It was a woman's handwriting, but there was no signature. *Good to see you. I'm glad Marta thought of it.*

Olga immediately popped into Grace's mind, and she thought back to the Fair. Could Marta have gotten the two of them together? She could well envision Marta coaxing Joseph to see Olga. Her intuition told her he hadn't taken up with her, but they could have met. She felt deprived of a conversation she couldn't have with Joseph, and now never would.

The following day, the note still churning in her mind, she called her mother.

"Now, you don't know for a fact. That note doesn't say much," Lorna said. "No need confronting the carline. She'll deny whatever you say."

"I know he loved me."

"Love has nothing to do with it. Four children take a lot out of you, and marriage makes a lot of men feel constrained— maybe like his parents made him feel."

"You're taking his side."

"As I've told you before, I've seen a lot. Men will never refuse what's offered to them, if you get my drift. Listen, I know you're hurt to think he might have seen another woman, regardless if it was nothing. But you were busy with the children and house and didn't have gobs of energy to deal with his ego. Could be he didn't want to pressure but needed a release, only if it was talking with another woman."

"I think I'm angrier with Marta than him."

"That knucklehead isn't worth it. My dear girl, life is not always the way we want. Forgiveness is yours to give."

After Grace hung up, she pondered her mother's words. She was right. It would do no good to dwell on it. Her eyes settled on a watercolor she'd sketched of a young woman, dressed in a red blazer and white brim hat, and holding a set of golf clubs. She thought back to when she and Joseph talked about taking golf lessons. Remnants of a life not lived.

Benedict ran in, out of breath. "I got the sign. It's blue."

"What's blue?"

"Remember, you said to ask father what color to paint our racing car?" Grace nodded.

"I was walking past the hardware store with my friends, talking about it. A man came out of the store and put a can of paint in the trash—it's blue and still good."

Sára came over the following day and told Grace and the girls, "Marta's giving a baby shower next week for the baby."

Surprised, Grace wondered what prompted Marta's nice gesture.

"She invited lots of people but only wants Vivienne and Erika to come."

Grace's composure cracked. She instinctively placed a hand on her stomach.

"Why isn't she inviting Mother?" Erika said.

"I don't know. Maybe so the gifts will be a surprise?" Sára said.

"That's cruel," Vivienne said. "If mother doesn't go, we won't either."

"They'll be happy to attend," Grace said to Sára.

After Sára left, Grace said to the girls, "I don't want you to miss out on treats and some fun."

"I'm going to tell Aunt Marta off," Vivienne said.

"Don't you see what she's up to?" Grace said. "People expect her to do it. Heaven forbid someone criticizes her for not giving one."

"It's not right," Erika said.

"If it means getting things I'll need for the baby, I'll swallow some pride. It's not fattening."

Grace gave birth to a third son later that August. She hadn't discussed names with Joseph before he died and decided to call him Victor. He was a survivor and came into this world robust and lively—a victor. A handsome child with curly light brown hair who smiled all the time, Grace showered him with an extra dose of love; he'd never know his father.

When Victor was a week old, Frank came round to see the baby and brought Grace a bouquet of peppermint pink English roses, along with *The Velveteen Rabbit* and *Bambi* books for the children.

"He's got your hair and eyes."

"He reminds me of Erika when she was a baby, except he's stronger."

He caught her eye and smiled. "If you need anything, I'm here to help."

Frank continued to visit, always with bags of goodies: See's candies and lollipops, Tom Tinker toys, a gyroscope and a bird whistle that sounded like a canary. He'd stay on after the children went to bed and conversations usually turned to local and world events.

"I'm still on the national desk. Tomorrow we're leading with a story about the Democrat presidential nomination, Al Smith from New York. Someday I hope to get on international. Wish I could travel and see a bit of the world. Don't you, Grace?"

"Joseph and I talked about going places. He was excited when people started flying and said one day we would." Her eyes settled on one of her seascapes she'd framed and tacked to the wall.

"Don't mean to pry, but how are you doing?" Frank put his hand on hers. It surprised her, but she didn't move hers away.

She looked at Frank's lean face, partially obscured by his limp hair that fell over his forehead. "You and others help and I'm grateful. Clara does so much and Quincy brings things from the market. Brought us some nice veal chops the other day." She sensed she shouldn't tell Frank that Xavier, now a practicing attorney, stopped over often, always leaving an envelope with twenty dollars when he left. She moved her hand away. "I have the small pension and Anton's investing the insurance money in the stock market, so I'll have income."

"They say you never get rich with money sitting in a bank. You have to invest."

"You think he's doing the right thing?" Grace said. Frank nodded. "Then I'll have to trust."

CHAPTER 26

♦

*The magic of Christmas lingers on, though childhood days have
passed upon the common round of life, a Holy Spell is cast.*

The Christmas after Joseph died, the *next doors,* as Erika
started calling them, invited Grace and the children for
dinner on Christmas Eve. They'd stop extending an invitation for
the holiday meal when Benedict was born; they hadn't wanted
young children spoiling their dinner. It then became customary
for Joseph and the family to stop by after dinner to wish everyone
a happy holiday and exchange gifts. They celebrated Christmas
Day at home as Grace's family had always done.

After a light lunch of curried egg sandwiches, Grace ironed
the girls' dresses, moistening her fingertip with her tongue to test
the heat of the iron so as not to singe the white ruffles along the
collars and sleeves.

"I wish Father were here and coming with us. He'd make it
more fun," Erika said, turning up the volume on the radio. "He
was so handsome."

"Grandmother Susanna was pretty," Vivienne said as she
wrapped a book for Pauline.

"Uncle Dan said a look from her could sour wine,"
Benedict said.

"He was kidding," Grace said. "You girls take after her with
your smooth alabaster skin."

"Aunt Marta looks like the pelican in my science book,"
Benedict said, stuffing his hands in his pockets.

"She's an old crab," Leo said, curling his lip. "Doesn't like our
toys in the yard."

"It's Christmas," Grace said. "Let's think only of nice things."

Bundled in their wool coats and caps, Grace and the children walked across the yard to the *next doors*. Light falling snow gave a glow to the fresh precipitation. Vivienne, her hands buried in her furry white muff with a holly twig on top, stuck out her tongue to catch snowflakes. Benedict and Leo did the same while Erika held out her hand to catch the crystals. Grace held Victor close, shielding him from the wind whistling around them. An air of anticipation enveloped the children, and Grace hoped this year the Tschidas would spoil them.

Anton opened the back door in his formal white bowtie and motioned them inside as an icy wind blasted through the door. The aroma of roasted meat drifted out from the kitchen.

"The girls made Susanna's recipes," Anton said as Clara and Marta joined them, "roast goose, *spätzle*, cabbage strudel."

"And for dessert," Clara said, "apple fritters and cheese dumplings with plum jam."

Seven-year-old Benedict rubbed his hands together and Leo mimicked him until Vivienne shook her head at them. Clara took Victor from Grace while she removed the wool wrap coat Joseph bought her the previous Christmas.

"Rubbers off in the house or you'll go blind," Marta said, pulling off Benedict's billed cap and placing it on the coat rack near the door.

"Blind?" Benedict said, crinkling his nose. "Mother says we'll get a headache."

"It doesn't matter," Grace said to him as she helped Leo out of his boots. "The important thing is to take them off." She pulled up Leo's cotton stockings bunched at the ankle.

"Clean your shoes on the mat before you come in and stand up straight," Anton said, patting Benedict on his head. He was still nearly six feet tall, with a frame like a bear; the children were always on their best behavior around him and afraid to ask him much. "Careful of the candles on the tree. We want no fires." He took Grace's elbow and led her and the children into the parlor.

He sat on the high-back sofa; the soft glows from the candles around the room made his light-blue eyes sparkle.

"Pauline, Sára, Grace's kids are here," Marta called out.

Grace gave an inaudible snort. *Before Joseph died, the children were "Joseph's kids" and now, they are "Grace's kids."*

Everything was as it was when Susanna was alive. The wooden crèche under the tree, the pine boughs over the windows and on the sills, and on the tables, dishes of ribbon candies and oranges pierced with cloves. But now there were more photos of Pauline sprinkled around the room.

Draped between the parlor and the dining room was the white sheet Anton put up on Christmas Eve. "No peeking," he said, "wait till Pauline comes down."

Time passed glacially for the children before Pauline sashayed down the stairs and into the parlor, hands wedged in her pockets, her cylindrical auburn curls bouncing with each step. "I want to open my presents now," she said to her mother.

"We have to wait for Sára," Marta said as she straightened the bow on the back of her dress. Pauline crossed her arms and stuck out her lips in a pout.

"No *Krampus* this year, right? You've all been good," Anton said, referring to the wicked furry devil that gives coal or sticks to bad children. All the children nodded. "We do it now. Pauline doesn't have to wait." Anton peeled back the sheet, revealing a pile of gifts on the sideboard. "Marta, hand them out."

Marta, with her new finger-wave hairdo, wore her garnet necklace and a stylish crepe-de-chine dress with ruched ribbon trim and a drop-waist sash buckle. Grace recognized the dress from a Sunday Bon Marche advertisement for socialite holiday wear. What she lacked in physical attributes, she made up for in glamor. She started handing out the presents, one to each of Grace's children and six for Pauline.

"Why does she get so many and we get only one?" Benedict said.

"It wouldn't be right if we gave many gifts to your family and only one to Pauline," Anton said. "Six for your family and six for Pauline."

"That's not fair," Benedict said.

It raised Grace's hackles. She'd hoped it would be different this year. They'd lost their father, and she didn't want them to feel more injustices and deprivation. She wanted to say something, but disgust stole her words. What did she expect? These were the Tschidas, and they were *Grace's kids.*

Vivienne tore the paper off her gift, unearthing white cotton undershirts, panties and socks. She tried to put on a smile, her eyes slightly mocking.

Erika's face fell when she saw she got the same as Vivienne.

When Benedict unwrapped his white shirt and underwear, his face crumpled. And when Leo opened his gifts, similar to those of Benedict, he said, "Santa got it wrong. I didn't want this."

"Santa knows what's best," Anton said. "You should be grateful."

Grace gave herself a moment to get her voice under control. "Still, it would've been nice for them to receive a fun toy or gift."

"We never had fun gifts when I grew up," Anton said.

Grace's mood permeated the room, ensnarling them in silence while Pauline opened her gifts. She first unwrapped white underwear similar to what Vivienne and Erika received. And then she opened a wooden puzzle, a powder pink coat and matching hat, and two books, *The Adventures of Doctor Dolittle* and *Winnie-the-Pooh*.

Envy coated Erika's eyes as she watched Pauline show off her musical merry-go-round. It ached Grace to see her younger daughter pretend it didn't matter that Pauline got things she would have liked.

Aunt Clara, the scent of Shalimar surrounding her, told the boys how handsome they'd look in the new shirts. To the girls, she said a lady must always have nice undergarments. She gave Grace a knowing look and then leaned in closer to each of the children, one at a time, and said, "I'm taking you shopping and you can choose whatever you want."

After dinner, the family gathered in the parlor. Anton stood next to the fireplace and tapped the barrel of his long-stem pipe against the sole of one of his high-top laced shoes. He sprinkled burnt tobacco over the hearth. Before he could take out his pouch and refill his pipe, Marta rushed over and brushed the strands into the grate. "There's a plate for that. Like mother used to tell you, you're not in the old country."

As he smoked his pipe, Marta took out the cut-glass decanter of homemade plum brandy and poured it into tiny mauve glasses rimmed in gold for the grownups. For the children, Sára brought out hot chocolate and candy apples. The family roasted chestnuts and sang songs until midnight to greet the Savior's birth.

Getting ready for bed that night, Erika buttoned up her flannel nightgown and said, "I couldn't taste dinner tonight."

"Bile must have tainted your mouth," Grace said.

"Aunt Marta kept frowning at me. I was afraid I'd spill something on my dress. I don't think they really wanted us there."

"If you think that way, you've no one to blame but yourself, Lady Jane."

"It wasn't right that Pauline got six gifts, and we only got one."

"You're right, it wasn't." Grace brushed Erika's hair back. "Think what it must be like for Pauline living with all grownups. Doesn't she say you're lucky because you have fun playing with your sister and brothers? And isn't she always asking you to play with her?"

The ends of Erika's mouth turned down. "I don't care."

"You may think her life is better than yours, but it sounds like she wishes she could change places with you."

Erika scrunched up her face. "I don't want to change places with her."

Later, as the back-porch light from the *next doors* spilled into the hallway through a crack in the curtains, Grace overheard the girls as they lay in bed.

"I don't believe Pauline would want to change her life with ours," Erika said.

"Stop caring about Pauline. We're going to get presents from grandmother and Uncle Daniel, and more from Aunt Clara. She has no one else to give her things. You're always whining about something." Vivienne pulled the white raised-leaf design coverlet up under her neck and turned on her side.

Erika's resentful silence followed.

Grace closed the girls' bedroom door and braced herself against it. *Will they ever forget?*

Looking through the frost patterns on the window the next day, Grace saw the snow-clad yard shimmering in the sun. "It's beautiful outside," she said to the children. "We should build a snowman to greet grandmother and Uncle Daniel when they come."

"Yeah," Benedict said, while Leo jumped up and down.

"Put on your coats," Grace said. "Vivienne, get one of Victor's blankets. We can put him in the wagon."

They went outside; the glistening sun on snow momentarily dazzled them. As their eyes became accustomed to the glare, Erika and the two boys plotted out a spot to start the snowman. Vivienne and Grace sat on the porch steps next to Victor and watched. As they'd finished with the largest lump of snow for the body, Pauline, in her new coat and hat, came out the back door of the *next doors*. She sat down on the steps, a freshly baked cinnamon bun in each hand. The children stopped rolling and watched Pauline lick the white frosting off one bun and then the other.

"Why does she have buns and we don't?" Leo asked.

"You'll spoil your appetite for dinner," Grace said.

Benedict stuck out his tongue at Pauline as he watched her eat.

When she finished the buns, Pauline came and stood near her cousins. "I want to play."

"Can't," Erika said, flicking her muffler around her neck.

"Why not?"

"Mother says too many cooks spoil the broth."

"You're not cooking."

Erika stood frowning, her gaze like a knife. "We don't need any help."

Pauline dug her patent leather shoe into the snow, trapping ice crystals in the pink fabric flower clipped to the top.

"Let her play with you," Grace said with a nod.

"Why should we?" Benedict said. "She's always eating cake or something and never offers us any."

"You never ask me for a bite," Pauline said.

Erika glanced at Grace briefly. "All right. But you have to do it on your own. You can make the head."

Pauline scooped up snow and formed a ball. She knelt with her arms extended and pushed it forward, gathering bulk. Her arms traveled faster than her body and she fell on her face, getting snow in her mouth.

"Mrs. Rice's dog peed on it," Benedict said, laughing. "You ate dog pee."

"Don't tell her that," Grace said, expecting her to cry. But Pauline only spit it out and continued rolling the ball with a determined look.

A few minutes later, Marta appeared at the back door. "Pauline, you're ruining your clothes. Get in here immediately." She shot an angry glance at Grace.

Pauline brushed frozen snowflakes off her coat and walked away, her head hung low.

"That's what she gets for not sharing," Benedict said as Pauline shuffled home.

Marta held the screen door open for Pauline. "Look at you. You shouldn't play with those ruffians."

"A fox smells its own hole," Erika shouted.

CHAPTER 27

◆

It is sweet to drink but bitter to pay for.

Victor was fourteen months old when Black Tuesday befell the country on October 29, 1929. The following morning, when Grace stepped out to collect the bottles the milkman left on the porch, she grabbed the *Tacoma News Tribune* without glancing at the headlines. She heard Mrs. Gartner shout out something about turmoil. But she didn't pay attention and only waved, not wanting to get trapped into listening to the prattler. It was only when Frank came over after work and told her what happened that she realized what the woman was trying to tell her.

"I've been worried about you," Frank said, his expression grave, as if talking about the loss of a beloved pet. "Anton put your funds in the stock market, didn't he?"

Not understanding at first, she only nodded. "Except for what I keep in the bank for expenses."

"Have you read the newspaper?"

"Not yet. Got busy today."

"The bottom dropped out of Wall Street. Everyone started selling stocks—couldn't get rid of them fast enough. There was panic and prices crashed." He rubbed his collarbone. "Some lost so much they committed suicide."

The word suicide reminded Grace of something her mother said. Once someone decides to commit suicide, there's little anyone can do to stop them, selfish as it was. Her mother had seen her share: depressed seamen after long voyages, injured men suffering after a mine accident, and men who lost their jobs and couldn't feed their families.

"Wait. Are you saying I lost Joseph's insurance money?" Grace's thoughts swirled as she tried to digest what she heard.

"You need to talk to Anton and find out what's happened to your investments."

"It's all I have," she said, her voice tight.

After Frank left, Grace found Anton in the parlor, slumped in his overstuffed chair, a pensive and distant look in his eyes. She haltingly asked him about her investments, her words dissolving in her throat as if eroded by acid.

"I thought it was best," he said, his voice barely audible. "Charlie agreed with me. We thought you'd earn money."

"Don't tell me I lost anything?" There was a fear she could smell as the rapid thrum of her heart echoed in her ears.

He looked down and tugged at the cuff of his shirt sleeve, avoiding her gaze. "I also lost. Times will be tough, but we'll manage."

Grace put her palms together and nervously slide them up and down as resentment and fury built up inside. "I have five children. How am I going to care for them?" She moved closer and stood in front of Anton. "I told you I wanted to keep it in a saving account, but you said you'd take care of it and make good investments. I expect you to make up my losses."

Small beads of sweat glistened on his forehead. "After all I've done and given you, you dare say that. You're better off than many."

A recent conversation she'd had with Anton replayed itself in her mind. *Joseph was my only son. I raised him to take over the family. I did everything for him, and you, and the children.* It wasn't true. Anton wanted Joseph to do everything for him.

"You can never admit you're wrong." Grace's face hardened. "If you hadn't asked Joseph to move that stone, he'd still be here."

"It wasn't my fault." He grabbed the arms of the chair. "It's not fair for you to keep accusing me."

"Life is never fair."

Grace knew she'd have to reign in expenses, starting with the children giving up their after-school activities. It was important they be part of the decision. One evening she gathered them in the parlor.

"I don't know if you've heard, but things are difficult for many people now."

"Dennis told me his father lost his job," Benedict said. "Is that what you mean?"

"Yes. More people will lose their jobs because companies can't pay them, and without jobs and money, they won't be able to pay rent and eat." Grace looked down and twisted her wedding band. "We lost your father's insurance money. We won't have much for extras."

"Will we be able to eat?" asked Leo.

"We'll always eat but we won't have money for extras. You girls will have to stop your dance and painting classes, and Vivienne, you won't be able to take riding lessons. You boys will have to give up your clubs that require dues."

"I can get a paper route like Willy," Benedict said. "I'm old enough."

"If you can, that'll help." Grace looked at the children to gauge how they were taking the news. The two oldest boys appeared unfazed; the girls sat with downcast eyes.

"Let's put our heads together and think of other things we can do." Her smile was wearier than she intended, but it was difficult to pretend cheerfulness when the fear of how she'd manage gnawed at her.

"My friends love the dresses you make," Erika said. "You could make and sell them."

"And costumes," Vivienne added. "Everyone says your Halloween ones are the best."

"We can sell tussie mussies like we read about in that magazine," Erika said. "Grandfather won't notice if we take flowers from his garden—if he does, we say the birds took them."

"Those are old-fashioned," Vivienne said. "People used them because they didn't bathe."

"You always make fun of what I say," Erika said.

"All ideas are good," Grace said. Victor waddled over and pulled at her skirt; she helped him scamper up onto her lap. "Let's keep thinking."

"You could sell your drawings, Mother," Vivienne said.

"Or tint photos like I did in Everett." And she wondered what she could barter. There was her jewelry—but for now, she wouldn't consider pawning anything.

The children tackled their new life as a game, finding ways to pitch in and cope with shortages. Benedict got what he thought was one of the best paper routes in town, with deliveries to Sears, the shops along Pacific Avenue, and the Merkle Hotel. He and Leo picked watercress at the Tacoma Avenue Gulch and scrounged for onions in nearby fields. After memorizing train schedules, they scoured the tracks to collect coal that fell from the open-top hopper cars. Nothing went to waste. They even used the wax paper the Alber's Mill violet bread came in to coat pans to prevent food from sticking when cooked. And they cut up and fried garter snakes.

When no one was home at the *next doors*, Erika snuck into Anton's root cellar. She filled a canvas knapsack with potatoes, carrots, beets and turnips from her grandfather's garden, careful to take only a few of each so no one would notice. One day, as she was crawling out, Mrs. Gartner yelled, "Does your grandfather know you're stealing from his cellar?"

Erika froze.

"No need to bother yourself," Grace said, coming down the porch steps.

"No way for you to treat the man who takes care of you."

Grace let out a humph. "You know not of which you speak." Glancing up at the branches of the maple tree, she spotted a puff of mocha- and white-hued feathers. "Look, a barred owl."

"Chase him away. I don't want to listen to his hoots at night."

"It's a good omen. We should be glad he chose us."

Later, Mrs. Gartner told Anton his grandchildren were pilfering. He came over to talk to them.

"Stealing is against God's commandments. It's a sin to steal as much as a penny." He narrowed his eyes as he looked at each of them. "You've been raised better than that. If I had to say, I think it was you, Benedict."

Benedict blew out his cheeks and sputtered, "It wasn't me."

"Lying is as bad as stealing. You must confess your sins and be sorry and intend to never do it again, or it doesn't count."

"We're not fibber Magee's," Leo said, "are we mommy?"

"He said he didn't do it, Anton," Grace said, feeling a spark of anger. "You're quick to judge and blame . . . tell me, you have plenty . . . why aren't you bringing us extras from your cellar?"

"Don't change the subject. Stealing is a sin and I cannot excuse it."

"The real sin is not helping those in need." Grace pressed her lips together. "Good deeds are the best religion."

After Anton left, Benedict again protested he didn't do it.

"I know you didn't," Grace said. "He figures it would be difficult for your sisters, and Leo and Victor are too small."

"Gee-whiz, if I'm going to be blamed, I'm going to help Erika."

"'Tis only a stepmother would blame you." Lorna's voice echoed in Grace's mind as she uttered her mother's words.

The pilfering continued, with Erika and Benedict going after dark to avoid Mrs. Gartner's gaze. Grace taught Vivienne to fry the thinly sliced purloined potatoes in oil and it became a favorite treat. Quincy still brought meat and fish from the market, but not as often, as business was tough with many customers buying on credit. After Grace's pension ran out at the end of the month, she cooked up a large batch of porridge in a double boiler and left it on the stove all day. When it was hard, she cut it into squares and put maple syrup or jam on it for lunch or dinner. She reminded herself of her mother's words: *Enough and no waste is as good as a feast.*

One afternoon, after putting the boys down for a nap, Grace looked for some of the other pan watercolors she used in Sonora. She found them tucked away on the top shelf of a bedroom closet. As she mixed them with water, the pigment did not separate from the binding agent. They were still usable. She warmed up her hands by drawing flowers on yesterday's newsprint. As she painted, she felt a calmness she hadn't known for weeks. Maybe she could translate her sadness into something lovely, something she could sell. As she recalled how Joseph would praise her drawings, that all too familiar sense of loneliness overwhelmed her. She started crying as she always did when these feelings showed up at the strangest times, like when she was vacuuming, or washing the bathroom sink—the sink where she used to watch him shave. *All the things I wish I'd said that last night.*

If the depression that started after the crash wasn't bad enough, that winter a severe drought left the streams and rivers low. The water the city collected in the reservoirs froze. With no water in the dams, the city couldn't provide electricity for homes, street lights, hospitals and businesses.

One evening, Grace placed candles in the middle of the kitchen table for the children to do their homework. As the candle wicks burned to nubs, Grace searched in the pantry for more. There were none.

As she walked over to the big house, soft white light spilled out from the side windows onto the frozen ground. She peered inside. The Tschidas were all in the parlor, each one sitting next to an Aladdin table lamp.

When Anton answered the back door, Grace said, "I need to borrow an oil lamp. I don't have more candles and the children have homework to finish."

Anton beckoned her inside. "Grace needs one of our lamps," he said, accompanying her into the parlor.

"You can have the one I'm using," Clara said. She turned the wick knob, extinguishing the glow. "Don't touch the chimney," she told Grace as she handed it to her. "It's still hot."

Grace thanked her and took the lamp.

"I filled it earlier," Clara said, "so there's at least ten hours left."

"Keep it until the electricity comes back," Anton said. "I'll bring you more kerosene tomorrow. The children must do their homework."

When the electricity still hadn't been suppled weeks later, it endangered the local economy. The city sought help from President Hoover. After much wrangling, the government permitted the aircraft carrier *U.S.S. Lexington* to come to Tacoma and pump electricity into the city transformers.

Frank came over one evening after the Navy agreed to send their new electric-drive ship.

"It's my byline on the front page," Frank told Grace and the children. "Navy didn't want to send the ship. But after Cascade Paper stopped lumber production, other companies followed suit. The governor, mayor and a state delegation took action and helped cut the red tape."

"It was a fine article," Grace told Frank. "And it was good of Camp Lewis to turn off lights at four in the afternoon to help other places get electricity."

"But it's not enough," Frank said. "The ship's due to dock at the Baker and Shaffer Docks, near Stadium High. I'll be covering it. Since the kids are on Christmas break, why don't you all come with me."

"We get to see the big ship?" Leo said, bouncing on his feet. "Please, Mommy."

Grace nodded and smiled. She was glad the children would have something to look forward to, and to serve as a substitute for the clubs and activities they'd had to give up.

The morning the ship steamed in from its berth in Bremerton, Grace got the children up early to go with Frank. As the ship appeared on Commencement Bay, a band started playing and the crowd that had flocked to see the ship cheered and waved.

Frank was authorized for an in-depth tour of the ship, and he took Benedict and Leo with him. When they returned, Leo was bursting with information. "It's big, Mommy. We got to sit on the guns."

"The captain told us there are fourteen hundred sailors," Benedict said. "They sleep in small beds down below."

"Airplanes can land on it," Leo said. "They paint their tails yellow and that means they're from the ship."

"We watched the crew connect the ship's power plant to the city's power grid," Frank said. "They still have to test it before they can start pumping electricity."

"This was a special day," Grace said, patting Leo on the head. "Thank you again, Frank."

The Lady Lex, as the town nicknamed her, remained in Tacoma one month and the city adopted her. Citizens feted the sailors like heroes and held dances, socials and dinners to keep them entertained. Benedict and Leo spent many afternoons after school down by the ship, taking every opportunity to speak to the sailors. And Leo filled his sketchbook with scenes of the ship.

In March of the new year, Ellen visited Lorna and Daniel. After she'd been in Everett a few days, she telephoned Grace.

"Mother shouldn't be alone. It's getting difficult for her to do things and Daniel's working most of the time. It'd be too much for her to come to California. I was thinking she could stay with you. You're closer and it would be easier for Daniel to visit."

"Oh, Ellen, I don't know. I . . . I'm just getting by as it is. Our stove went out last week. You know what Marta said? *Let them do without.*"

"She's wicked that one. Listen, Mother could help. She's a good crack and the children would love to listen to her yarns."

Grace fiddled with the seam on her apron as scenes of her mother unrolled in her mind. She saw Lorna traipsing around her garden and yelling at the hens as she scattered corn. She heard echoes of her bickering with Grace's father as they lovingly hurled sayings at each other; her inviting the neighbors in for a game of whisk; her tossing out a lodger at the boarding house when he came home drunk. She really was as her father used to say, *feisty and full of fire*, a dynamo.

"We'd love her to come. She can have my room and I'll sleep on the sofa."

"Daniel will help. He can send you what he usually gives her. And I'll try to send you something each week. Oh, I'm not going to tell her we discussed this. I'm going to say you mentioned you need help and wished she'd come live with you."

At first, Lorna resisted Grace's invitation to move in with her and the children, insisting she wanted to stay in Everett. Then in short order, two of her friends died, and another moved to Bellingham to be with her daughter.

"All right, I'll come," Lorna said, with a curse under her breath. "Never scald your lips with another man's porridge."

Grace laughed. "I'm not another man. I'm your daughter."

CHAPTER 28

◆

Everyone lays a burden on the willing horse.

Preparing for Lorna's arrival, Grace reorganized her chest of drawers and closet to make room for her mother's belongings. Outside, it was nippy and rain lashed against the windows. After she'd finished, she prepared a cup of tea to warm herself. "Putting on the Ritz" was on the radio as a loud knock on the door jolted her.

"Your drain pipe is plugged up," Anton said as he entered. "I'm about to clean it out." He pointed to the sofa. "Smart to have sturdy furniture. I always tell my workers they must use the best materials. Whatever they make must last five hundred years."

Grace thought back to how disappointed she was when the furniture arrived. But it was for the best. It would last them many years; she'd never be able to replace anything now.

"Before you go, Anton, there's something I want to talk to you about."

He placed his rain slicker on the coat rack and sat at the kitchen table, next to Grace.

"I know you want the children to go to Holy Rosary," she said, "but all of them tell me how the nuns hit the kids over the head with rulers, pull their ears and lock them in dark closets. Benedict tells me Tommy in his class is so scared of them, he wets his pants." Grace ran her fingertips over the tablecloth's moiré-weave and pulled on a loose thread. "It's hard for them to get up early every day to attend Mass before classes—and it's cruel they have to go to funerals and see the open caskets."

"The nuns are strict for their own good. They're learning discipline. They're getting the best education."

"How, when they're always ringing bells and interrupting their studies so they can pray some nun will be canonized? And it's not only the nuns. The monsignor comes and asks them what the Sunday gospel was about. He can't expect young children to remember."

Anton squinted. "Children exaggerate. They need a good Catholic education like my children had."

"Mrs. Olson says the public school is good. She's thinking of sending her boys there."

Anton's body tensed. "I built that church. My name is on the base of the cross. Because of me, the Benedictine fathers came here. How would it look if my own grandchildren didn't attend the school I helped build?" He knit his brows. "They must stay."

Grace gazed at the cedar bark basket on the counter near the stove; she reminded herself to put more apples in it for the children. Fleetingly behind this thought was a vision of the day she and Joseph visited a Snoqualmie Indian community, the day he bought her the basket. *Look how tightly it's woven,* he'd said, *and delicate like you.*

Anton brought Grace back to the moment. "Now that Vivienne's at Lincoln, you'll see how better prepared she is," he said, referring to the high school Vivienne had entered after her eight-grade graduation from Holy Rosary.

As silence hung over them for a few minutes, Grace thought, *Well, here goes.* "There's something else." Anton gave a quick nod. "Erika had a school assignment to write about family and she wrote you were Czech."

"That's right."

"That's not what the nun told her." Anton's gaze intensified. "Sister said you're really Hungarian. Is that true?" She raised her eyebrows as a challenge.

Anton cocked his head to one side as if uncertain he'd heard correctly.

"She's confused, Anton. I told her I'd ask you. They have a right to know." Grace thought she could see his mind whirling.

"It doesn't really matter if you're Czech or Hungarian. You're American now." *Unless you think Czechs have more prestige than Hungarians. We know how hard you tried to be German until they fell out of favor.*

"The old people in the village used to say they didn't know where we came from—originally." Anton's lips moved, but no words came out. He fiddled with his pocket-watch fob. "It's complicated."

No, it's really a simple question, Grace wanted to say, *no need to concoct some myth.*

"Three, four hundred years ago, the Turks went on raids from Constantinople to the gates of Vienna. There were plaques around town that told of their comings and the battles," Anton caught her eye for a moment before turning away. "They kidnapped children along the way to work as shepherds, milkmaids, servants. When they retreated, they abandoned them. The Hungarians took them in and cared for them." He cleared his throat. "Called them Tschidas—means rider, or so they say. That's why there were many Tschidas in our area. Susanna was also a Tschida, but we weren't related."

"Riders?"

"The Turks came on horseback." He inhaled deeply, as if relieved he no longer had to fabricate and embellish his ancestry. "It may or may not be true, but it's our story."

"So, you're really Hungarian. Why all the lies?"

"We lived in the Austro-Hungarian Empire. There were many cultures. When I was young, we were called general Austrian citizens. Does it really matter? That's the past."

Finally, Grace thought. *But how can I be certain this is the true story?* Something lingered in her memory. "What about that Sudetenland story?"

Anton froze. He seemed unsure of what to say next. He looked down for a moment and then stood up. "We . . . we came from towns near Vienna." He glanced toward the door. "Have to go. Need to clean out that drain." After taking his raincoat off the rack, he turned around. "Keep the children in Holy Rosary, Grace."

After Anton left, she rang up Lorna. "Another fib. Now they're really Hungarians."

"Did you ever tell Joseph? Or did he go to his grave thinking he married a lass his own age?"

Grace ran her hand along the wood grain of the telephone box and was quiet. "Must go. The children will be home from school soon."

While Grace thought having her mother with them might add to her burdens, the opposite was true. Being around the children gave Lorna an injection of life. It was as if she forgot her infirmities. Her presence became a joy and her singing filled the house. She delighted in telling the children her stories, sprinkled with words of wisdom, and the occasional bawdy joke. She insisted on sleeping in the parlor so she could take over the kitchen. Once again, she made meals out of nothing, as she had done many years ago in Michigan and Montana.

One Saturday, as Lorna stood over the stove, making her version of Hoover stew, a mixture of macaroni, hot dogs, corn and canned tomatoes, she said. "I'm proud you're all working to help your mother."

"Vivienne doesn't work that much," Erika said.

"Who irons the clothes?" Vivienne said. "And my school jobs." She'd starting working after school as secretary to the high school principal, and she also took dictation from the journalism teacher. "This summer I'm picking strawberries, Miss Smarty Pants."

"I'm a better cook than she is." Erika said under her breath.

"'Tis often a person's mouth that broke his nose," Lorna said before tasting the boiling ragout. She added a pinch of salt.

"Mrs. Gartner asked me what I wanted to be when I grew up," Erika said. "I said a nurse like Aunt Clara."

"You'll have to empty bed pans all day," Lorna said. Erika wrinkled up her nose. "Gives you something to think about."

"I get the biggest tips at the Merkle Hotel, Grandmother, and I give them all to mother" Benedict said. "The ladies are really nice there."

"Bejeebers, bet they are. Handsome boy like you. Don't let one of those fallen frails get you up to her room." Lorna gave Benedict's shoulder two short pats.

Benedict pulled a pack of cards out of his back pocket and shuffled them. "Mr. Rinke from the candy store is teaching me magic tricks." He lowered his voice and glanced sideways at Grace. "Want to know a secret?"

"Love secrets," Lorna said, putting the Alber's Mill bag of rolled oats in the cupboard.

"Sometimes I go to Nalley's and sneak pickles and chips."

Lorna placed both fists on her hips. "That sleight of hand comes in handy then."

Benedict again glanced toward Grace. "I also go to Brown & Haley and swipe as many chocolates and candies I can stuff in my pockets"

Lorna bent down and motioned for Benedict to come closer. "Think you could get me some steak scraps from the butcher? Would be good in the stew."

"Mother," Grace said, "don't put them up to more mischief."

"Wouldn't do that." Lorna laughed as she sliced the salt-rising bread she'd made earlier.

"When I get big, Grandma," said Leo, "I'm going to work two jobs."

"Child, don't be wishing your life away."

As Benedict was about to leave, Lorna grabbed his arm and whispered. "Snatch some yeast from the grocers—if you can find some. Mighty scarce these days."

When they were alone later, Grace said to Lorna, "Please don't encourage them. What if they get caught?"

"They're doing it to help. And with those hollow legs they've got, best they get as much as they can." Lorna let out an *Osti*. "There are worse things."

"If their grandfather—"

"These hard times make you realize how much worrying you waste on little things."

One night when Frank came over, he and Grace stayed out on the porch, talking, after the children went to bed. He took his tobacco pouch from his shirt pocket and rolled a cigarette.

"Joseph was such a good actor. He should have gone to Hollywood."

"I've often wondered how things might have turned out, had he listened to you."

Frank shuffled around the porch and took a few puffs on his cigarette. In a voice weighed with apprehension, and pausing strangely between words, he said, "I don't know how you feel about this, or thought about it . . . do you think you'll remarry?"

It was a simple question, but it startled her. "It's never entered my mind."

"I've always liked you, Grace." He cleared his throat. "If you think you could . . . if you would consider marriage, I'd like to discuss it."

She felt crimson blotches spring up on her face. She liked Frank, but she'd never thought of him as a romantic partner. "I have five children. That's a lot—"

"I know." He removed his glasses and rubbed the indented spots on each side of the ridge of his nose. He stole a glance at Grace. "Please think about it."

She gave him a warm but not-too-familiar smile. "I will, Frank. I will."

The next morning, she told Lorna what Frank said.

Lorna slapped her thigh. "You thought he was being nice. But he was thinking of his own self-interest—like we all do."

The next night, as Grace washed Marta's uniforms on her hands and knees in the bathtub, Lorna said, "I hate seeing you hunched over and laboring for that biddy. And a measly ten cents for each one."

"Every bit helps." Loose hairs stuck to the sweat on her brow; she pushed them away with the back of her hand. "I do it at night so the children don't see me."

"Children are smart. They know how things are." Lorna scooted to the edge of the chair she'd brought into the bathroom. "Didn't you know how difficult it was for me when your father died?"

Grace rubbed the bar of soap over the white garment stretched across the washboard. "We wanted to stay strong so you wouldn't worry about us."

"Of course you did. You hid your feelings." Lorna let out a sigh. "And you've carried that misbelief all these years—hiding your true feelings so people won't be bothered or get upset."

"That's not true. I show my feelings. I let people know when I'm upset."

Lorna re-tied a lace on her low-heel oxfords. "Look how well all of you turned out after your father died. And yours will be fine, too."

"The boys keep outgrowing their clothes and they need school supplies."

"That old prig, living like some sherry-sniffing robber baron. *Osti*. And bought himself a new car."

"At least he pays their tuition. This year it's four dollars a month for each one. And he finally agreed to pay for utilities."

"You're too proud and not playing it right. Tell him if the kids go around with cardboard soles in their shoes and wrap inner-tube strips around them to keep them from falling apart, people will find out. Put silk on a goat, and it's still a goat."

Grace let the soap fall into the water and sat on her haunches. "How do you remember all those sayings?"

"Grew up with them. Learned more from your father and the miners." Lorna rubbed behind her ear. "We laugh outside about the things that bring us sorrow inside."

"I should consider Frank's proposal. He'd be good to the children."

"Seems you've got some thinking to do."

"No advice? You usually aren't hesitant to speak your mind."

"You're asking for advice but you really want approval." She pulled a thread from her frayed hem. "We're all condemned to loneliness and sadness. Love is the cure, and you've got that in spades with these young ones. Maybe you could find some with Frank, too. I don't know. Remember, a shack with food and love is better than a hungry loveless castle."

"When father died, did we give you solace?"

"You kept me going. Had to get you out of that boarding school."

"Isn't it time to admit it wasn't a boarding school?"

"No one must ever know. Promise you'll never tell."

"You shouldn't be ashamed. You may think you had a choice, but things happened that forced you."

"Still, you must never tell anyone."

Grace gave a slight nod. "The children are reading the books by Dickens you had Daniel bring."

"Thought it might be good for them to see others have struggled and known heartbreak."

"After Joseph died, I was afraid I wouldn't be able to keep us together. I feared I'd have to make the same decision you did."

"It was different then. And look at all you've learned and done—and during a depression. You're resilient. Sure, you changed but you're still yourself. If that isn't triumph over adversity, I don't know what is." Lorna drew a long breath. "Maybe this is how it's supposed to be so we learn how strong we are."

The furnace creaked and groaned. "Lights out at the *next doors*. They're all cozy in their beds and you're slaving away." Lorna slapped her thigh. "A widow's curse upon you."

"You're incorrigible." Grace laughed and wiped her forehead with the end of her apron. "Anton once told me I should have family nearby. I discounted his advice. But he was right. I'm happy you're with us."

Lorna was pensive for a few moments. "Wasn't doing that much up there. Days revolved around me and the girls discussing if we had a poop that day." She held out her hand. "Give me the one you finished. I'll start the iron." As she took the garment, she moaned, "*Dá fhada an lá tagann an tráthnóna.*" However long the day, the evening will come.

CHAPTER 29

♦

*Dance as if no one's watching, sing as if no one's listening,
and live everyday as if it were your last.*

On a lazy Saturday, when rain clouds crisscrossed the sky and glided in front of the sun, Vivienne and Erika snuggled up on the sofa, studying. Grace painted at the kitchen table while Lorna sat at the opposite end with a magnifying glass, squinting as she read an old issue of *Ladies' Home Journal.*

"Mother, you're straining your eyes. Stop worrying about how you'd look and get reading glasses."

"Haven't a vain bone in my body. Can see fine, thank you."

"Get round tortoiseshell ones like the movie stars wear," Vivienne said, extending her feet and wiggling her toes. "Or a lorgnette like the flappers. You'd look glamourous."

Lorna became quiet with a faraway look in her eyes. "My father read gothic novels. He'd sit in his rocking chair and light his pipe . . . our tabby cat nipped at his trouser legs until he cradled him. Then the two of them rocked away while he read."

A loud clomping sound on the porch announced Benedict and Leo's arrival after an afternoon with Anton.

"Don't let in the cold," Vivienne said. "Hurry. Shut the door—if it's still on its hinges."

"Jeepers," Benedict said, slinging his knapsack on the chair. "Don't blow your wig." He sauntered over to Lorna and asked what she was reading.

"Were you playing in mud?" Grace said, seeing the dots of dried dirt speckled on the boys' legs.

"Puddles in Proctor," Benedict said. "Grandfather said it was poor drainage."

"Thunderation. What's in your mouth making all that noise?" Lorna asked. "It's about as bad as the racket from those cards you stick in your bike spokes."

Benedict put a hand over his mouth and mumbled, "Dubble Bubble."

"Where did you get the money for that junk?"

Benedict smiled his lopsided smile. "Grandfather gave us money for the church collection." He raised his hand to the corner of his lips to shield his mouth from view. "But we went to Mr. Rinke's and got candy."

"Good," Erika scoffed. "Makes me mad when Father Gerhard or Father Francis praises him for all he's doing to take care of us. One day, I'm going to get up and tell the entire church the truth."

"No, you won't," Grace said. "Embarrassing your grandfather won't solve anything.,"

Leo pulled a pack of candy cigarettes from his back pocket. "We hid behind the store and ate most of it. Did you know, if you get a pink center in the chocolates and not a white one, you get a free candy bar? Benedict breaks them with his nail to find one."

"No, you don't do that, do you, Benedict?" Grace said. "You could contaminate them."

"Oh, people can survive a nail prick," Lorna said.

Grace frowned at Lorna and mouthed the words, *Don't encourage them.* She turned and asked the boys, "How was your walk today?"

"They take forever," Benedict said. "Every twenty steps he stops and talks to someone. And he tells us the same things— have to appreciate fine material. Buildings should last five hundred years. Jesus Christ, God Almighty."

"What did you say?" Lorna asked.

Benedict wedged his hands in his pockets with his thumbs sticking out. "Cheese and crackers got all muddy."

"Saying I've wax in my ears? I heard you right the first time. No cussing in this house."

"Mother says those French words you say are cussing and we shouldn't use them," Leo said.

"Why do you cuss in French?" Vivienne asked Lorna.

"Was my first language. We lived in Quebec before New Brunswick. It's better to cuss in another language."

"Did you learn anything else today?" Grace asked Leo.

Leo puffed out his chest and lowered his voice. "You should be proud of those men on Mt. Rushmore, sculpting George Washington's head."

"Yeah, and he said if he were younger, he'd go to South Dakota and work on them," Benedict said. "He also told us some Pope thought coffee was the devil's drink. But they had a lot of coffee houses where he studied and he drank it."

Leo tapped Grace on the arm. "He said to watch the mountain. When clouds are sitting on the top, it means low pressure's coming and farmers can harvest their hay. And when there's a north wind, the mountain is clear."

"But we must never call it Rainier," Benedict said as he rummaged through the cookie jar, pulling out a ginger snap. "Rainier was a British admiral and had a prison ship. He took American prisoners and tortured them."

"During the Revolutionary War," Leo added. "He said we must call it Mount Tahoma. That's the name the Indians called it for hundreds of years."

"Then that's what we must start calling it," Grace said. "See all you learn when you go with your grandfather."

Leo nodded. "We had cherry cokes at the soda fountain."

"Why are you limping, Benedict?" Lorna asked.

"Got a blister from all that darn walking."

"Let me see." Benedict took off his shoe and sock. At the back of his heel, quasi-transparent slabs of skin had peeled away. "You've had this awhile. Starting to fester. Sit down so I can draw out that nastiness." Lorna cut an onion in half and heated one side over a burner.

As Benedict held the warm onion on his blister, Pauline knocked on the door and peered in. "Can someone play with me?"

"Leo," Grace said, motioning him towards her.

Leo scrunched up his face and kicked at some imaginary object. "It's always me."

Bending close to Leo's ear, Grace said, "She likes to be with you. You're the same age." Play here on the floor, next to me."

Leo held the screen door open. "What do you want to do?" he asked his cousin.

"Can we play jacks?" She held up a small mesh bag filled with metal jacks and a small hard red ball.

"I suppose." He walked with her to the far side of the table, near Grace and asked, "Do you know 'round the world'?"

She handed him half of the jacks. "I'm not good at that. Let's play regular."

They both tossed jacks in the air and caught as many as they could on the back of a hand. Leo caught more and played first. As Leo scattered the jacks, Pauline said, "I thought all families had a mom and dad and were always happy and lived together in one house forever."

Leo threw the ball up and picked up a jack.

"Onesie," Pauline said as Leo caught the ball before it hit the ground. "I said I'd be good and pick up my toys and never cause trouble, if Daddy came back."

"Did your mom and dad fight a lot?" Leo asked, picking up two jacks and repeating the sequence.

"They talked mean. Sometimes I wanted to run away but I ran and hid under the bed. Twosies."

He handed the ball to Pauline. "Here, your turn."

"You didn't lose," she said, taking the ball.

"Doesn't matter." He extended his hand until she took it. "Are you mean to your mother?"

"Sometimes I make ugly faces."

"She yells at you a lot. Doesn't she love you?"

"Aunt Clara says she does."

"Mother doesn't yell at us, but she gets mad." Leo looked up at Grace. "Like when we ruin our school pants."

"It hurts because my father isn't here." Pauline sniffed and wiped her nose with the back of her hand.

"Mother says it takes time to stop the hurt." Leo scrambled after the ball as it got away from Pauline. "It's not fair that some kids have both mothers and fathers."

"Mother says at least we're not poor like you."

"We're not poor," he said, with a frown. "We don't have a lot, but we're not poor."

During the depression years, the boys became more ingenious, and they became known, along with other youngsters, as the 'gunnysack kids.' To clear up space, merchants gave them the sacks that potatoes, onions, carrots, corn and other commodities came in.

One afternoon, Benedict and Leo tucked the gunnysacks over their belts and prepared to leave for their excursions around town.

"Where you fixing to go today?" Lorna asked as she cleaned Leo's ear with her apron.

"Waterfront and Puyallup Avenue," Benedict said. "And the cannery to see if they have any peeled apples or tomatoes."

"I want to go to Nabisco," Leo said.

"Have to go soon, so we're there when the truck drivers return," Benedict said, sticking his slingshot into his back pocket. "Hope there's a lot of spoiled stuff today." The boys learned cookies and crackers couldn't take too much knocking around and were easily damaged.

"Got old newspaper, in case you get any pickled pigs' feet?" Grace asked.

"Don't know if we'll get there in time," Benedict said

The meatpacking plants on Commerce Street and Swift's near the Northern Pacific Railroad were on their search routes. Both had their own smoke rooms where they cured meats and the workers would slip the boys bacon or sausages.

"At least get some ice on your way home," Grace said, referring to Tacoma Ice and Storage where the workmen would chiff off large pieces of ice for the icebox. "But don't stop at Heidelberg. I don't like that man giving you beer."

As the depression wore on, the boys also took to junking, gathering up old rags, bottles and other throwaways to sell. Later, they broadened their reach, wandering around to find a City Light crew. They'd ask the puncher or foreman when the job would be done and later return and scout around for pieces of copper wiring they'd take to a vacant lot and dump into a bonfire to burn off the insulation, crunching it into piles to sell. All the money they collected they gave to Grace. It was not their money; it belonged to the family. On the days they carried home sacks full of loot, Grace had them share it with their neighbors, as the others reciprocated when they came upon a windfall. They knew that alone they didn't stand a chance.

Their forays weren't always successful, however.

"Got nothing today," Benedict said one day, collapsing onto a chair. "The truck drivers were in a bad mood and chased us off. And the smoke rooms were closed." His voice dropped as he continued. "We tried Medosweet—"

"But others beat us there," Leo said.

"Don't let slim pickings dash your spirits," Lorna said as "Brother Can You Spare a Dime?" played on the radio. "You might find treasures tomorrow."

"Yeah, some Mountain Bars or Almond-Roca ice cream bars," Leo said.

Without telling their mother and grandmother, Benedict and Leo would occasionally hop a freight train to Puyallup to see what they could swipe from the agriculture fields or Victory Gardens. They would also check out the aluminum collections for odd pieces they could resell.

One day they took the wrong train and ended up in Georgetown, in Seattle. A stationmaster turned them over to the police who asked what they were doing at the train yard. Benedict concocted the story they were on their way to see their Uncle Dan in Everett. The police took them to a school for troubled kids where the matron gave the boys red long johns for the night and told them they had to stay at the school until their parents came. It was Uncle Dan who picked them up the following afternoon and took them home.

"You had me sick with worry," Grace said when they arrived home, her relief overshadowing her crossness.

"I was afraid," Leo whimpered. "I thought we'd have to live there forever."

"You big sissy," Benedict said. "No, we wouldn't. I had a plan to break out."

"I know you want to help, but you must never do that again," Grace said. "Next time we just might leave you at that school."

They never again caught another freight train.

In early April, as a chorus of crickets chanted and a warm wind whisked across the yard, Marta came to see Grace.

"Cousin Silke died. Complications from strep throat we're told. Father would like you to attend the memorial service on Friday. It's in Fife." She handed Grace a piece of paper. "Here's the chapel address, time."

A window to the past opened and Grace saw herself at Aunt Ilona's farm, watching Silke climb trees, and turn cartwheels and somersaults around the yard, her short bloomers visible under her red-and-white checkered skirt. She was the daughter who took the horse and carriage to Tacoma to do the shopping.

After Marta left, Grace told Lorna. "Such a shame. So young."

"The way of the world. We all suffer, we all die." Lorna took two of her favorite lemon drops from her apron pocket and gave one to Grace. "I'll go with you."

"I was thinking you could take care of Victor."

"See if Sára can take him for a few hours. The wee one's too much for me to run after. Makes me a bit forswunk."

The luminous northwest day radiated through the stained-glass windows of the funeral chapel. It cast sunbeams around the votive box where lit candles dissolved into pools of wax. Vases brimming with peonies, lilacs and lavender tulips infused the room with a sweet, heady aroma. The open casket was in the aisle in front of the altar. After the eulogies, mourners came up one by one with bowed heads. They genuflected, made the sign of the cross, and kneeled near the youngster to bid their farewells. When it was Grace's turn, she heard Lorna behind her chuckle and say, "Holy smokes." Grace turned around and gave her mother a puzzled look. Lorna, a mischievous smile bunching up her cheeks, raised her eyes and put her hands in a prayer pose, feigning a pious guise.

As Grace stood to leave, she looked at Silke and blinked. Amid the pale ivory satin lay the young girl, a peaceful expression on her face. She held a lily the color of angel wings and she was wearing a fluffy organza dress with ruffles around the collar and sleeves—in candy-apple red.

As they left the chapel, Lorna muttered, "Flaming red at a funeral. Gadzooks."

"It could have been her favorite dress," Grace said, nudging Lorna with her elbow. "Why shouldn't she wear it?"

"Can't deny it now. That family's got gypsy blood."

"A fox smells its own hole, eh?"

"No gypsy or funny blood in our family. Scot and Irish through and through. Haven't you ever wondered about Vivienne's and Leo's narrow eyes?"

"Please don't say that, especially around them. They don't need another story about where they came from."

"Don't get your knickers in a knot." Lorna clasped Grace's arm and hugged her close. "I'll just say—good for ya, Silke. You went out in your party dress."

Lorna wasn't able to respect Grace's wish. When Daniel came that weekend with two bags of groceries, several fish strung together through their gills, and packs of cards to teach the children how to pay pinochle, she told him, "You better bet someone in that Hungarian family mixed it up with a gypsy. Those bloodlines never leave you."

"Mother, you promised," Grace said, a peeved look on her face.

Erika hovered in the hallway, one foot on top of the other. "Did father's family have gypsies?"

Lorna looked at Daniel who looked away, and then at Grace who had an *I told you* look on her face. "My darling grandchild, anything's possible in that part of the world they came from. Invaders from all over. Don't they teach you that in school?"

Erika's eyes narrowed. "We're not gypsy."

"Get that pained look off your face. We're all a hodgepodge and all that matters is your precious self. Hey, what's that dead man's pinch on you?"

Erika stroked the bruise on her arm. "Victor rammed me with his truck."

"The things boys do. Come here, let your grandma hug you." Lorna dried Erika's tears with her apron. "Now take one of those Hershey bars your uncle brought and go twirl among those roses and dahlias in the garden. It'll make you feel better."

CHAPTER 30

♦

The last Saturday in April was blustery and cold, with intermittent rain slashing across the window. All were stuck inside, except Benedict and Leo who were off on a gunnysack quest. As Lorna stirred a pot of homemade Navy bean soup with a plethora of tomatoes, celery and onions, she sang, "I wandered today to the hill, Maggie."

"I used to make this for Sunday dinners at Kearny Court. People loved it."

"Why do you always sing that song?" Erika asked as she put her school book aside.

"Was my mother's song. Maggie McIntosh she was. Maiden name O'Brien. Irish, like my Patrick. In the mornings, when I was snuggling in bed, her voice came up from the kitchen while she prepared porridge." Lorna scooped up a spoonful of soup and blew on it before tasting. "Bless her soul. Never imagined I'd go against my father." She grabbed the salt shaker with her arthritic fingers and gave it a few shakes.

"What did you do?" Vivienne asked.

"Do you really want to tell that story?" Grace said with a reproachful look.

"Oh, Mother," Vivienne said, "we want to hear."

Lorna gave Grace a smirk. "Ran away from home when I was eighteen."

Before she could go on, Erika and Vivienne in tandem said, "Why?"

"Oh . . ." She let the word trail, implying a long remembrance. "My father didn't want me to pick up with a seafaring man like him. He thought he'd made the deal of the century when he agreed rich old Mr. Winthrop could marry me." She cocked her head to the side. "He said, 'Better an old man's darling than a young man's slave.' Eh, that's what he said."

"How old was he?" Erika asked, wrinkling up her nose.

"Now that I think about it, not that old—thirties." She forked a bean, testing its tenderness. "Fiddlesticks, what would I've done with servants?"

"Weren't you afraid?" Erika said.

"Whole town was talking—*Did you hear? Maggie Mackintosh's daughter ran away on Tuesday, leaving only a note that said she couldn't marry Mr. Winthrop.*" Lorna gave another stir to the pot before putting the lid on to simmer. "My father was on his way home from Portugal and didn't know I'd left—he was the captain of the frigate *Halifax.* Hauled cargo from the local lumber and pulp mills."

She shuffled over and sat down next to Vivienne and Erika on the sofa. "Stop touching your face, Vivienne. You'll grow a mustache."

Vivienne put down her hand and asked, "What did your mother say?"

"Later she told me she was terrified something foul would come upon me, like poor Mary Ann Nickols in London. Killed by that 'Jack the Ripper.'"

Grace cleared her throat. "Your feet and ankles are swollen. Is that why you're still wearing your slippers?" Lorna nodded. "Erika, put the stool under her feet."

"Didn't you miss your parents?" Erika asked, lifting up Lorna's feet.

Regret passed across Lorna's face. "Sure did. Later my mother said she wished she hadn't made me so independent."

"Mother wants us to be independent," Erika said.

"It'll mean heartache for her, but . . . you girls have it easy. Life was hard for independent women in the old days. Take Bridget Cleary."

Lorna told them of the Irish lass, who was called a 'new woman,' because she did what she wanted. An educated seamstress, she also sold eggs. When she married, her husband didn't like her going off alone, especially when delivering eggs because she had to go by the fairy fort.

"People in those parts said nothing was more certain than fairies and everyone knew they snatched people. One day, Bridget got sick after delivering eggs. Her husband thought an evil fairy from the fort had taken Bridget's form. One night, he and some village men forced her to drink a concoction of herbs to drive the fairy out. She got better, but when she asked for milk, her husband panicked—fairies crave milk, you see—and he killed her."

"That's terrible," Vivienne said. "She was only sick."

"That's what happened to women who didn't do what society expected. Like they burned those witches here."

"Sister Joan says fairies are superstition," Erika said. "Was your family superstitious?"

"A wee bit. There was the *Sidhe,* an Irish spirit mother blamed when things went wrong. And when I irritated her, she'd call me *Leanhaun Shee*—the Faery Mistress who inspires love, but sucks your life out. Oh, lordy, my mother's imagination was always at full gallop. She never liked the townsfolk knowing the goings on in the family. And then I ran away." Lorna took a deep breath and closed her eyes.

"Why did you go to Michigan instead of staying in Canada?" Vivienne said.

"Heard there were good jobs there. Didn't need papers to cross the border. Only had to be healthy, no criminal past, of good moral standing and willing to work."

"Are you sorry you didn't marry that man?" Vivienne asked.

"Nope. Let me tell you girls, once you're married, you're married for a long time. Buy what you need now, new hairpins, new corsets, new—"

"We don't wear corsets." Erika said. "How fuddy-duddy."

"Don't make fun of grandmother," Vivienne said.

"I'm not and don't tell me what to do?"

"What's that thing sticking out of your blouse?" Lorna asked Erika.

Erika's hand flew up, covering her Madonna Sacred Heart Badge. "Sister says we have to wear these to protect us from temptation and impure thoughts."

"Honey, a picture—not even of the Madonna herself—isn't going to ward off temptation." Lorna let out a laugh. "I suppose they tell you there's a guardian angel on one shoulder and the devil on the other."

The soup boiled over, spilling onto the stove, making a sizzling sound; the flames flickered and hissed. "Erika, honey, turn off the soup. Oh, the stories they tell."

Her plump herrings soaking in saltwater brine, Lorna helped Grace pick up toys strewn around the yard. Mrs. Gartner popped her head over the fence. "How are the kiddies getting on?"

"It's like the Katzenjammers, but we're managing—like everyone," Lorna said. "The boys have it the worst. Kids at school tease them, saying they don't have a father. As if that's a crime."

"Kids can be cruel." Mrs. Gartner's head bobbed. "Vivienne's turning into a fetching young woman. I see boys flocking around her."

"She's a fine lass. Got a job in Sumner, picking berries. Going with two friends."

"Lots of strawberry and rhubarb fields there. In spring they grow daffodils."

"Twenty-five dollars for the summer. Working from seven in the morning till five in the afternoon. Gave them a cabin to live in. Has a stove so they can do their own cooking."

"Mrs. Gabler's from there, the one whose husband ran off. Says she's lonely and in dire need of company. No wonder he left with all the blabbering she does"

"We live with the burdens the good Lord gives us."

"Did you hear old Miss Nora's taking the soup?"

"Going to the other side, eh?" Lorna rubbed her foot across the trampled grass near the fence.

"Never thought she'd convert, but she's done stranger things." Mrs. Gartner waved Lorna closer to the fence. "One time she roamed the street in her nightdress, howling about how *Perchta* stole into her house, hidden in a jug of milk."

Lorna listened to more of the local goings on, told in a chirpy tone. She understood Grace's reticence to speak with the woman, as anyone who disdained gossip would.

A high-pitched bird on the fence warbled with a defiant tilt to his beak as if daring the women to shoo it away. "You have a good afternoon, Mrs. Gartner. Mighty glad my girl has a friendly neighbor like you."

As Lorna walked back to the house, a bee buzzed around her. "Get away, you nasty bug." She swatted it away and quickened her step.

"Don't believe everything she says," Grace said as Lorna joined her. "We shouldn't be messing in other people's business."

"Only doing some ear wagging. Best to hear what a person has to say. There's no tax on talk."

After a dinner of baked beans with salt pork, the family listened to the latest episode of *Laurel and Hardy* on their Crosley radio. Victor wagged his head and hummed "The Dance of the Cuckoos," the song he'd heard at the end of the program.

"Tell us one of your stories, Grandma," Leo said.

"Need to cut Benedict's elflocks first," Lorna said.

Benedict shook his head, his eyes glued on the *Washington Tubbs II* comic strip.

"Then comb that tangled mass. You look like a bum." Lorna adjusted herself on the sofa. "My father told stories in rhyme, the way sailors do to help remember them. He said a long time ago in Scotland they'd tell stories in the castles. They'd begin at the ground level and tell each following part, one level up. The children would run from floor to floor to hear all the parts. He said that's why levels in homes are also called stories."

"Is that true?" Erika asked.

Lorna shrugged. "My father said it was."

"Are you going to tell us a story?" Leo said, putting aside his wooden sailboat.

"Did your mother tell you where her name came from?" The children shook their heads. "Her father wanted to name her after the pirate queen of Ireland. He was full Irish from Tipperary and had the gift of the bard."

Lorna told the story of the Irish patriot and clever merchant, who was also a hard-hearted pirate that raided foreign ships, especially those of the English.

"Aw, that's a foolish story," Benedict said, miming a gagging sound. "Girls can't do those things."

"If you aren't careful, I'll have the púca come for you," Lorna said.

"What's a púca?" Leo said.

"A monster, a ghost that takes children on a frightening ride." Lorna splayed her fingers over her eyes.

"Another stupid story," Benedict said with a sneer and a snort. He looked around the room warily as he bounced on the balls of his feet.

"They told us about St. Patrick in school," Leo said. "He used the shamrock to tell the story of the Holy Trinity. But he didn't chase the snakes out because there weren't any."

"We're studying about Europe," Benedict said. He opened his history book to a picture of the Eiffel Tower.

"I remember when they built that," Lorna said, sweeping stray hairs into her bun. "Said it was the world's tallest structure. We thought it was monstrous and useless. And now here it is in books. You never know. But there's one thing I know—it's getting late and the best sleep you get is the sleep before midnight—your beauty sleep."

"And only whores sleep after eight in the morning," Erika said.

"And only pigs sleep after they eat," Leo said, smiling at Lorna.

"Where did you two hear that?" Grace said, titling her head with a frown.

Both children looked at Lorna.

"Don't be tattling on me," Lorna said. "All I said was no hurkle-durkling."

"That means staying awake in bed and doing nothing," Benedict said.

Early March the following year was a slow time for fishermen in Puget Sound. Crab season was winding down and the salmon wouldn't be running for months. The threat of rain started each morning. One afternoon, as a storm raged against the windowpanes, a delivery boy from the market dropped off a package of ham and sausage from Quincy.

"We can have this with the peas tonight," Grace said as she rejoined Lorna to finish shelling the first of the season's peas.

"Victor's taking a long nap," Lorna said.

"You kept them up late last night with your stories." Grace snapped off the end of a pod. "You've told them a lot but you've only mentioned Andrew a few times."

"Still hard for me to talk about. I miss that boy every day and with every breath I take."

"And you never mentioned Max."

"He wasn't real family."

"Did you love him?"

"I married him to get you home." Lorna opened a pod and raked out the peas. "And I liked the sex."

"Mother." Grace let out a slight moan. "Do you ever wonder what happened?"

"Thought hard about it, but memories aren't fixed. He never gave an inkling he was unhappy or wanted something else. Guess taking on another man's family is a bit much for any man."

"Might have met another woman."

Lorna gazed at the ironing board inset on the wall. "Could've been." Lorna placed her hands on the seat of the chair and heaved herself up. "Eh," she muttered, "you'll never plow a field by turning it over in your mind." She took the peas Grace shelled and dumped them in with hers, placing all in a colander.

"We're all slaves to our past in one way or another, aren't we?" Grace said as she picked a fallen pea off the worn green-and-white checked linoleum floor. "But if you lose it, do you lose a part of who you are?"

"Sometimes we think the past isn't beautiful—only the future is." Lorna ran water over the peas. "Illusion and hope."

"Is happiness an illusion?" Grace mused. "We always want more."

"Got to be satisfied with yourself. Can only really count on yourself," Lorna sat back down. "This chair's wobbly. Tell that miser to fix it." She straightened the faded and frayed blue and white toile de Jouy tablecloth that had bunched up in the center of the table. "Thought more about Frank?"

"I think I'll marry him. The children need a father. But one thing nags me. I wouldn't want him treating my girls better than my sons, like Max did."

"Many times, when you get what you want, it may not be what you thought. Things change. Max was kind until he wasn't."

"Frank's never given me reason to think he'd be anything but kind—to all the children." Grace went to the sink and shook the colander. She transferred the peas to a dish while glancing at the raindrops pinging into the puddles in the yard.

There was a knock at the back door and Grace greeted a hobo, one of many who came round. She put some slices of bread and baloney in a bag with an apple and gave it to him.

"Shame the government can't find work for those men," Lorna said.

"The boys see them down in the Gulch in the sheds they make from packing boxes," Grace said. "Guess they boil eggs in their coffee and toast bread over metal wire."

"Hmmm," Lorna said. "Leo was talking how they sneak over and look in the windows when the *next doors* are eating dinner and say, 'So this is how rich folk eat.'"

Grace gave a slight nod. "One day he said Pauline has the life he was supposed to have—they miss their father."

"Ah, *a father's worth more than a hundred schoolmasters,* 'tis true."

"There are so many little things I miss, like his musings in the evening." She paused. "I felt his presence last night—his hand on my shoulder. I leaned into him."

"Brings you comfort for sure," Lorna said. "Need all the comfort we can get—humph, soon they'll knock off five dollars from your pension when Vivienne turns sixteen." She touched Grace on the shoulder. "Give her an education like I did for you and Ellen."

"Unless Anton helps, she won't be able to study after high school."

"You'd think he'd want her to follow in his daughters' steps." She took the discarded pea pods and put them in the compost bin, along with the potato peelings. "Shame Benedict can't play football. Giving up so much to work." Lorna pushed the curtains aside. "Eh, those winds kicking up a bunch of nastiness."

Grace placed a few pieces of silverware back in its box and laughed. "Do you ever think how we don't have much but we eat off silver?"

CHAPTER 31

♦

God is good, but never dance in a small boat.

The next time Anton stopped over to see Grace, he handed her a stack of *American Girl* and *Calling All Girls* magazines. "Pauline finished these. Maybe the girls would like to read them."

After thanking him, Grace asked him to sit down; she had something she wanted to talk to him about.

"Joseph's friend, Frank, asked me to marry him. It's a good idea. The child—"

"You cannot marry a friend of Joseph's." Anton recoiled, a look of shock on his face.

"I thought you'd be pleased. The children would have a father, a male figure. And we'd be more financially secure."

"It's . . . it's not done. They have me as a male figure. You must honor my son's memory," he said, clipping his words. "I won't permit it. How dare Frank suggest such a thing."

Grace felt her body stiffen. "It's really my decision."

"If you do it, you can no longer live here and I will not help you."

"Damn old penny-pincher," Lorna said as she came into the parlor, marching toward Anton and waving a wooden spoon as if ready to strike.

"Mother, no." Grace reached for the spoon.

Lorna blocked her and continued, "Your grandchildren, Joseph's children. You'd throw them out like that, you boot-faced old goat? What do you do anyway, pay school fees, pontificate, begrudge them food from your cellar?"

"Don't interfere. This is between Grace and me."

"I'll interfere all I like," Lorna said, shaking the spoon in his face. "Always knew you were a scoundrel, you old blackguard."

"That's enough," Grace said, putting her outstretched arms between them.

Lorna pushed Grace's hand away. "You want to rule everyone's life, take no responsibility and dole out punishment—like a military junta."

Anton stared at Lorna, babbling, unable to get a coherent thought out.

"You've nothing to say because you know I'm right." She gave him a dismissive humph and yelled after him as he left, "*Junte Militaire.*"

After he left, Grace plopped on the sofa and stroked her brow. "That was some performance."

"I should've landed him a good one." Lorna put her hand on an out-thrust hip. "Would've served him right." She let out a humph and then laughed. "Guess I got a bit riled up."

"A bit?" Grace said with raised eyebrows. "He didn't mean all he said. It was the heat of the moment."

"Heat of the moment. Phooey." Lorna dusted off the side table with her apron. "Time for some O-be-joyful." She took a bottle of Anton's plum brandy from the cabinet and filled two glasses three-fingers high. She clinked her glass with Grace's and took a swig. "That man dresses like an undertaker."

Before school one morning, Lorna tottered around in the kitchen. She washed eggs and checked for blood spots before scrambling them to put in sandwiches for the children's lunches. "Look at that sky," Lorna said, glancing out the window. "Red sky at night, sailor's delight. Red sky in morning, sailor's waring— that's what my father always said."

"I remember you saying it, too," Grace said from the parlor as she put Leo's schoolbooks in his bag.

Vivienne and Erika, hunched over mirrors as they applied the Maybelline cake mascara Clara gave them, asked Lorna what it meant.

"Wish you'd do that thingamajig in the bathroom," Lorna said, "not at the table."

"It's easier sitting down," Vivienne said.

"Your teachers going to like you all . . . d . . . doll . . .ed—."

Vivienne looked at her grandmother, mascara wand poised in midair. "What's wrong?"

"Tingling in my arm." Lorna grabbed the counter edge as her legs wobbled. "I think I'm having a wee. . ." She lost her balance and slumped to the floor.

Grace hurried into the kitchen and found Lorna with a small trickle of saliva running from her mouth. When Lorna tried to speak, only garbled words came out.

There was an unnatural silence as Vivienne and Erika stood motionless, dread fluttering in their eyes. Grace's voice quivered as she told Vivienne to finish the sandwiches and to give each of them a box of animal crackers before hurrying to school. She placed a pillow under Lorna's head and remained by her side for all but the few minutes she was on the phone with the doctor. She held Lorna's hand and tried to comfort her as she gazed transfixed at the dense clouds skirting across the kitchen window. Twinges of regret engulfed her as she thought back to the last few days. Her mother had had trouble breathing and doddered around, often shooing Victor away and telling the four-year-old she needed to rest. She should have seen the signs.

"She had a stroke," the doctor told Grace. "She's sixty-five and I don't think surgery is wise. I'm prescribing a painkiller and a diuretic to reduce the swelling. We'll see how she progresses." He also wrote up a prescription for an anticonvulsant, in case she had seizures. Grace asked if there was anything she could do for her, and the doctor only said, "Make her comfortable."

When the children returned from school, Grace told them what the doctor said. Viviene offered to stay home and help. When Grace said she didn't want her missing classes, she said, "Ruth can bring me my assignments. I want to do it."

Vivienne stayed home the next two weeks, helping Grace tend to Lorna's needs, reading to her, and keeping her company. Sometimes she'd sit on the floor with her knees drawn up and encircled in her arms, humming along with songs on the radio. "When the Blue of the Night Meets the Gold of the Day" and "Lady of Spain" were two of Lorna's favorites. Vivienne would tell her grandmother that when she was better, she'd take her to Puyallup to see the daffodils in bloom, and to the tugboat races on Harbor Day.

When Lorna felt chilled, Grace or Vivienne would heat a brick and wrap it in dishtowels to place at Lorna's feet.

"This should keep you snug as a bug in a rug, as mother says." Vivienne moved the covers closer to Lorna's chin and asked, "What are you thinking?"

"So, this is how it ends. In Tacoma, Washington, throwing my daughter out of her bed."

"You're not throwing me out," Grace said. "I wanted you to have it from the beginning." She stroked Lorna's forehead. "Would you like me to call the priest so you can confess?"

Lorna's chin jutted out. "I'll confess, but I won't repent."

Grace glanced at Vivienne and smiled.

"My mother's jewelry is in my underpinning drawer," Lorna said. "I want Vivienne to have the gold-oak-leaf-and-acorn broach. And Erika, the posy-holder pin."

Grace remembered her mother's words from when she was a child. *Every young woman should wear a posy holder on her dress to keep away disagreeable odors, and each flower you put in it has a meaning.* All she could remember was that azaleas signified temperance. She wished she knew the flower for grieving.

"Don't leave us," Vivienne said.

"Listen. Each time you hear Mr. Owl hoot, know it's me telling you I'm here."

"I used to think such a thing was preposterous." A tear formed in the corner of Vivienne's eye; she blinked and it ran down her cheek. She dug for a handkerchief in her sleeve. "Then I read a passage in a book at school where an Indian elder said, 'All that separates the living from the dead is the width of the edge of a leaf.' I'm trying to believe, Grandmother." She dabbed her cheek with her handkerchief. "Are you afraid?"

"My darling girl, the way to survive is to not be afraid. Listen to your heart and do what makes you happy." Lorna motioned for Vivienne to come closer. "Never let anything go to waste. Can't tell when hard times are around the corner. And remember, idleness is the devil's playground."

"No need to tell her that," Grace said. "Her dance card is always full."

"Are there things you wanted to do that you didn't?" Vivienne said.

"Like fly in one of those new contraptions?" Lorna scoffed. "Only crazy folks leave this good earth that way." Memories passed in front of her eyes. "I had a happy home, a good home, and I wanted the same for my children. But I made decisions that made it difficult."

"You gave us love," Grace said, "the most important thing."

"That's what I want you to remember—how much I loved you and how I never stopped fighting for you."

A short while later, Lorna looked paler and she dozed off, her breath erratic. Before the clock in the parlor struck the next half hour, Grace whispered to Vivienne, "She's getting cold. I think she's gone."

Grace had known her mother might not live long, but she was not ready to accept the reality. She felt an emptiness that was all too familiar, the same hollowness she felt when Joseph died. Again, she wondered how she could go on.

"I wish I could've taken her places, the Pantages theater, the steamer to Victoria," Grace said with a catch in her voice. "She only stayed home and helped."

"She was happy with us," Vivienne said. "We loved her and she knew it."

A small gasp that held back tears escaped from Grace's mouth. "We think things will never end."

"I loved hearing about her life," Vivienne said. "I don't know if I could have done and survived all she did."

"You could. Did you ever think it's from her you get your independence, your charm and enjoyable companionship, your abilities?" Grace stroked Vivienne's head. "It must be."

The family held a funeral at Holy Rosary. Ellen came from Long Beach, and Uncle Daniel took a few days off work to be with Grace and the children. Mrs. Gartner and Betty attended the service, along with other friends and the *next doors*, who sent a funeral cross of ivory roses and daisies. Daniel paid for the funeral and a headstone for her resting place in Calvary Cemetery, not far from the Tschida plot. But far enough away she never had any concerns about their spirits dampening hers.

A few days after the funeral, Grace helped Erika fix her hair with the curling iron Clara gave the girls.

"The house is so empty without grandmother. She was loving, like you," Erika said. "Hugging us and telling us how special we were. Grandmother Tschida never did that."

"She loved you. But she didn't know how to show it."

Grace felt her mind fog up. There were days she felt numb and struggled to concentrate. At other times, early remembrances of Lorna vanished the confusion: her mother collecting driftwood at the lake; her pulling off the brambles stuck to the hem of her skirt after they hunted mushrooms; her pumping the water outside their cottage on the coldest mornings. Small things that held so much.

There was a knock at the door and Clara came in with two large brown paper bags of groceries. She pulled out two loaves of Wonder bread, three boxes of Jell-O, two boxes of Birds Eye frozen peas, Heinz beans, a tin of peanuts, a bunch of bananas, a jar of peanut butter, a box of Bisquick, and a bag of Toll House chocolate chip cookies. "I have one last surprise," she said to the boys, who barely acknowledged her, engrossed as they were in their game of Chinese checkers. "Nurses at work told me about these."

"What is it?" Benedict said, without looking up as he placed a marble in a circle.

Clara held up a small package of yellow cakes. "Twinkies. Have you tried them?"

Under his breath, Benedict said to Leo, "Haven't had a chance to steal any."

"I'm leaving one for Vivienne. Save it for her. And if you all stay skookum, you can come with me next week when Old Ironsides is here."

"Really, Aunt?" Leo said.

"I'm one of the nurses tending the aid tent on the wharf while she's here." She looked over at Grace. "You should all come and be part of the welcoming party." She moved next to Grace and whispered, "It'll be good after so much sorrow."

The day of the ship's arrival, Grace and the children stood for hours with the crowd on Stadium Way. In spite of the long wait, the day was full of excitement. They first caught sight of the *USS Constitution* as it came around Point Robinson and into the harbor, towed by a minesweeper. The children joined in with the cries of "There she is!"

During the ship's one-week visit, Leo awoke earlier than usual and stood beside Aunt Clara's car to ensure she didn't leave without him. He'd spend each day roaming the vessel. One day he couldn't resist and climbed a lower ratline on one of the three masts. A bucko mate caught him and escorted him off the ship, warning him if he tried anything again, he'd be barred.

"I trust you learned your lesson," Aunt Clara told Leo. "You can only come from now on if you're extra good and keep out of the way of the crew." She gave him an understanding smile. "I see you nodding, so, I guess we agree."

In the late days of summer, Grace and Clara traipsed through the yard as warm whispering winds scattered blossoms, leaving a dotted carpet of pink, blue, and white petals.

"Have you thought more about marrying Frank?"

"I told him I couldn't. He's a lovely man but I don't see myself making a life with him. He said he understood. We'll still be friends."

"I hope Father didn't influence you."

"He didn't." Grace was quiet for a moment as she pondered whether Max's treatment of her brothers had influenced her unconsciously. "I made chicken soup for your private patient. I'll bring it to you later."

"That's so good of you." Clara lowered her voice. "There's something else I need to talk to you about. I hesitate . . . especially since you're still grieving for your mother."

"I miss her so much." Grace pressed her lips together. "I used to think we were different. I wasn't as outgoing and humorous as she was. But we were similar—our children are the most important things in our lives."

Erika came outside with the boys. "We're going over to Bichsel's for a while."

Grace turned to Clara. "You wanted to tell me something."

"I don't want to upset you, but they found something in my colon and they think it's cancer." Grace let out a gasp. "I know, no one ever says the word 'cancer' aloud—totally taboo, but that's probably what I have."

What Grace thought would be a lovely idle chat with Clara turned devastating. She realized the illusion she'd been living under, thinking no more tragedy would descend upon them. They'd had more than their share.

Clara fingered her pearl necklace. "I read a lovely thing that said, 'We can't prevent birds of sorrow from flying over our heads, but we can prevent them from building nests in our hair.'"

Grace grabbed Clara's arm, squeezing it so hard it left a red mark. "Can't they do something, operate?"

"I'm taking treatment, but I fear it's too advanced."

"I'm not going to tell the children. It'll shatter them—you, their favorite aunt."

A ripe apple plunked to the ground and rolled toward them.

Clara wrapped her arm around Grace's. "I'm sad I might not be here to help you. You shoulder so much alone. If Joseph . . . he was always saying how much he loved you. An angel on earth, an extraordinary wife." Clara stroked Grace's arm; the light spilling between the apple trees bathed its hairs with a golden sheen.

"Before I forget, I started a bank account for Victor when he was born. Remind me to give you the deposit book. It's under the name Baby Victor."

Grace thanked Clara and looked off in the distance, where gray profiles of hills and evergreens stood against the backdrop of the afternoon sun. She felt her life unraveling again.

"Vivienne's coming," Clara said. "I want to give her something. I'll see you tonight." Clara slowly let her hand slip away from Grace as she strolled towards her niece. Grace followed her with anguished eyes until she turned and walked back to her house with a gaze that saw nothing but her own thoughts.

Grace busied herself reorganizing a kitchen drawer, her back to the door so Vivienne wouldn't notice her red-rimmed eyes when she came in.

"Aunt Clara's giving me her antique powder box, the one with painted flowers. She said I've always been her favorite."

"Keep it to yourself. You know how hurt Erika gets. Did you go to the Bon?"

"Yes. Ruth and I saw the new styles and got some ideas." Vivienne tossed her fan-shaped red pochette on the sofa. "She always jokes we're so poor we shouldn't even go window shopping. But I did buy some Mary Garden Rouge. The color's called rosebud."

"I need some fresh air. Let's take a walk and you can tell me what you saw."

As they strolled down the street, Vivienne said, "I saw Aunt's friend, Olga, at the Bon. She asked how you were."

The simple mention of the woman's name made Grace brood. After so many years, this woman still got under her skin. *The past pursues us like an angry wasp.* "What did you say?" Grace asked, as if hardly giving it a thought.

"That you were fine. Oh, I told Aunt about *Boy Meets Girl* and she's coming opening night. She said she enjoyed seeing me in *Spanish Onion* when I played Delight and the lead in *Little Nell.* Such a melodrama, especially when I had to kiss the stove and everything goodbye."

"You're a good actor, like your father. You never flub your lines."

"It's easy to memorize them. But remember how I couldn't stop giggling when Bobby couldn't get the friendship ring on my dress?"

"I thought it was part of the play. That's how good you were."

"I'm the soubrette, the lead again. I play Susie Seabrook."

"I'm glad you encouraged Erika to be in it. She might not have tried out otherwise."

As they walked around the corner, a squirrel climbed up a tree and nibbled on branches. A few steps away, Mrs. Aiken, in a faded striped housedress, rocked on her porch. Grace called out and asked how she was.

"Wonderful," she answered. "Lovely day, isn't it?"

"It certainly is."

Back in the front yard, Vivienne stooped and picked up a bronze mechanical lighter.

"Where did that come from?" Grace asked.

"Leo found it. He was playing with it the other day."

"It's full of kerosene. He could start a fire. Give it to me. I'm going to hide it."

Vivienne handed the lighter to Grace. "My Cardinal Club meeting is Thursday night, so I'll be home late."

"You take after your grandmother Susanna with all your clubs and associations."

"But nobody will ever say I'm a good cook and housekeeper," Vivienne said. "Didn't pass Home Ec, But I got an A in Palmer handwriting."

For Vivienne's graduation from Lincoln High, Clara made her the dress of her dreams. The yellow organza sheath had a pinched waist and ruffles descending half way down the back. Grace saved up and bought her a heart-shaped gold locket with the engraved letter V encircled by delicate scrolls. As Vivienne tried on the dress the night before graduation, Grace said, "Your father and I wanted you to go to college."

"I know but I'm happy with my job." She held out both sides of the dress like a fan.

Vivienne secured a job as an account manager and bookkeeper at Hunt & Mottet on Pacific Avenue, an industrial hardware company that supplied ship and railroad parts. Like her father, she was good at numbers and having worked after school for the principal and journalism teacher, she had office and clerical experience.

The opposite proved true with Erika. She dreaded starting her senior year without Vivienne nearby; the anticipation alone made her nervous to the point of nearly having a breakdown. She'd never felt comfortable in school. While she no longer had to put up with the nuns, the fear they instilled in her contributed to her anxiety. In her sophomore year, her male classmates teased her, often chanting, 'Erika has *the* vapors. "This and their other affronts wounded her. Grace voiced her concerns to Ellen.

"She's not outgoing like Vivienne—she masks her fears and feelings. It's upsetting, as she's a beautiful young woman with the soul of an artist, and everyone's fond of her." Grace paused. "Unless Vivienne insists she join in activities, she prefers to stay home with me. But when she goes out, she has a good time." Grace let out a sigh. "Vivienne told me if she sees someone coming down the street, she crosses to the other side. She also said Erika sneaks into the bathroom to eat her lunch so others won't see what she brought. There are days I don't have much to give them and—"

"Have her come here. She can attend the local school."

It surprised Grace when Erika welcomed the idea. They made plans for her to move to California for the new school year. Clara paid her travel expenses and bought her several new outfits. Grace was certain she'd love California. Memories of an unfilled dream still lingered on the peripheries of her mind—and in the background, her mother's words: *Don't dance with dreams, lassie.*

Before Erika left for California at the end of August, Clara died. The nursing staff of District 3 wrote a loving tribute: *A wonderful nurse, loyal to her profession and beloved by all, a genuine friend to those who were privileged to know her.*

For Anton, losing his eldest daughter was one death too many. He withdrew. He stopped taking the boys on walks and visiting Grace. He'd wander around the yard, sometimes mumbling to his bushes and flowers.

"What's wrong with Grandpa?" Leo asked Grace one day. "He acts crazy. Marches back and forth like this," he said, strutting from one side of the room to the other.

"He's not nuts," Erika said. "He's sad."

"I want him to fix my bike."

"Let him be," Grace said. "Don't bother him."

CHAPTER 32

◆

It is easy to halve the potato where there is love.

As the depression lingered, FDR instituted the WPA and social security. Households kept making popular depression-era recipes, like slugburgers, and sandwiches of mayonnaise with either peanut butter or thin layers of relish. Anything to help them fill their stomachs.

One morning, Betty came over with one of her applesauce cakes, Green River soda for the children, and her used copy of the *Prohibition Punches* book.

"I was going to bake a tomato soup cake," Grace said. "But now we'll have yours." She took a dishtowel from the drawer to cover the cake and saw the mechanical lighter. She made a mental note to hide it in a better place. "Last week I didn't have anything for dessert, so we had pieces of bread in milk."

"I remember your mother saying one good chocolate after a meal was all you need."

Grace smiled at the memory. "We loved the bubble and squeak you made with your Sunday leftovers. What was in it?"

"Roast beef, cabbage and mashed potatoes. They fry up well."

Grace opened the book Betty brought.

"Keep it. Don't need it now that alcohol is legal. It's got fruit-juice drinks the kids may like." Betty picked up the newspaper resting on the table and looked at the front page. "A shame about those Dust Bowl people. Our lives are hard, but we may have it easier than they do."

"Do you think they'll find work here?" Grace asked.

"Hard to say with so many having it tough. They say that's why we have all these crazes—swallowing goldfish, sitting on pole tops. Or rooting for Jesse Owens and Seabiscuit. Anything to distract people. Gosh, first-run films are now twenty-five cents."

"They're only five cents at the Rose. Each week I give the boys their nickels so they can go there."

"This weekend I'm seeing *Mr. Smith Goes to Washington.*" As Betty fixed the back strap on one of her shoes, she let out a laugh. "I always know what time it is each morning by how fast Vivienne runs down the hills in her high-heels."

"I tell her she's going to sprain her ankle, but she won't wear anything else."

"Sounds like her job's going well. She told me she also handles the Alaska orders now."

"She does and she's the youngest by ten years. But she likes her coworkers and gets along well with them." Grace shook her head. "She's out every night—dances at the Spanish Castle, Ft. Lewis, and Century Ballroom with the big bands—she's fond of Eddie Duchin. Or they go for cokes and fries at the Poodle Lounge Restaurant."

"Can't keep track of all the guys asking her out," Betty said, straightening the belt on her navy pleated dress. "That music store owner, the policeman, the professional wrestler from the University of Washington."

"I tell her and Erika what my mother told me—not to go out with only one. It's better to go out in groups and learn about different types than be stuck with one guy who may get jealous and not want them to see other people." Grace raised herself on tiptoe to put a carafe away on the top shelf. "They're busy now with the amateur theater group and Vivienne's talking about taking tennis lessons."

"She told me she wanted to join the rifle club but didn't because she's afraid of guns," Betty said. "Wasn't it grand she won the 'Miss Transportation' beauty contest—and in a wet bathing suit."

"She didn't want to do it but her friends encouraged her. She got a silverware set." Grace laughed. "The other night, she had a bit too much to drink. Came in weaving and pirouetted through the living room. Then she ran through the other rooms, pretending she was a train and singing, "Choo-choo. Here I come on the *Wabash Cannonball.*"

"Wish I could have seen it."

"It upset Erika. But I told her she wasn't hurting anyone and she shouldn't let little things bother her."

"How's Erika?

"She's more self-confident after her year away, and she likes her job at Kreiss's. She walks to and from to save on car fare. One of the boys usually meets her after work to walk her home, like they do with Vivienne."

"She told me she won some dance contests."

"Yes, at the USO dances on the base. One boy asked her to join him in a dance marathon. I know she wanted to do it because of the prize money. But I discouraged her. Most get nothing."

"Some last over twenty-seven hours. Takes a terrible toll on contestants."

"I'm encouraging her to draw more. She's good at it. Like Leo and Victor." Grace pointed to a pile of paper on a chair. "Boats Leo drew last week. He's happy when he's around boats."

"Erika told me you sold more of your watercolors."

"Mr. Walbaum at the print shop put them in his store window. Everything helps, especially with bread going to ten cents. Frank told me people are faulting on their mortgages— over fifty percent."

"How is Frank? Do you see him often?"

"Less and less. I think he met someone." With a wandering gaze, Grace said. "Joseph's friends have helped so much—as you have."

"You know how much you've done for me." Betty placed a hand on her chest. "Hate to ask but did Marta take you to Calvary Cemetery on Sunday like she said she would?"

Grace bowed her head and paused. "I waited in my one good dress and she never came."

"Again? If I had a car, I'd take you instead of you taking three streetcars." Betty clicked her fingernails on the countertop. "I don't mean to be harsh, but isn't it time to stop trusting and tell her off."

Grace kept her gaze down. "I'm tired of fighting. And they're the only family the children have."

"Some family." Betty fluffed up her hair on the sides. "I hear a man in the South End offered Benedict a job at his casket and monument business. Liked his confidence and outgoing personality."

"I fear I ruined it for him. I said if girls found out he worked there, they wouldn't want to go out with him. That did it."

"He could always tell the man he changed his mind." Betty put her clutch bag under her arm. "He said he met a train porter from back East. Told him Mrs. Roosevelt takes the train to Florida to see a psychic. Guess she goes down often."

"We could all use a psychic. It'd be nice to know when things will get better."

Grace and the children never again spent Christmas Eve at the *next doors*. Marta sent holiday cards but neither she nor her father offered to help in any meaningful way, not even stopping in their cars to offer a lift when they saw Grace or one of the children climbing the hills, loaded down with packages.

Marta oversaw everything now, reigning like an imperial commandant, ordering everyone around, including Anton. She gave away all his gardening tools because she didn't want him helping the neighbors and his friends with their yards. She told him he shouldn't be toiling away when they could hire a gardener; there were plenty of men looking for work, as witnessed by the hobos who begged for handouts or any menial task. Grace would see Anton outside, pulling up a weed with his hands, or trimming a stem with kitchen scissors. Marta treated Pauline like an indentured servant and had her run to the bakery each morning to get her a walnut and maple Danish.

Years slipped by and global turmoil continued with the rise of totalitarian regimes in Germany, Italy and Spain. With memories of World War I still fresh in Grace's mind, she, like most Americans, was concerned about threats to peace. Through the newspaper and radio, she followed Germany's invasion of Poland, the bombing of Warsaw and the rounding up of Jews into ghettos. As horrific as it was for the Polish people, Grace was relieved when President Roosevelt declared neutrality. The country was still in the depths of the depression, and Grace feared if the country intervened, Benedict could be called up to fight.

One evening, as she was listening to a broadcast, Marta came to see her.

"We're selling both houses and moving uptown to Yakima Avenue," Marta said in a matter-of-fact tone. "You'll have to find another place to live."

Grace's thoughts swirled as she tried to digest what Marta was telling her. "What are you saying? Your father gave us this house. He said it was mine for life. You're kicking us out?"

"I understand it's a shock. But my father's seventy-five. The stairs in front of the house are too dangerous for him. I want to make it easier for him."

"You're the one enfeebling him. You took his tools and now you're taking away all he knows—including his neighborhood."

"This area's not what it used to be with these new immigrants."

"Your parents were immigrants." Grace scoffed and turned away in disbelief. "Where will we go? We're barely getting by as it is."

"Your daughters and Benedict are working. Your brother and sister can help more." Marta crossed her arms. "It'd be hard, but you could send Leo and Victor to an orphanage."

Hearing the word orphanage, the vision of Lorna crumpled on the floor flooded Grace's mind. "How can you do this? We're your family."

"Joseph was my family, and he's gone."

"Your nieces and nephews are not?" Grace felt as if she were standing on the edge of quicksand, the earth around her sinking. "I'm going to talk to your father."

"It won't do any good. He already signed the papers." Marta shifted her weight. "You act like you're the only one who's had hardships."

Grace jerked her head. "You've never known hardship. Everything was your choice—even letting your parents drive David away. Much of what happened to me was not my choice."

"It wasn't like that." Marta started walking away, signaling an end to the conversation.

"Yes, it was," Grace said, following her. "And as for David, Benedict stopped to see him at the tavern where he works. He said we're the only ones who didn't desert him. You tossed him out of your life like you're doing to me and my children." Grace felt tears welling. "You're so miserable. You'll do anything to make everyone else miserable."

The next morning, Grace's unfocused gaze fell upon a sparrow as it strutted across the yard, pecking for worms. Observing the hardworking creature, she mulled over what her sister-in-law had done, bitterness clouding her mind. She didn't see how she'd manage with rents around twenty-five dollars a month. It was more than what she received from her pension now that Erika and Benedict were over sixteen. It helped her three oldest contributed to the household, and it was fortunate Daniel was sending her more. He'd been working at Grand Coulee Dam, near Spokane, as part of a WPA project. But she wanted them to keep much of their earning. They had their own lives to live.

Grace intended to confront Anton, as soon as Marta left for work. But before she could, she saw Marta come out the back door in her nurse's uniform, carrying a large paper bag. She set fire to the trash barrel and began tossing papers and what looked like photographs into it.

Grace sprinted outside. "Are any of those photos of Joseph and us?"

"I don't have time to go through this junk."

Grace grabbed Marta's arm, her nails digging into her skin. Marta tossed off Grace's hand and looked at her as if she were a lowly servant girl.

"You have copies of our wedding photos. Photos of my children." Resisting the urge to knock Marta to the ground and pummel her, Grace only pushed her away from the barrel.

Marta stumbled and yelped. "I'll report you for assault. They'll put you in jail and take your kids away." Marta pitched the bag into the fire. Ashes and embers flew into the sky.

Grace tried to stick her hand inside to retrieve something, anything. But it was too hot.

Marta didn't break stride as she marched toward the house. Before she went inside, she turned. "If you won't consider an orphanage, take Victor to court. Tell them you need help."

"A low-down trick only *you'd* think of."

After Marta left for work, Grace found Anton in the parlor, smoking his pipe. "You said the house was mine for life. You gave me your word."

"Marta . . ."

"Don't give me Marta. You're her father."

Anton's eyes were vacant, as if spellbound, his gaze directed toward a far corner. "I don't want to leave my home and my friends. I want to end my years here."

"Then why didn't you stop her?" Grace's heart beat like a wasp trapped in a jar. "You're leaving the neighborhood you love, and throwing out your grandchildren from the only home they've known. But you don't care. They're *Grace's kids* now."

His left eye twitched. In a limp voice, he said, "I've helped you."

"You tricked us into staying here, having Joseph move that rock, losing our money." Grace spewed out all her pent-up anger and hurt. "Your grandchildren went without—while you did everything for Pauline."

"Pauline was all alone."

"How you justify your actions. Your words change nothing." Grace felt her hands quaking. "You had the responsibility to treat all your grandchildren equally. Oh, yes, you pretended to be good and generous with us. But we both know the truth. My mother warned me about people like you."

Grace flew out the back door. She kicked the smoldering barrel, toppling it over. It spewed glowing, red-hot embers on the grass. Incandescent sparks flew in the air. *Damned if I'll pick it up.*

Back home, she slumped in the wingback chair, using its arms to steady her. She looked around at the house that had been her home for twenty years as if seeing it for the first time: the faint pencil marks on the wall where Victor scribbled; the green sofa with Erika's mending basket perched on a cushion; the Canterbury magazine rack filled with old newspapers and *Life* and *Photoplay* magazines. It was the house she'd criticized and wanted to leave. But now it held memories she didn't want to lose. In her mind's eye, she saw Lorna holding court as she told one of her stories, Leo licking the lead of his pencil while doing homework, and Benedict, asleep on the sofa, snoring like a warthog.

Mrs. Gartner shook her reverie when she ran in. "Smoke's coming out of Anton's house."

Grace slowly turned. "Come in. I'll put on some tea and I have some icebox cookies."

"Anton's house is on fire."

"Are you going to your Altar Society meeting?"

"Grace, what's wrong with you?"

"I've done everything I can." She stared into the distance and let out a weary sigh. "As mother used to say, 'However long the day, the evening will come.'"

CHAPTER 33

◆

If you give the loan of your britches, don't cut off the buttons.

S moke inhalation inflamed Anton's lungs and airways, causing them to swell and block oxygen. He died in hospital a few days later, due to respiratory distress and failure.

"You—you killed my father," Marta screamed, her forefinger stabbing at Grace. "You always took from us and now you've taken my father."

"You're wrong. I'm sorry he died," Grace said. "It torments me to think about it."

Marta scrunched up her face. "You wanted to get back at us for selling the houses."

Grace raised her hands in a warding gesture. "No. I was upset but I had no desire for revenge. I would never hurt him or anyone like that."

Marta filed a wrongful death suit against Grace.

"There are no reasonable or factual grounds to support her claim," Xavier told Grace. "Besides, it's a civil offense. Not criminal. If won, it awards a settlement and you have no assets."

Her gaze down, Grace fidgeted with the zipper on her bag. "She's angry. She's wants to sully my name."

"You didn't cause his death."

She glanced up hesitantly. "I kicked over the barrel."

"That wasn't enough to set the house aflame. Something else caused it."

"What will happen? Will they put me on trial?"

"It lacks merit. I'm going to file a no-merit brief and a motion to dismiss. Marta only wants to harass you."

"I have nothing but what if she tries to take the children's wages?"

"That won't happen." Xavier placed his hand on Grace's shoulder. "Try not to worry. I'm confident the judge will find the suit frivolous."

The judge did not dismiss the case. He requested an in-person hearing of facts with the parties and their witnesses and he scheduled it for the following month.

"Wear an ordinary housedress with no accessories or adornment," Xavier told her. "I want the judge to see you as the epitome of the average, everyday woman people relate to."

"So, I should leave my strings of pearls at home," Grace said, allowing a smile to creep up her face.

Members of the trade guilds, Holy Rosary parishioners, neighbors of the Tschidas and the serial trial watchers filled the courtroom on the day of the hearing. Tension hung in the air as if awaiting news from the war front, mingled with a festive mood, as if attending a Roman Forum debate. Betty and several other friends of Grace sat behind the Defendant's table with Grace's three eldest children. Grace twisted her wedding ring as she looked around the room, intensely aware of Marta's presence.

The hearing started with Marta's attorney giving his opening statement. As Grace listened to his assertion that she caused Anton's preventable death, the tightness in her chest felt suffocating. She clutched her bag in front of her, holding it like a shield.

Xavier followed with his opening statement. "Your honor, I submit this case has no merit. My client admits she kicked over the barrel. But we will show that its position at the back of the house, was not close enough, nor hot enough to cause a house to go up in flames the way the Plaintiff's house did. With expert testimony, I will demonstrate that at the most, it would singe the surrounding area, which contained grass. Grass which was still damp from the previous day's rain. Damp grass is not conductive for fires. Our expert testimony will also detail how another spot inside the house showed signs of fire. It's possible the fire started there. We will also hear testimony that at the time of the fire, my client was in her own home."

Marta's attorney called her as his first witness, after which Xavier cross examined her. Waves of nausea rolled over Grace as Marta relayed what happened the morning of the fire.

"It's possible then," Xavier said, "you burned things pertaining to the Defendant. Now, Mrs. Marsh, was there another reason the Defendant was angry with you, besides the burning of papers—specifically, the fact you sold her house along with yours?"

"We had to sell both." Marta looked to the side, averting Xavier's gaze.

"Both houses, you say. One was the large house where you lived with your father and the other was the smaller house alongside it, correct?" Marta answered in the affirmative. "Isn't it true that after the Defendant's husband died, your father told the Defendant it was hers for life and she and the children would always have a place to live?"

"She misunderstood." Marta blinks became rapid. "It was for when my brother was alive."

Grace rammed her nails into her palms. *That's a lie.*

"But she lived in it eleven years after her husband died. I remind you, Mrs. Marsh, you are under oath." Xavier proceeded to ask Marta if she could've sold only the house she lived in and left the Defendant's out of the sale.

"No one buying ours would want her and all her kids living so close, sharing a yard."

Grace remembered the names Marta called her children. How long she put up with the unacceptable—with the hope of making life easier.

"You knew it would displace your sister-in-law, who with her children has lived in the house for nearly twenty years," Xavier said. "Did you offer any compensation? Or offer to find them another place?"

"No." The vein in Marta's forehead throbbed.

"Was your father pleased with the move uptown?" Xavier asked.

Marta squirmed in her seat and looked around as if searching for someone to answer for her. "He agreed the move was best."

"You filed a wrongful death suit against your sister-in-law. What do you hope this will achieve?"

"My father and all my family have been very good to her and her children for years. We did much to help her and she repays us by killing my father. She has to be held accountable."

Xavier stated what Marta testified to was conjecture. She couldn't assert if anyone else was at the house after she left for work. He also brought up the fact the two days before the fire, there was a heavy downpour.

Grace thought Xavier was doing well. Still, she dared not be optimistic because what she thought wouldn't matter. *Hope,* as her mother used to say, *the last thing in us to die.*

The Plaintiff's lawyer called a doctor from St. Joseph's who testified to Anton's smoke inhalation. Xavier did not cross-examine, stating the cause of death was clearly defined. When it was time for Xavier to call his witnesses, he called Mrs. Gartner first. On the stand, the woman looked at Grace and smiled, kindness radiating from her eyes.

"She was in her house when the fire started. When I told her about it, it was like she was in a trance. She was oblivious to what I was saying."

Grace vaguely recalled Mrs. Gartner coming to tell her about the fire; her words had rolled off her like rain on a window, without meaning.

The next witness Xavier called was the local postal carrier.

"I was on my rounds and saw flames coming out of the lower front window. I told a delivery boy at the next house to tell the family to ring the fire station."

"Did you see anything or anyone else?"

"Only Leo standing near a tree in the yard, between the two houses. Yes, it was Leo. Been delivering there over ten years. I know all the kids."

Grace cocked her head. Why wasn't Leo at school?

"He was watching the fire," the postman said, "like young kids do."

Xavier faced the judge. "This confirms my client was not seen near the fire. I call my next witness, Mr. Charles Fahey, to the stand."

Grace watched Anton's friend, the bank president, come to the stand. After all these years, there was still something inside her that blamed him for her loss. But how do you rail against fate?

"You were close friends of Mr. Tschida for over fifty years," Xavier said. "What kind of man was he?"

"Honorable, a man of integrity. Contributed much to the building of Tacoma. Helped establish the Guilds, a talented artist. He was also prominent in the church and spearheaded the new building."

"What was his relation like with his daughter-in-law and her family?"

"He took care of them. Provided them with a house and furnishings, helped his son establish a market."

"You state he provided them with a house and furniture. Did you ever hear Mr. Tschida say the house belonged to the defendant?"

"Yes. After his son Joseph died. We discussed placing the insurance money in the stock market. He told me the house was hers for life and she'd always have a place to live. He also said he was paying for the children's school tuition."

"He must have discussed the selling of the house and the move uptown with you?"

Mr. Fahey looked briefly at Marta before answering. "He did."

"Was he pleased about the move?"

"Well, not really. He lived many years in that house . . . and had many friends in the neighborhood. Said he'd miss his garden—he was a master gardener, you know."

Grace closed her eyes and tipped her head back. He'd contradicted what Marta said. A happy tear escaped and rolled down her cheek.

Next, Xavier called his expert witness, Mr. Green. The fire and arson investigator testified he reviewed the evidence. He determined the overturned barrel could not have started the fire.

"Due to recent weather conditions leading up to the fire, the fuel moisture content of the surrounding grass would make it improbable to support combustion, let alone allow fire to spread to the adjacent structure."

"Is it also possible the fire started inside the house?" Xavier said.

"Yes, the Fire Department reports state the front door was ajar when they arrived and they determined a possible origin was a living room curtain," Mr. Green said. "The report also stated Mr. Tschida smoked a pipe and would occasionally drop lit ashes. One theory is a spark caught in the curtain, igniting the fire that eventually killed him. Still, arson was not ruled out."

"As we heard, your Honor," Xavier said, "it's possible the fire that set the house aflame started in the living room. It had nothing to do with the overturned barrel." Xavier looked behind him and then turned back to the judge. "I would like to call my next witness, Miss Erika Tschida."

Grace whipped her head around. She watched Erika, eyes drilling into the floor, come to the front of the room. *If Xavier had to call one of her children, why did he call her?*

Erika took the stand and made herself small, like a snail escaping into its shell. After her swearing in, Xavier asked her, "Erika, did you ever see your grandfather toss lit ashes around, on the floor, on the rug?"

Erika said nothing for a few moments as her eyes roamed the room. "All the time. My aunts would scold him and run and get a dish."

"Erika, you've heard the witness say your grandfather did much for the family. He took good care of you."

She held her gaze on Grace for a moment. "It's not true. We struggled to live."

A murmur rose in the courtroom. Grace put her hand over her mouth, trapping a gasp.

"You're saying it was a façade." Xavier said.

"Aunt Clara helped us the most. And our friends." Rubbing her hands on the front of her skirt, Erika continued, "Grandfather gave us the house and paid for school, but not much else." She looked down for a few moments. "My mother protected them. She never wanted anyone to know how they treated us. She said we had to respect them because they're family. But what kind of family lets their relatives eat cold porridge while they ate large meals? Or buy a new car while we wore threadbare clothes and missed out on school activities?" Erika looked at the judge. "We called them the *next doors* because they didn't act like family. Others treated us better."

A muttering filled the room. The judge slammed down his gravel again, ordering silence. But the buzz went on for another minute.

Grace surreptitiously glanced at Marta. Scowling, her shoulders nearly reached her ears. Turning back, Grace gazed straight ahead. It was as if the world had shifted, uncovering all that had remained hidden for so long. She'd worried her name would be sullied, and it was the Tschidas who were tarnished—something she never imagined, or wanted.

In Xavier's closing statements, he said all evidence presented by the Plaintiff was circumstantial. There was no proof Grace had set the fire inside the house, and no one could aver if another person started the fire or if Anton himself started it.

"Testimony demonstrated Grace tried to protect the family. It would be out of character for her to harm them. I again submit this case has no merit."

The judge retired to his chambers and returned in an hour to render his verdict. He dismissed the case.

Grace turned to see Marta motion for Pauline to follow her. Her footfalls' sharp thuds echoed throughout the room as she left.

Xavier came and stood next to Grace. "I'm still concerned it's far from over," she told him. "She might try something else to get back at me."

"She won't," Xavier said. "Erika did a good job, didn't she?"

"Why call her? She gets so nervous and doesn't like speaking in front of people."

"I knew she'd be the most believable. Vivienne always puts a positive face on everything and Benedict wouldn't have been able to quell his anger."

Grace smiled. "I didn't realize you knew my children so well."

Erika joined them, linking her arm in Grace's.

"It must have been hard," Grace said. "But you told the truth."

"I kept remembering how I wanted to get up in church and tell everyone what they were doing," Erika said. "This was better. Now everyone knows."

"We can be more generous, darling." Grace squeezed Erika's hand. "Do it for your father. He'd want us to be good to his family."

Erika bent close to Grace's ear and whispered, "I can't be like you. I know I shouldn't hate them, but I'll never be able to forget what they did."

A few weeks after the hearing, Grace and the family moved into a rented house set on an incline outside town. A large wraparound porch set with large stone boulders overlooked the road below. Evergreen and hemlock trees surrounded the house, and whimsical elf statues stood among the abundant foliage.

After they settled in, Ellen told Grace. "Why don't you and Victor come to Long Beach? You've been through a lot. You could use a change."

"It would be good to get away and I haven't seen you for so long," Grace said. "California . . . just think, after twenty years."

After she returned home, Grace took the streetcar into town to have lunch with Betty.

"The house sounds spacious," Betty said as she set napkins and silverware on the table. "And how fortunate Benedict's friend's uncle gave you a deal. But it's too far from town."

"The streetcar stops in front. You must come visit."

"Did I tell you Mrs. Gartner asks about you and said she'd like to see you? She misses having you nearby, like I do." Betty took the salt and pepper shakers from the credenza and placed them on the table. "The soup needs to simmer longer, so let's sit on the sofa and you can tell me about your trip."

"Ellen took us to the Griffith Observatory, Venice Beach— and she treated us to lunch at the Brown Derby. We also saw the float Shirley Temple rode on when she was the Grand Marshall of the Rose Parade." Grace reached over and touched Betty's arm. "My mother once told me it was different down south from where we lived in Sacramento. I didn't believe it. But it was."

"Sometimes we hold on to an idea and later find it's not what we thought it was." She raised her eyebrows into a question. "I take it you're not planning on moving down there any time soon."

"All that matters is my children, not whether I'm in Tacoma or California."

Another year passed and Grace maintained close contact with Betty and Mrs. Gartner. One day when they came to visit, the city was still abuzz about the collapse of the Tacoma Narrows Bridge.

"People are still stunned," Mrs. Gartner said. "And to think it opened only four months ago."

"I read its deck flexed and rolled and then tore apart," Betty said. "Blamed it on the winds—forty miles per hour."

"With the winds we get here," Mrs. Gartner said, "you'd think they'd have calculated for them."

"The kids love her nickname—'Galloping Gertie'," Grace said.

"Well, it takes our minds off the war for a while," Mrs. Gartner said. "Germany went into Czechoslovakia." She shook her head. "Can't stop thinking about what's going to happen to all the people there."

"Let's change the subject," Betty said, "especially with Benedict in basic training."

"It helps to talk and not worry alone." Grace glanced out the window. "He wrote there are rumors his unit's going to ship out to North Africa."

"I'll light extra candles at church and tell Father Gerhard to pray specially for him," Mrs. Gartner said. "Did you hear Marta bought a new DeSoto sedan? Paid over nine hundred dollars for it."

Again, the Germans had fallen out of favor and Grace remembered how the Tschidas sought to be what they deemed desirable immigrants. She thought back to the old house and its family dinners, holiday celebrations, weddings, funerals, and foibles. They were nearly all gone now, with only Marta and Pauline left in the house on Yakima Avenue.

She'd been free of the Tschidas for a while. But it still hurt that as hard as she tried to be a part of the family, she never really was. But was it her responsibility or the fault of the Tschidas? She'd always wonder if Joseph hadn't died, what would her children have been able to do and accomplish? In spite of all the obstacles and heartaches they endured, she was proud of the people they'd become.

A few more years passed and one afternoon as Grace weeded the garden, she thought of Anton and how he doted on his plants and flowers. The freckled toad lilies, hollyhocks and lavender-blue asters she saw when she arrived in Tacoma that September, were as vivid in her mind today as they were then. She wished she'd asked him to teach her how to do more than weed and water. Her thoughts floated to the stories he told about his early years. The responsibility he felt throughout his life led to the mistaken belief he had to take care of everything and everyone. *It's hard to judge others, but it would have been nice if he'd opened his heart wider.*

Starting back to the house with the lilacs she gathered, she saw Leo on the porch steps, staring into space. He was flipping open and closed the old brass mechanical lighter. Her mind flashed snapshots behind her eyes: her finding the lighter in the grass; the mail carrier's testimony; Mr. Green averring they could not rule out the fire started in the house. After the hearing, she'd asked Leo why he wasn't in school that day. He told her he forgot his homework and Sister let him run home to get it. She hadn't thought more about it.

Leo looked over and saw her. He furtively placed the lighter in his jacket pocket. "Hi, Mom. Know what I heard today?"

"Hope it was something nice."

"It's sad. Remember *Lady Lex* that came the winter we had no electricity?" Grace nodded. "She sank in the Battle of the Coral in the Pacific." He tugged at his jacket collar. "I still have the drawings I made of the ship. I'll never forget her."

"None of us will. Saved us from much misery." She started to say something, and hesitated. It was difficult to believe Leo would've caused his grandfather's death. It still could've been that Anton accidentally started the fire. He said he wanted to die there. Still, if Leo did something so terrible, she'd want to understand what he was thinking.

Walking up the front steps past Leo, she placed her hand on his head, leaving it there momentarily, as if deciding something. She let it slowly slip away and went inside.

After Grace tucked the last lilac stem in her mother's old Redwood pottery vase, she lingered at the window, staring into the distance.

We go through so much in life. We never know all the answers but we learn as we go down our paths. We persevere, never losing hope that something better lay ahead.

There was a knock at the door. Grace ignored it, thinking Leo would let the person in. But when it resumed, she wiped her hands on the dishtowel and went to answer it. After swinging open the door, Grace gripped the doorknob and stood frozen.

Marta slowly looked up. "May I come in?"

KJ KELLY

KJ Kelly grew up in the Pacific Northwest. After living abroad and across the United States, she now resides in the Midwest.

ACKNOWLEDGMENTS

This novel is a work of fiction. It weaves together actual events, family lore, and myth, transformed through the lens of narrative imagination. Though some characters are based on real individuals, their portrayals, actions, and interactions have been fictionalized to serve the story and should not be read as factual accounts. Similarly, while scenes are set in real cities, these locations have been reimagined, and any departures from historical or present-day realities serve the story rather than strict accuracy.

My research drew upon press reports, articles, and advertisements from the time, but the heart of this work beats with the voices and memories of my family. I am indebted to my aunt and uncles, whose rich and vivid stories inspired some of the narrative. Special gratitude goes to my uncle, Robert Tschida, whose insightful articles about life in bygone times, written for the Tacoma Historical Society, provided invaluable historical context and inspiration in shaping some of the novel's backdrop.

I am grateful to Pam Hickey for generously sharing her family stories, which added authentic texture to the narrative. My siblings and cousins also contributed vital threads and input.

My writing group deserves extraordinary recognition. Linda Marsh and Sandy Carp have been more than critique partners. They have been my steadfast companions through the years, offering not only their keen insights, but also their time and encouragement. Their commitment helped transform many raw drafts into meaningful storytelling.

For their generosity and thoughtful feedback on early drafts, I thank Beth Bauman, Lori Strang and Betsy Wald, whose constructive critiques proved invaluable in refining the manuscript. I am also grateful to Battalion Chief Casey Novak for reviewing an excerpt to ensure technical accuracy. Any remaining errors are entirely my own.

Additional thanks go to Julie and Melissa Baur, and Pat D'Alessandro for their unwavering support, and to the editors at History Quill, whose expertise and suggestions helped shape this book into its final form.

This work draws inspiration from Ireland's rich folkloric traditions and customs whose mythic character and cultural depth have been an endless source of inspiration.

Finally, this book stands as a testament to the collaborative nature of storytelling—a convergence of memory, imagination and shared experience that brings these pages to life.